SUSPICIOUS ACTIVITIES IN PLAIN VIEW

Published by East Bay Publications

Copyright © 2020 Helen and Morna Mulgray

Authors' website
www.the-mulgray-twinsonline.co.uk

Helen and Morna Mulgray have asserted
their right under the Copyright, Designs and Patents
Act 1988 to be identified as the authors of this work

ISBN 978-1-84396-619-7

Also available as a Kindle ebook
ISBN 978-1-84396-618-0

A catalogue record for this
book is available from the British Library and
the American Library of Congress.

All rights reserved

This book is a work of fiction. Names, persons
and the Pear Tree Farm Creative Arts Centre are inventions of
the authors. Any resemblance to persons, living or dead,
or events, is entirely coincidental.

No part of this publication may be reproduced, stored
in or introduced into a retrieval system or transmitted in any
form or by any means electronic, photomechanical,
photocopying, recording or otherwise without the prior written
permission of the publisher. Any person who does any
unauthorised act in relation to this publication may be liable
to criminal prosecution.

Pre-press production
eBook Versions
27 Old Gloucester Street
London WC1N 3AX
www.ebookversions.com

*Other books by the authors in
the DJ Smith and Gorgonzola series*

No Suspicious Circumstances
(Scotland - Edinburgh and the Lothians)

Under Suspicion
(Tenerife)

Suspects All!
(Madeira)

Who Would Suspect!
former title *Above Suspicion*
(Scotland – Islay, the whisky island)

No. 1 Suspect
(Scotland – Fife, St Andrews, Edinburgh)

Acting Suspiciously
(Scotland – sites associated with Mary Queen of Scots)

*This book is dedicated to
Shirley
in friendship and admiration*

SUSPICIOUS ACTIVITIES IN PLAIN VIEW

The Mulgray Twins

EAST BAY PUBLICATIONS

CHAPTER ONE

November.
Puerto Colon marina, Playa de las Americas, Tenerife

Liz read aloud the words of the newspaper headline:

BIG CASH REWARDS FOR
INFO ON TOBACCO GANGS

Totally absorbed, oblivious of the presence of the man cleaning the café windows behind her, she was unaware that the squeegee paused momentarily in its arc across the glass.

Again, her eyes avidly devoured the newspaper article.

Tobacco smuggling gangs based in Tenerife finance drug barons in Britain... millions of pounds of tobacco tax revenue lost... UK government urges Brits in Tenerife to tip off HMRC. Big cash rewards. Phone 062 to contact UCO, the Guardia Civil's unit that deals with Organised Crime. Anonymity guaranteed. It's easy.

Big. cash. rewards. Anonymity. guaranteed. Liz paused a finger under each word just as she'd done all these years ago as a child learning to read.

The window cleaner slid his bucket to the window behind her and sprayed the glass with soapy water.

Big cash rewards. That money would finance the course of the water-ski lessons she'd set her heart on. Lost in thought, she stared down towards the neat lines of catamarans, cabin cruisers and powerboats jostling in the slight swell. Ski Reg's eye-catching slogan 'From Beginner to Winner in Minutes' had certainly come true for her. She couldn't believe the progress she'd made. She was now definitely ready for the challenge of pointing her skis at an angle to cross the wake of Reg's boat. But water-ski lessons didn't come cheap, and it would take a good few lessons before she'd have improved enough to rise effortlessly out of the clear blue waters and skim across the waves on a mono-ski with her long blonde hair streaming in the wind. That was her dream.

'Anonymity guaranteed,' she murmured.

Should she make that phone call to the *Guardia Civil*? Risky, though. More than risky if the smuggling gang had the faintest suspicion that she'd contacted HMRC. Despite the sun, hot on her bare arms, she shivered. She took another sip of coffee.

Behind her, the window cleaner made another pass over the glass with his squeegee.

Undecided, she bit her lip and looked across to *Pantalon* 4 where Reg was preparing the boat and skis, making them ready for her. Without that cash, this could be her last ski lesson. Decision made. There'd just be time before her lesson to tip off HMRC. If she was careful, what could go wrong? And she'd be very careful, very careful indeed. At this time in the morning there were no other customers at the terrace tables, no one to overhear.

She picked up her phone. 'HMRC hotline? I've a tip-off for you...'

The window cleaner laid aside his squeegee, felt in his pocket for his phone, took her picture and tapped in a number.

With a light heart Liz hurried down the stairs towards Reg's boat moored at *Pantalon* 4. She'd done it. Those water ski lessons were in the bag!

Email to Gerry Burnside, Chief Controller Undercover Agents (Scottish section):

UCO, Tenerife's Unit Against Organised Crime, has received a tip-off from a resident of Playa de las Americas giving important information on a cartel smuggling drugs and tobacco into the UK. See attachment.

December
Puerto Colon marina, Playa de las Americas, Tenerife

Arms straight, knees bent, ski tips up, Liz crouched low in the water, running through in her mind Ski Reg's instructions. With the cash reward from HMRC she'd been able to practise seven days a week, so she was confident that today her dream to mono-ski would come true.

She focused on keeping the mono-ski in the deep V of the

device that held it in the correct position behind the boat. The engine powered up. She rose out of the water, light as a feather, skimming along the surface, blonde hair streaming out behind her. Just as she had imagined.

A few seconds was all it took for the marksman to rest his high-powered rifle on the villa's balcony rail, line up the distant water-skier in the crosshairs of the telescopic sight and squeeze the trigger. Job done.

The change in the feel of the rope told Reg she'd fallen. He spun the wheel and circled round, the towrope bouncing along in the wake. Liz was floating on her back, eyes half-closed, quite relaxed, with no hint of disappointment that she'd managed a run of only fifty yards.

'Good show, Liz, you've got it licked! Just a lapse in concentration, there. Next time, when you hit a rough patch, bend the knees, don't lean back and–'

From her, no answering smile, no effort to reach out for the mono-ski drifting slowly off in the direction of shore. No response at all.

He frowned. 'She's gone and knocked herself out!'

He reached down and lifted her into the boat by the straps of her life jacket. His eyes narrowed in shock. Blood was welling out from a wound in her back and forming a small pool in the bottom of the boat.

Pale beneath his tan, Reg spoke urgently into his ship-to-shore radio.

CHAPTER TWO

Edinburgh, Scotland

The first hint of trouble ahead – though I didn't realise it at the time – was a letter telling me to bring my sniffer cat, Gorgonzola, for a reassessment of her sniffing ability. Frowning, I reread the letter. What was all this about? My ability as an experienced trainer had never before been questioned. Fuming, I addressed my audience, the Red Persian cat snoring gently in a patch of sunlight.

'A human has no difficulty in detecting tobacco. A dog's nose is far superior to a human's, and yours is better than the best sniffer dog's, isn't that right, Gorgonzola?'

The large ginger mound twitched an ear and purred agreement.

'So what's all this bureaucratic nonsense about appraisal? The Powers-That-Be want proof that you can detect something as strongly scented as tobacco! What do you think of *that*?'

The snores continued, if anything louder than before, delivering her answer. 'Of course I can detect tobacco! Haven't I proved it each time you tested me? It's not worth losing a moment's sleep over.'

That was my reaction too, until I read on and noted that taking personal charge of the appraisal would be none other than HMRC Assistant Controller Andrew Tyler – or Attila, as he was unaffectionately known to myself and my fellow undercover agents for his 'My Way Or No Way' stance on, well, everything. That should have alerted me that something unusual was going on.

And on the day of G's appraisal, there he was, clipboard in hand, expression sour, waiting in the warehouse adapted for all types of sniffing tests.

'What's all this about, Mr Tyler?' I made no attempt to hide my irritation.

'Agent Smith, I'll be blunt. In these days of austerity, the taxpayer must have value for money. To that end, all sniffer animals are to be reassessed and regraded and only the best will be kept in the service of HMRC. In my view, of course, your sniffer cat – and indeed, all sniffer dogs – are old technology. The way forward for HMRC in the detection of drugs lies in EDDA, the Electronic Drug Detector and Analyser, discreet, hand-held, capable of instantly detecting twenty different substances. It is by far superior to even the nasal powers of the Great African Pouch Rat, though this splendid rodent is capable of eight sniffs a second and has the ability to differentiate two separate smells in one sniff.'

Foolishly, I paid little attention to his mention of the electronic device. Inwardly amused at his notion of employing a Pouch Rat for undercover work, I was unable to suppress a smile. However efficient the Pouch Rat was as a sniffer, there'd certainly be nothing undercover about the unwelcome attention drawn to it by the hysterical screams of anyone who even glimpsed a rat, let alone a giant rat.

Observing my smile, he snapped, 'For the taxpayer, an additional consideration is the cost-saving in fodder. Food eaten by a rat, even cheap food, is unnecessary expenditure which *must* be avoided at all costs in this time of austerity. Your creature is exceedingly wasteful, demanding gourmet cat food, as is all too evident from those exorbitant claims you submit for feeding it.'

Riled, I burst out, 'Unnecessary expenditure, Mr Tyler! Her record shows she's an ace sniffer-out of drugs, and of tobacco now I've trained her. Your test is an expensive waste of time. It's a one hundred per cent certainty that she'll detect the substance well within the set time limit.'

I might as well not have spoken. He continued, 'I have here a list of timings already achieved by dogs and if your creature takes longer, she will fail.'

Despite her past successes, he'd never accepted the concept of a sniffer cat and would have great satisfaction in finding Gorgonzola deficient. He'd make the test as tough as possible. She would be rated on the time it took to detect a substance, so a few seconds too slow would be enough for him to downgrade her into the 'to be dispensed with' category. She wouldn't fail, of course, but despite my confidence I felt an inexplicable sense of unease.

Tyler stared coldly down at Gorgonzola who was peering out of the cat carrier, then equally coldly at me, no trace of warmth in his briskly businesslike manner. 'It is mere *assumption* that your cat will pass this test. Assumption, I'm afraid, is one of your flaws, Smith. A *major* one. And as Assistant Controller,

I must take that flaw into account. Any weakness in an agent should be drawn to the attention of management.' He made a note on his clipboard. 'The test will take half an hour. You cannot be present as you may – *unintentionally*, of course – signal by your demeanour that the creature is approaching the hidden substance.'

After the test I returned, confident that G's performance had made him eat his words. I was looking forward to him being forced to admit that G was indeed one of HMRC's best sniffers.

With a thin-lipped smile, he passed me the clipboard. 'To be blunt, agents prone to making assumptions do not understand that assumed certainties may not turn out to *be* certainties. And the outcome of this test is the *perfect* example.'

Puzzled, I skimmed down the page. All the boxes were marked with a cross, signifying 'Fail'.

Stunned, I stared at him. 'She *failed*!'

Attila took back the clipboard. 'Exactly that! This feline shows no aptitude whatsoever for detecting tobacco. It made no finds within the time limit. Indeed, it made no finds *at all*.'

He was enjoying my consternation. Payback for the times when, contrary to his instructions, I'd acted on my own initiative and been proved right.

My shock turned to anger. 'A sniffer often only responds to its handler,' I snapped. 'I demand that the tobacco test is rerun.'

'Facts are facts, and however unpalatable have to be faced.' Another thin-lipped smile. 'And what is more, in my opinion, the creature's failure to sniff out tobacco, surely an easy substance to detect, certainly raises serious doubts about its ability to detect drugs. She must now demonstrate to me that she still has this skill. But, so that it cannot be claimed that its failure was due to a stranger giving the 'search' command, this time *you* will be its handler.'

Outside, while waiting for the drug-detecting test to be set up, I had a stern face-to-face talk with G. Holding the carrier aloft, her copper eyes staring into mine, I ranted, 'I don't know what you were playing at, pretending you couldn't detect a strong smell like tobacco!' I wagged an accusing finger. 'You couldn't be bothered, that was it, wasn't it? Too easy for you, eh? Even *I* can smell tobacco when someone rolls a cigarette or fills a pipe! You *do* realise, don't you, you've played right into Attila's hands? And if you don't sniff out drugs this time, he'll have you thrown out of HMRC in disgrace. We're a team, and if you go, I'll have to leave too. And that's just what he wants – a loose cannon out from under his feet.' I summoned a tear, a talent I've often found useful in tricky situations.

She stared back at me, unblinking. I was sure she had understood, but there was no way of knowing what she'd decide to do. Cats are a law unto themselves.

'Smith!' Tyler's shout summoned me back into the warehouse. A brusque, 'Follow me!' He stalked off to the far corner which had been fitted out as a rather untidy bedroom: clothes flung carelessly on bed, box spilling over with children's toys, wardrobe hung with coats, dresses and trousers, and discarded on the floor, paint-stained cotton overalls reeking of turpentine.

Arms folded, he took up position. 'Perhaps this time you will accept that the creature is past its sell-by date. It will fail yet again. There is no doubt *whatsoever* about that.' He raised the stopwatch. 'Ready... The time taken to detect the substance starts *now*.'

I gave G the command, 'Search!'

Her reaction was a long, slow, y-a-aw-n-n. Nail-bitingly slowly, tail erect and twitching, she strolled into the test area and jumped onto the bed. After a cursory sniff, she jumped off again, then after a mere glance into the open door of the wardrobe, the box of toys ignored, sat down beside the smelly overalls where she began a leisurely wash-and-brush up with her paw. Gorgonzola had shown no interest in anything else in the room other than those overalls. Attila consulted the stopwatch and made a note on his pad.

'*Search*!' I repeated desperately. But the result was the same. No drugs detected.

Tyler made another note on his clipboard. 'It is an absolute requirement that a sniffer animal is able to detect a required substance. Sniffer Cat Gorgonzola has miserably failed *both* detection tests. Therefore, my recommendation is...' tense pause before the guillotine blade fell, '... is that HMRC dispense with the feline's services.'

I hot-footed it to Controller Gerry Burnside, and after a cursory tap on his door burst into his office. He looked up from the papers he was studying, and courteous as usual, didn't comment on my abrupt entry.

Face flushed and voice trembling, I flung the report down on his desk, blurting out somewhat incoherently what had occurred.

He frowned. 'Take a deep breath, Deborah, slow down a bit, and tell me exactly why Mr Tyler has decided that Gorgonzola is no longer of use to HMRC.'

I stabbed my finger down on the word *Fail*. 'G unable to

detect a strong-smelling substance like tobacco! I trained her myself so I can't believe the result. And as for being unable to sniff out drugs! *Nonsense!*'

He doodled a big question mark on his writing pad and avoided my gaze. 'Don't fly off the handle, Deborah. Think carefully, could your tobacco-training of her have been deficient in some way?'

'No!' I shrieked. 'It definitely *wasn't*. I built up the scent association exactly the way as I always do: tobacco shreds positioned beside her food bowl; the scent of tobacco present at each opening of the carrier door; her toy mouse rubbed with tobacco; a pack of cigarettes hidden in her bedding.' The words came tumbling out. 'At home, she detected tobacco, not just once, not twice, but *every* time, no matter how difficult I made it. Yet today at the test I saw with my own eyes that she didn't detect either tobacco or drugs. There *must* be a physical explanation. I demand that she sees a vet.'

Gerry Burnside made a show of studying the report, then looked up with a sigh. 'I'm as upset as you are for Gorgonzola, but facts are facts, I'm afraid.'

His repetition of Attila's words sent me into a fury. 'You know of G's *excellent* record. Yet, as a result of this *one* lapse, HMRC gets rid of her, a star sniffer-out of drugs. Gets rid of her without further investigation.'

Obviously uncomfortable, again avoiding eye contact, he delivered his verdict. 'I have to agree with Mr Tyler. As you must be well aware, if a cat decides it doesn't want to do something, it doesn't do it. A sniffer cat has to want to sniff on *every* occasion. So I'm afraid I can find no grounds for a reprieve for Sniffer Cat Gorgonzola.'

As a signal that there were more urgent matters to attend to, he slid the report into the Out tray and picked up the papers on his desk. As if G's fate didn't merit another moment's thought.

'You're no better than Attila! That's it! I resign!' I stormed out of the office slamming the door.

For years G and I had been a team. To work undercover without her would be inconceivable. That very day I handed in my notice, forfeiting the due amount of salary, packed a small suitcase, cajoled G into the cat carrier and drove off into the sunset, or more precisely, to my hideaway in Portobello, one of Edinburgh's seaside districts.

CHAPTER THREE

April

Trrr-ing. A loud prolonged ring at the doorbell woke me with a start. *Trrr-ing.* I pulled the duvet over my head and prepared to go back to sleep, muttering, 'Go away! No hawkers. No circulars. No doorstep sellers!'

'Special Delivery! Need a signature.' An imperious, not-to-be-denied rattle of the letterbox.

Still half asleep, prising open one eyelid, I shuffled along the hall and called through the door. 'Not for me! Wrong address! Go away!'

'Right address.' He read it out.

'Well…' I said, uneasy. Whatever it was, it couldn't be for me. I'd disappeared from HMRC's radar – or so I'd thought. I made no move to open the door.

Another rattle of the letterbox. 'It's for Smith.'

'Smith?' I said cautiously.

When I'd resigned as an undercover agent with Her Majesty's Revenue & Customs drug detection unit, some months ago to be exact, I'd thought I had cut all contact with HMRC.

'Deborah Jane Smith. That you?'

'Ye-es,' I said slowly.

To friends and colleagues I'd been known merely as DJ Smith. Only one person – my controller, Gerry Burnside – knew what the J stood for. I still felt bitter at the way HMRC, and Gerry Burnside in particular, had dispensed with the services of my cat Gorgonzola, star sniffer-out of drugs.

'Right person, then. Come on, mate. Don't keep me waiting, I've a job to do.'

Wide-awake now, I opened the door, signed on the slippery electronic screen with a spidery signature bearing little resemblance to my own, and took possession of a thin white envelope.

Holding it gingerly as if red hot and might burn me, I returned to the bedroom and sat on the bed, pushing aside Gorgonzola who had taken immediate advantage of my temporary absence to curl up on the warm mattress. I tore open the envelope and pulled out a postcard.

Portobello Edinburgh's Seaside Resort. The view was of blue sky, golden sand and the frontage of Portobello promenade with its sedate grey or red sandstone Victorian tenements – and bizarrely out of keeping, an intrusive, starkly white, twenty-first-century block of flats that had brashly elbowed its way into the line of buildings. At the right- hand edge of the postcard, above a red neon sign marking the position of an amusement arcade, the sender had inked in a large black X.

I'd been so sure nobody knew where I was living now, and certainly nobody at HMRC, even Gerry Burnside. I could be living anywhere in the UK. How then, had the sender of the postcard managed to track me down to my self-catering holiday accommodation, the garden flat of a Georgian cottage in the Portobello district of Edinburgh?

I turned the postcard over. On the reverse was written, *Saturday 11 a.m.* Underneath was the doodle of a cat's head, unmistakably the handiwork of Gerry Burnside. In the past, when I was with HMRC, the anticipation of a new mission would have set my heart racing. Now all I felt was mounting rage. Only a crisis would have made him pull out all the stops to track me down. Had it not been a crisis for *me* when Gorgonzola had been so summarily dismissed from HMRC? And what support had Gerry Burnside given *me* then?

Saturday 11 a.m. That gave me three days to think about the message from Gerry. My first reaction was to ignore it. I owed HMRC nothing. After all, had not HMRC denied one of their star undercover sniffers a second chance? The postcard was tossed *prontissimo* into the wastepaper bin.

Saturday dawned grey and blustery with a spatter of raindrops on the window. At 8 a.m. I poured milk onto my porridge and with some satisfaction imagined an HMRC agent – perhaps even Gerry himself – loitering among the arcade machines as the minutes crept towards eleven o'clock... quarter past eleven... half past eleven... until the agent was finally forced to accept that I wouldn't be coming.

It was around 10.30 a.m. that an inconvenient niggle of conscience began to worm its way uncomfortably into my warm glow of satisfaction. By sending the postcard, Gerry had been making it clear he knew my Edinburgh address, but he had also made it easy for me to refuse his request. He'd been considerate enough to ensure that there need be no embarrassing face-to-face encounter. So he was leaving me free to do exactly what I intended to do – and that was *nothing*. I firmly suppressed the niggle of conscience and leisurely leafed through the morning newspaper that had noisily thumped its way through the letterbox onto the mat.

A few minutes later, yet another niggle, stronger than before, forced its way between me and my perusal of the newspaper. At a moment of crisis, Gerry was relying on me, as so many times during a mission I had relied on him. How could I possibly refuse to help? I couldn't. 10.50 a.m. There'd be just enough time to make that rendezvous.

With minutes to spare before the appointed time, I made my way along the promenade, battling against a biting north-west wind that forced the breath from my lungs. Today, no picture-postcard blue sky, no sapphire sea sparkling in the sun, no lacy-edged wavelets washing lazily up the beach. Instead, threatening dark clouds sped across a leaden sky, and a relentless succession of waves thundered onto the sand.

The yellow-and-black façade of the Tower Amusements signalled an incongruously sunny presence from afar. The international flags above the entrance flapped briskly above paintings depicting heroic victories, battles to stir the Scottish heart, Bannockburn, Prestonpans, Stirling, and Spanish-American Puerto Bello from which Portobello took its name. The doors stood optimistically open to welcome the few hardy enough to venture out on such an unpropitious day.

Inside was a cosy dark underworld: black-painted ceiling crossed with lines of tiny bulbs, walls topped with red and blue neon fluorescent strips, carpeted floor crowded with machines each fighting for attention with *tings*, *beeps*, flashing lights and tinny music. The place didn't appear to be particularly busy for a weekend, but the height of the closely-packed machines made it difficult to see past them in any direction.

I lingered at the entrance, allowing time for the HMRC agent to recognise me and make a move. After a couple of minutes I went to the kiosk and exchanged a £2 coin for a supply of copper two pence pieces, then wandered over to one of the machines and tried with varying success to nudge a line of coins to spill over into the collecting tray. The agent would make a move when the time was right.

Five minutes later, still no contact. That agent was being ultra-careful. I moved on to Lucky Loco, a glass box with the jaws of a crane dangling over a colourful heap of soft toys. By gambling the last of my dwindling stock of coins, I might win a very realistic furry mouse, ideal for G to toss and shake when the mood took her. Pitting one's wits against a machine is curiously addictive. Four times I manoeuvred the crane into position. Four times the jaws grasped the tiny body, only for it to slip out as the crane rose and my game time ran out. I fed in the last of my coins.

'Concentrate!' I muttered. The closing jaws gripped the toy... raised it high...

Behind me, Gerry Burnside said quietly, 'I was counting on you not to let me down, Deborah.'

Training prevented me from drawing attention to our meeting by whirling round, but couldn't prevent an involuntary jerk on the controls of the crane. It swung sideways in a violent arc. Time up. The jaws opened – and dropped the toy neatly into the collection box.

His hand reached past me and retrieved it. I kept my face averted hoping to conceal the flush brought on by guilt: he'd been counting on me not to let him down, and I'd so very nearly done exactly that.

I turned round ready to add a biting comment, then stopped, stunned. I'd heard Gerry's voice, had expected to see Gerry. But the man standing there looked nothing like him.

'Oh, I'm sorry,' I said. 'I thought you were someone else.'

He handed me my prize. 'No mistake, Deborah. I'll explain in a minute. All I ask is that you hear me out. Then you can decide whether to walk away.'

Reluctantly I trailed behind him as he moved from machine to machine, pausing at each one as if contemplating whether to play, then strolled on. The promised explanation didn't come. I had the uneasy feeling he was steeling himself to tell me something that I wouldn't like to hear.

At last, I couldn't bear the tension any longer and pulled him round to face me. 'Explain *now.*' He had taken great care to disguise his appearance. I didn't breach security by addressing him by name.

He didn't reply, just stopped beside a dual-seat car rally machine sandwiched between two machines blaring out loud tuneless music. He slid into a seat, motioning me to take the other seat and fed a £1 coin into the slot for each player. 'Ideal for a conversation, safe from eaves-dropping. Select a car.'

I couldn't resist snapping, 'What's so vital that you have to call on an *ex*-agent? Did everyone else turn it down?' Mean of me to respond like this, I know, but it just came out.

'Wait.' No irritation, just the calm even tone of Mission Control handling a critical situation.

The video screens changed to show our choice of car: his Mitsubishi and my Ford Escort lined up side by side for the start of the race. Count down, ten seconds… five… zero. An uncomfortably loud soundtrack of revving engine assailed my ears as the Mitsubishi sped away in a macho cloud of dust.

Unenthusiastically I pressed down the accelerator and followed at a slow speed calculated to annoy him, my Escort making no attempt to catch up with his Mitsubishi as he blasted round the twists, turns, and dizzying drops to the sea of the Corniche French Riviera. No screaming tyres and wrenching at the steering wheel for me, just the sedate pace of an elderly lady's leisurely Sunday afternoon drive in the countryside. Irritatingly, he didn't seem to notice, just launched into the long-awaited explanation.

It was a strange one-sided conversation between us, our eyes staring straight ahead, hands turning the steering wheel in response to the changing images on the screen, his lips moving, mine pressed together in a tighter and tighter line as I listened.

'This drug ring has established a nationwide smuggling network in the UK,' he said quietly. 'For more than a year we've set up raids on businesses suspected to be acting as a front for the smugglers, only to find the premises hastily abandoned with no evidence either of tobacco or drug smuggling.'

So what was new about that? I shrugged dismissively, my expression making it evident that this in no way justified the unforgivable treatment of G and myself.

'Just hear me out, Deborah.' The quiet desperation in his voice shocked me. 'A Number One Priority justifies what must have seemed to you my brutal handling of your appeal for Gorgonzola to remain with HMRC. Recently, an undercover agent has been found dead within a short time of being placed in position to investigate the drug organisation in question.

He was as experienced as yourself, had brought many previous missions to a successful conclusion. It is vital to find out what blew his cover – a mistake made by the agent himself, or a leak from within HMRC. He was silent for a moment. 'And this is where you and Gorgonzola come in. *If* you take on this mission, your task would be to keep the new operating agent under surveillance, to report anything he has said or done that could arouse suspicion, so that I can recall him in time. You would report directly to me. For complete security, *no one* except myself, and that includes the new agent already in place, would have any idea that another agent has been assigned to the mission. You are no longer employed by HMRC, indeed have lost all contact with the Department, so there would be no risk of inadvertent leakage from that quarter.'

He fell silent, eyes on the screen, hands on the wheel, all his concentration seemingly on performing a neat manoeuvre. I wasn't fooled.

I didn't turn him down immediately. His choice of 'if' and 'would be' was a point in his favour. He was giving me a choice, was accepting that I might very well refuse a dangerous mission where others had failed and paid with their lives.

'And in worst case scenario?' I murmured.

'In worst case scenario, if that agent meets the same fate as the others, you would stay in place, your mission to find out what went wrong, and of course, provide the evidence I need to nail whoever is controlling that drug ring.'

An awful suspicion dawned. 'Let me get this straight. Was my resignation *necessary* for the new mission…?' The thought unacceptable, improbable, *incredible*. I narrowly avoided crashing my virtual car into a group of spectators lining the route. 'You couldn't have *known* G would fail to find the tobacco?' A long pause as suspicion became certainty. 'And you couldn't have *known* that I would resign. Could you?'

He didn't reply.

I stared at him. '*Could* you?'

There was only one explanation for his silence.

'Did you *know* that G would fail the assessment test?'

'I didn't know *in advance*,' he said quietly.

The nose of the Mitsibushi came into view, level with my back wheel as he came zooming up preparing to lap me. At just the right moment I spun the wheel and sideswiped him. With considerable satisfaction I watched his car crash into the cliff face. 'Game Over!' flashed up, followed by 'Winner – Ford Escort.'

With my eyes on the screen, I said slowly, 'So…there *was* no tobacco, no drugs, for her to find.' I made no effort to keep the bitterness out of my voice.

'When you came to me begging for a reprieve for Gorgonzola, I *did* investigate,' he said somewhat defensively. 'You were not the only one who found it incredible that Gorgonzola had suddenly lost her sense of smell. On close examination of the report, I noted a discrepancy between the chemical analysis of substances used in Tyler's test of Gorgonzola and those used for the Electronic Drug Detector Analyser test. This could only be accounted for if the packets labelled 'tobacco' and 'heroin' did not contain these substances. Of course, the sniffing test assessor had no reason to check. You too were guilty of being misled in that way. I've pointed out to you on several occasions, have I not, Deborah, the folly of making assumptions?'

When I ordered Mr Tyler to rerun the tests, he reluctantly

admitted that in a desperate desire to promote the EDDA machine, he had rigged the cat's test, and run another for the machine with the correct substances in place. Mr Tyler had been, shall we say, a little too enthusiastic in his promotion of the twenty-first century pocket-sized electronic drug detecting gismo to replace the traditional, and in his view expensive and time-consuming use of sniffer dogs, and particularly of course, a sniffer cat'

'Yet you let the result stand! How *could* you!'

His hands clenched on the wheel. 'The over-riding priority for me was that an operative has died on a mission. Your resignation gave the opportunity for a new mission, this time eliminating the possibility that our agent could be betrayed by a leak from within HMRC.'

'I see,' I said bitterly, 'the end justifies the means, eh?'

A long silence, then quietly, 'I'm afraid that sometimes the end does indeed justify the means when lives of agents are at stake. You and Gorgonzola are, of course, still on the payroll of HMRC.'

I have never known Gerry exaggerate or lie to his agents. And it was this that finally won me over.

I sighed. 'Agreed, the end *does* sometimes justify the means, Gerry.'

'I'm glad you're taking it so well, Deborah.'

I said nothing.

He turned from the screen. 'I have to make you aware that the Tenerife informant who gave us a tip-off has been murdered. This, and the deaths of two agents, gives you the option to refuse this mission.'

I didn't need to give the matter any further thought.

Determination not to let Gerry down was definitely the main factor in accepting. And another, I have to admit, was the adrenalin rush I get from danger. I met his eyes. 'I'll take care.'

From Gerry a quiet, 'Thank you.'

I made my way back along the promenade, the briefing file he'd slipped me hidden under my coat, safe from the weather and prying eyes. The rain had stopped. A pale sun was fighting its way through massed ranks of black clouds, but the north-west wind felt not one degree warmer.

With some relief I closed the door of the Georgian cottage behind me, switched on the kettle, and sank down in one of the armchairs to warm my hands at the fire. The other chair had been claimed by Gorgonzola curled up, nose buried cosily in her tail, eyes half-closed, ears alert to read my mood from my tone of voice. Since the disaster of the appraisal, though I'd tried to hide my disappointment, she'd sensed that in some way she'd failed to come up to my expectations. In the past four weeks there had been much twining around my legs as I stood at the sink doing the washing up. Much looking up at me with plaintive *miaow* unconnected with the quest for food, and most difficult of all to ignore, the presentation of little gifts in the form of a (fortunately) dead mouse and a goldfish scooped from someone's pond (only half-eaten to underline the sacrifice it had been to give it up).

I was overwhelmed with guilt. She hadn't failed at all! The appraisal had been rigged and her behaviour at the time, the puzzled stare, the bored yawn, had been an understandable reaction to being set to search for substances that were not present.

I jumped up and gathered Gorgonzola in my arms, whispering in her ear, 'Sorry, sorry, sorry, G!'

Gorgonzola purred and licked my hand, surprised, but taking my apologies as well-deserved and as only her due for being falsely accused of something, though she had no idea of what.

Suddenly remembering the silky-furred mouse I'd won in the arcade, I pulled it out of my pocket and dangled it by its tail. She reached up a paw to tap at it. I tossed it onto the carpet. Pounce…swipe…pounce. The soft silky creature was an instant success, the much-chewed rubber version now relegated to ex-favourite.

As I watched her play, I agonised whether at any point I could have exposed Tyler's underhand plan. He had told me outright about his enthusiasm for the electronic EDDA gadget, but no, I couldn't possibly have foreseen that he would stoop so low. Or that Gerry would spot the opportunity to use my resignation to launch a new mission. But now that I knew about the deaths of two agents and the Tenerife informant, I understood just why he had had to resort to these underhand tactics.

For the past months I'd been upset, more than upset, but I had to admire how Gerry had read me like a book after my resignation, knowing I'd react by cutting off all contact with HMRC and leave no means of contacting me.

My eye fell upon the Portobello postcard propped on the mantelpiece. To use me in his planned secret mission, he'd been absolutely certain he could find me. But just *how* had he traced me? Suddenly I had the answer. The inbuilt tracking device hidden in G's collar. I hadn't been out of contact with HMRC at all. For three months Gerry had known exactly where I was!

That reminded me that it had also been three long months since I had asked G to sniff out tobacco. I assumed she could still detect it and give a signal, but no more assumptions for me. I pulled on my coat and hurried round the corner to the newsagent to purchase a packet of cigarettes. This time G would be looking for something that *was* there and I made it as difficult as possible, half a cigarette hidden in the vegetable rack beside some strongly-smelling onions.

So that she would know she was on duty and make a proper effort, I rummaged in a drawer for her working collar, fastened it on, and gave the command 'Search!'

She opened one eye, stretched lazily, and jumped to the floor.

The strong-smelling onions had no effect on her sniffing ability. Within ten seconds a low croon rumbled in her throat. So much for Tyler's, 'No aptitude for detecting the substance.' G was ready for the mission.

I was ready too. Gerry was relying on me and I was *not* going to let him down. I spent the evening memorising the briefing notes of Operation Smokescreen, then as requested, sent Gerry the coded message to set up another clandestine meeting.

CHAPTER FOUR

I hadn't expected a library to be the chosen rendezvous but Gerry Burnside had done his research and Portobello library at this time of day was ideal. The two youths hunched over computer terminals in the far corner and a pensioner reading a newspaper beside the coffee machine were out of earshot, and chatter from the parents' and children's session supplied convenient cover for a private conversation. Gerry in the same disguise as before, was sitting at a table hidden by one of the bookcases making a show of thumbing through some booklets from a cardboard file labelled *Old Portobello*.

'Have a look at this.' He held up a map of 19th-century Portobello then slid it across the table. Hidden underneath was a glossy brochure entitled *Pear Tree Farm Enterprises*, presumably the briefing for Operation Smokescreen. The front cover featured an old farmhouse – grey sandstone walls weathered by the harsh Scottish climate, grey slate roof, grey gravel driveway, and just visible at the rear, grey outbuildings. Standing guard near the front door was a solitary pear tree from which the farm presumably took its name. A couple of out-of-scale pears had been inexpertly inserted courtesy of Photoshop onto one of the three grey-lichened ancient limbs, thick as the trunk itself, that struggled their way skywards in shaky zigzags dwindling to a cluster of wispy twigs.

The text beneath the illustration trumpeted:

A once-in-a-lifetime chance for artists working in a variety of media to experiment and develop their skills! Our renowned Creative Art Centre offers residencies of one to three months at Pear Tree Farm in peaceful countryside a mere short drive from Edinburgh's world famous art galleries and museums.

In answer to my unspoken question, Gerry murmured, 'Intelligence leads us to believe that Pear Tree Farm is in reality a front for the distribution throughout the UK of drugs financed by the proceeds of smuggled tobacco.' He pointed to a black-framed box on page two. 'Read that and comment.'

He has an irritating practice at the start of a mission of asking an agent to deduce from the given information what their undercover role is to be. He calls it 'exercising the brain.' I find this habit of his somewhat tiresome and usually cannot resist appearing to be puzzled, thus forcing *him* to explain. It's a battle of wits as to who surrenders first, a little game that lightens the tension.

To give me time to think up a suitably irritating response, I made a show of thinking deeply about the paragraph.

A unique and exciting feature, offered nowhere else in the U.K. will be the opportunity for our resident artists to submit works for inclusion in our Best of 21st Century Art Exhibition, now touring major cities in the UK and abroad.

I paused with my finger on the word 'artists' and looked up, brow-furrowed. 'I take it my undercover role will be to wave an arty-farty paintbrush about and produce canvases of Jackson Pollock-type random splashes?'

He pursed his lips. 'That is not at all what is envisaged.'

'Ah!' I unfurrowed my brow as if enlightenment had suddenly dawned. 'In the course of a previous mission I actually sold one of Gorgonzola's abstract paintings to an art gallery. It's *her*, not *me*, who is to be the artist! That's it, isn't it?'

Not as silly an answer as it appeared. Gorgonzola is one of those rare cats that can produce abstract works of art. When blank paper and saucers of acrylic paint are put in front of her, if and only if, the mood takes her, she'll dip a paw in the paint and dab it on the paper in random and very pleasing abstract patterns.

A sigh of defeat from Gerry. 'It's not the cat that's to be the artist. It's you.'

'Me?' I exclaimed loudly, drawing from him a warning glance. Now I was genuinely puzzled. 'The sum total of my artistic ability is splattering paint in the style of Jackson Pollock, so if that's not what will be required, what other skill will I have to master?'

'I have enrolled you at the Farm as up-and-coming sculptor Tamsin Kennedy. You seem to have forgotten, Deborah, that on a previous mission you posed as a sculptor by using a ceramic work of art you made yourself. A somewhat bizarre clay statue, if I may say so.' A faint twitch of his lips. 'Supported, of course, by the photographic evidence in your portfolio.'

That ceramic Work of Art had been the disastrous outcome of my beginner's attempt to create an elegant reclining figure in true Greek classical style. It hadn't turned out quite as envisaged.

Suffice to say, Barbara Hepworth, Picasso and Henry Moore would have been proud of it.

He passed over another booklet, the fictional Tamsin Kennedy's portfolio. Beneath my photograph, smiling enigmatically back at me was the White Lady, my first and last attempt at sculpture. The portfolio contained a further eleven photos of statues and other artistic artwork – creations I had never seen before and couldn't hope to replicate. I stared at them with a rising sense of panic.

'But, Gerry,' I hissed, 'my White Lady was a fluke. I couldn't hope to reproduce *anything* like those genuine works of art. My cover will be blown almost immediately.'

'Nonsense, Deborah! With Modern Art anything goes – the more bizarre, the more acclaim. Take as an example, some winners of the Turner prize.'

'But… but…' I thought for a moment, then played my trump card. 'Gorgonzola was trained to sniff out tobacco, presumably especially for this mission, yet I'll have to leave her behind. Pets won't be allowed.'

His smile, not a frown, told me I'd somehow miscalculated. 'If you care to take a look at the Terms and Conditions, you'll see that paragraph 3 states that pets are indeed allowed. This being the case, your artistic ability and your cat's ability to detect drugs and tobacco make you the most suitable agent for the mission. As we discussed, your resignation eliminates the possibility of a leakage from HMRC, and who at the Farm would ever suspect your cat is a sniffer cat?

'One more thing you need to know. Baxter, the maintenance man, is our agent in place at Pear Tree Farm. He is the one I want you to keep an eye on. Let me know if any of his actions could compromise his cover.' He leaned forward. 'Be on your guard, don't take any risks. I remind you that one agent has already died investigating this organisation.' Unhurriedly, he pushed his chair back from the table and walked away. The library doors closed behind him.

I spent the next fifteen minutes leafing through the Old Portobello booklets, but the images on the pages were unseen as I selected and rejected ideas on how best to bring to life the fictional up-and-coming sculptor Tamsin Kennedy. At last, decision made, I swept the booklets back into the folder and made my way back to the Georgian cottage.

Twenty-four hours later I studied my reflection in the bedroom mirror. Goodbye, DJ Smith. Hi there, Tamsin Kennedy! Gone were the unremarkable features and short brown hair of unmemorable, forgettable, undercover DJ Smith. Tamsin Kennedy gazed back at me: blue eye shadow and blue-streaked spiky hair most certainly meriting a second glance. And to complete the wow factor, electric-blue fingernails. I spread my fingers out, studied the effect, and after a moment painted on a zigzag in emerald green. Satisfied, I turned my attention to Gorgonzola.

'You next, G.' I scooped her up and sat her on the chest of drawers. A new name for her… something to do with Art… Picassa, that would do. Now for her appearance… I stared at her thoughtfully. Pedigree ancestor on her mother's side, alley cat on her father's, her moth-eaten coat made her unremarkable, unmemorable, forgettable too – perfect for an undercover cat. But what was needed for this mission was something suitable for the companion of Tamsin Kennedy, a rising star of the sculptural arts, something a little out-of-the-ordinary but easily reversible on occasions when she had to go unnoticed... It would not be easy to give *her* a makeover.

Something arty... Something second-glance-worthy. A dog might accept wearing a jazzy multi-coloured bow or a cotton coat, but cats are sensitive creatures, unwilling to submit to such indignities.

Miaow. She shifted uneasily. No animal likes being stared at. A stare signals the threat of imminent attack – in this case she was expecting a verbal attack, a severe scolding for a misdemeanour not yet discovered. A few minutes of feeling guilty wouldn't do her any harm.

Recalling that some pet owners dyed their pets' coats, I switched on my phone to research the internet on the pros and cons of streaking her fur to match my hair. There were detailed instructions on how to do it. Easy. I smiled. Then I read the footnotes and the smile faded. *Do not attempt to dye the fur of a cat who puts up a fight when washed!* I pursed my lips and contemplated Gorgonzola. If I ignored that warning, I'd end up with dye over me and everything else, and for at least a week afterwards anything I wanted her to do would be met with resistance and non-cooperation.

Footnote 2, printed in bold font, delivered a definite *coup de grâce* to the notion of dyeing her fur: **IMPORTANT.** ***All dyes are potentially harmful to your pet and can even prove fatal. Your cat's well-being should always come first.***

Harmful to your pet! My turn to be overcome with guilt. I cuddled G, pressing my face into her soft coat. Somewhat surprised that she'd escaped the expected scolding, she graciously submitted to my affectionate hug.

What would she consent to wear to fit with my appearance? Her working collar would just have to do. She never made a fuss about wearing it and its miniature transmitter. As I pulled it out of the drawer, it caught on something nestling beside it, a working collar adorned with rubber spikes, specially made for a previous mission. All that would be needed was a small blob of cat friendly air-hardening putty glued onto each spike, each blob painted blue to match my blue hair and makeup. Wearing that, she'd be the perfect companion-pet for an artist. And G wouldn't even notice. I set to work.

That problem solved, I turned my attention to the transformation of the old banger of a car provided by HMRC as a suitable vehicle for a struggling artist. Forgettable, nondescript – in a word, dull. Tamsin Kennedy had other ideas. Clad in overalls, gloves and mask, and with a pile of newspapers under my arm, I headed for the garage where several aerosol cans of brightly coloured car enamels awaited. An hour later, I stood back to survey my handiwork. Little of the original dark blue paintwork was now visible under random streaks and splashes of red, blue, yellow, green and white. Fixed above the headlights were a pair of curved metal 'eyelashes'. Car transformed – or disfigured, according to one's point of view. And definitely not *dull*. If I ever needed a stealth vehicle, I'd contact Gerry for something less memorable.

Me fixed. G fixed. Transport fixed. Tamsin Kennedy was set to go.

CHAPTER FIVE

The tyres of my jazzed-up jalopy crushed a scattering of small wizened pears as I drew up at the front door of Pear Tree Farm with a cheerful *toot toot toot* of the horn. When there was no response, I got out of the car and beat a tattoo on the door with its fox-head knocker. Still no response. I stepped back and scanned the windows. No face looking back at me, the only sign of life a thin curl of grey smoke from one of the two tall chimneys. This was not the welcome I'd expected when I'd supplied the date and time of my arrival. I'd taken it for granted that Mr McClusky, Director of the Centre, would have arranged to have someone here to greet me. There I was again, guilty of making an assumption.

What to do now? No sound of human voices, no barking dog, only the sough of the wind plucking at a few tenacious leaves still clinging to the cluster of wispy twigs at the tip of the pear tree. Nobody about, the perfect excuse for a look around. The blue blobs on G's collar and my blue hair signalling 'artist' rather than 'snooper', I wandered towards the rear of the house and the stone outbuildings presumably now used as studios for the creative artists.

I drew a blank there too. Some of the studio doors stood open, but no sounds of activity drifted from within: no sharp *clink clink* of hammer on metal, no solid *thump* of wooden mallet on chisel, no tinny radio playing as background accompaniment to creative work.

Studio A was equipped with easels, stacks of blank canvases, pots of brushes, palette boards and tubes of paint. A typical artist's studio except for the baskets full of a strange assortment of everyday objects such as shoes, cutlery, and pots and pans. Above the baskets was shelving holding neat rows of spray paint canisters. Nobody there.

With Gorgonzola trailing behind me, I moved on to glance into Studio B, a workshop for stone and wood sculpture. Its heavy-duty tables were layered with grey dust, on the wall a rack of chisels and mallets. Blocks of grey stone were stored on a trolley, someone was in the process of carving a design onto a heavy block of green slate, and sections of tree trunk stripped of bark were stacked on slatted racks in a corner. Nobody here either.

Studio C was a surprise. It was fitted out with kitchen workstations, each equipped with turntable, moulds, bowls and utensils as for a cookery class, including, strangely, a bow-shaped wire cutter like the one I'd used for slicing through lumps of damp clay when working on my White Lady. Packets of fondant icing, foil-wrapped blocks of marzipan, and bottles of food colouring stood on shelves. Everything neat and tidy – and not a soul in sight.

Studio D, the last of the outbuildings, was the ceramic workshop where I'd have to work out how to fashion a striking Work of Art out of a shapeless lump of sticky clay. Occupying the centre of the room was a long, clay-streaked wooden table, and to one side a potter's wheel. Large plastic tubs of glazes and underglazes stood on shelves. Roped off from the rest of the room was a six-foot by four-foot kiln. Rectangular blocks of bagged clay were stacked several layers high against the back wall.

Normally the drying shelves would have held ceramic works waiting for space in the kiln, but these shelves were empty, a sign that a firing must recently have taken place. Curious to see the work of my fellow artists, I checked to make sure the kiln had cooled down before pulling open its heavy door. Empty, but the kiln shelving was evidence that sculptures smaller and lighter than my White Lady were acceptable. That was one less worry. I'm not a quick worker. Creating something the size of the White Lady had taken me three months of trial and error, mainly error, the end result fortunately misconstrued as originality and vision. There'd be no time for anything so large on this mission.

So far I had found nothing out of the ordinary at Pear Tree Farm – apart from the rather puzzling absence of artists, that is.

Miaow. I felt a tug on the lead. G was reminding me that *her* interest lay, not in boring studios, but stalking birds and rodents in the Great Outdoors. In the hope that her sensitive nose might pick up a scent of interest to myself and HMRC when I made a circuit of the house, I released the catch on the retractable lead to allow her freedom to wander ahead of me. Suddenly her ears pricked, she quickened her pace to home in on a large domestic wheeled rubbish bin at the back door. A receptacle like that would be the perfect way to conceal drugs or tobacco for onward transportation. Who would go poking in a rubbish bin smelling strongly of fish? Who would pay any attention to a refuse lorry collecting household trash?

I resisted the temptation to lift the bin lid to inspect the contents as I might be under observation from a hidden camera. It would be folly to risk blowing my cover within half an hour of arriving at the Farm. Sharply retracting G's lead in pretend irritation at her interest in the smelly bin, I attempted to continue on my way. Mistake. Miffed, she sat down on the flagstones and commenced a long, slow stre-e-tch, the cat equivalent of a dog obstinately digging in its heels, the opening shot in a battle of wills that I knew from experience could go on for some time.

'I don't have time for this, G!' I snapped.

Subterfuge followed by a pre-emptive strike was the solution to this impasse, fool her into thinking that she'd won, and that freedom awaited. I unclipped the lead, then pounced and scooped her up. Ignoring her struggles, I marched round to the front door, only loosening my grip in order to beat another fierce tattoo with the fox-head knocker.

Another mistake. Seizing her chance, G leapt from my arms onto an adjacent windowsill. Outwitted, I made a grab for her and pinned her down. With my face close to the glass, I could see clearly into the room. Perched on a chair was a pretty young woman. A sleek cap of brown hair was brushed forward to conceal nose and one eye, focusing attention on the eye, the champagne-pink lips, and the artistically pencilled-in eyebrow. A pink vest, one size too small, enhanced her curves, and skimpy denim shorts showed off her long spray-tanned legs to advantage. Pink toenails peeped through Roman sandals laced up her calves.

The Gorgeous Creature was totally absorbed, headphones plugged into her mobile, eyes fixed on the screen. She might well have been enclosed in a soundproof booth. No surprise that my tattoo on the front door had failed to register. I tried a sharp rap on the window. No effect. A pink-nailed finger continued to tap her thigh to the beat of music from the ether.

Sensing that my thoughts were elsewhere, G took advantage of my relaxed grip, bracing herself against the window preparatory to launching herself over my shoulder for the Great Escape. Under pressure, the hinged window swung inward without warning. With a startled *miaow*, she tumbled into the room, at the last second twisting round to land on her feet. She stared up at me, momentarily disorientated, then pretending her descent into the room had been part of a feline masterplan to attract the attention of the daydreaming Gorgeous Creature, she turned and stalked purposefully towards her. To Gorgonzola, human fingers tapping on a thigh signified an invitation to jump up onto a comfortable and friendly lap. G gathered herself and leapt.

'Aaa-aaah!' Still engrossed in the beat of the music and startled by the sudden arrival of a large well-fed cat on her lap, the girl jumped to her feet. The mobile clattered to the floor, dragging the headphones with it, and for the second time within a minute, G found herself falling to the ground.

'I'm *so* sorry!' I called out. 'Picassa was just trying to make friends.' A gross distortion of the truth. Uppermost in G's mind, I knew, was Comfort.

The girl picked up mobile and headphones and advanced to the window. 'Hi!' The one visible eye sized up my hairdo, the faintest of nods indicating approval. 'I'm Bev. You must be

Tamsin.'

As we shook hands over the window sill, she studied with the expertise of a connoisseur my electric-blue nails with their emerald-green zigzag design. 'Cool job.' A satisfying seal of approval of my DIY makeover. 'Pembrose said you would be arriving this afternoon. Ceramic sculpture, isn't it?'

'That's right,' I said. 'But where *is* everybody? The whole place seems deserted.'

'The art works for the next exhibition to be held at the St Andrew Blackadder Church in North Berwick were chosen this morning so the guys have gone off to celebrate. Except for me, of course.' She plugged the headphones back into the mobile. 'I had the rotten luck to have to stay behind to welcome you. Oh well, suppose I'd better show you to your accommodation.'

But it seemed she was in no hurry to do so. She peered at the screen, frowned, tapped it, peered again, then poked at it with an artificially-long pink nail. 'Shit! Broken.'

Nail or phone? I never found out, for at that moment Gorgonzola jerked the dangling lead out of its socket and leapt out of the window. My ineffectual grab and cries of 'Stop!' only added spice to the game with her new toy. Spotting that the pear tree would be a handy escape ladder from my wrath, she shot up one of the fissured branches trailing the lead behind her and stretched along the highest branch with the lead dangling just out of my reach clamped under a paw.

Spurred on by Bev's wail of, 'These headphones cost a fortune!' I made ineffectual leaps upwards with outstretched hands. G edged back, dragging the headphones further out of reach.

'Come down *at once!*'

The stern glare and tone of command did the trick. Digging her claws into the ridged bark, G edged cautiously down. The headphones, alas, remained up.

I was conscious of the farmhouse door behind me being flung open. Bev materialised beside me, face flushed, the one visible eye glaring furiously at G now sitting at my feet, the picture of innocence. The eye narrowed, signalling the arrival of An Idea. She turned on her heel and stormed back inside. The unmistakable sound of drawers wrenched open and banged shut, a cry of triumph, and she trotted out brandishing a booklet I recognised as Pear Tree Farm Enterprise's Terms & Conditions. The champagne-pink lips compressed into a thin angry line. A long pink nail stabbed down on a page, skewering Condition No. 3.

*Only **well-behaved** pets will be accepted. Any resident who cannot control his or her pet will be required to leave.*

'Oh dear!' I gazed down at G in genuine dismay. 'Is there a ladder somewhere? If we can't retrieve the phones, I'll pay the full price, of course.'

'Well... perha-ps, just perha-ps... I don't need to bring it to Mr McClusky's attention.' Bev looked at me for a long moment, £££ signs flashing up in the beautifully made-up eye as she calculated just how much she could extract from me. 'Two hundred pounds. You see, they're brand new, top of the range... Payment in cash.' She shot out a hand to receive.

'You're so... so...' mercenary sprang to mind, 'understanding!' I fixed on a grateful smile. 'Pay you when I make my first sale.'

Checkmated, realising my offer to pay was as bogus as the inflated price of the headphones, the champagne-pink lips formed into a magnificently petulant pout.

'The artists' rooms are this way.' She flounced off without looking back.

A somewhat chastened G, sensing that she had Gone Too Far, allowed herself to be attached to her lead, and we followed Bev through a gate behind the studios, through a small copse of birch trees, leaves already tinted yellow, and up a gentle rise in the ground. From the top, I looked down upon a picturesque scattering of black yurt-like tents and a wooden boathouse beside a small lake.

She jerked a dismissive thumb in the direction of the yurt nearest the lake. 'Yours is number six. Attached to your yurt is your own private bathroom, with solar-heated shower, sink, and toilet facilities.' Duty grudgingly done, she hurried away, calling over her shoulder, 'Information booklet with meal times and studio times is in the yurt. Jim the maintenance man is somewhere nearby. Just give him a shout if you need anything. Gotta go, things to do.' The slim brown legs hightailed it over the rise and were gone.

I grabbed G and stared her in the eye. 'Well, whatever Bev has in mind to do, it won't be listening to music on her mobile will it? That was very, very naughty of you to make off with her headphones. Unprofessional. In our business we can't afford to stir up animosity that will attract attention to ourselves, can we?' I tapped her blue-bobbled working collar. 'From now on, keep that in mind.'

Her copper eyes opened wide, signifying that try as she might – and she wasn't trying very hard – she understood not a word.

I was surprised to find my yurt had a wooden door fitted

with a proper lock, giving me a welcome sense of security. No hand would unzip the door as I slept. Though the 'room' was in essence a tent, it was cosily furnished with sheepskin rug, a small settee with cushions, and a proper bed with plump duvet. A metal pot, a couple of mugs and plates, and small camping cooker powered by a canister of bottled gas was available for the occasional tea or coffee. Propped against the gas canister, a notice, '*Use sparingly. When it's gone, its gone!*' One oil lamp stood on the table, another on the small chest of drawers. For G's comfort, a cat bed and litter tray had been provided, but after a very cursory inspection, she spurned both. What she had in mind was my duvet for sleeping, the sheepskin rug beside the stove for daytime relaxation, and a patch of soft earth in the Great Outdoors for toilet.

The autumn chill in the air had penetrated to the interior of the yurt in spite of the insulation on the walls. G felt it too. She took up position on the sheepskin rug, pointedly waiting for me to light the wood-burning stove. There didn't appear to be any instructions on how to do that, but it was already set with kindling and paper, so I envisaged no problem. I opened the glass door, lit the paper with the battery-lighter provided and closed the stove door. The flames licked the wood, flickered, and died.

Several attempts later, I gave up. It was probably useless to go in search of Bev. She wouldn't be in a receptive mood to help somebody who had seen through her little extortion scheme and outwitted her. Anyway, I couldn't imagine that Gorgeous Creature ever roughing it in what was, after all, just a tent, getting those perfect hands dirty setting up and lighting the stove. She probably knew as much about it as I did. Accommodation with central heating was more her style. The stove problem did, however, give me the ideal pretext to make the acquaintance of Gerry's agent, maintenance man, Jim Baxter.

I went to the door of the yurt and stood there looking around in the hope I would spot him. No luck. According to Bev, he was working nearby, but there was no answer to my shouts of, 'Hello... Hello... Jim?'

If she was right, there was a good chance he'd be in the boathouse a couple of hundred yards away. I left G busily creating a cosy hollow in my duvet, closed the yurt door and walked over the grass to investigate. A ladder leaning against the side of the boathouse and a brush dipped in a tin of varnish were hopeful signs of a man at work. The door was ajar. I peered inside.

At the far end of the boathouse, the double doors that gave onto the lake were open, framing a view of a fringe of reeds, a small island beyond, and on the grey water several over-wintering black-and-white Barnacle geese.

In contrast with the bright light outside, the interior of the boathouse was a dark cave, the wooden jetty stretching ahead and the rowing boat moored to it, reduced to mere silhouettes. The only sound was the gentle *slap* of water against the wooden piles. It was clear that there was nobody here.

The harsh cries of geese taking flight from the lake startled me. Curious as to what had alarmed them, I wandered towards the end of the jetty, eyes probing for loose boards and other hazards. Despite this precaution, my foot slid on a smear of oil invisible in the dim light. Instinctively I twisted away from the water below, flailing hand clutching at thin air, to lay sprawled on the slatted wooden boards, nose inches from the planking. Through a gap between the boards, I glimpsed the movement of a dark shape in the water, something floating half-submerged.

My first thought was that I'd found a drug cache. A frequented place, yet almost certainly overlooked in the dark, was an ideal way to avoid detection. Underwater, it would be safe even from sniffer dogs – and sniffer cat. An ideal opportunity for Atilla to demonstrate his EDDA machine – but only if it was waterproof. I envisaged Attila snorkelling beneath the jetty, headphones clamped to ears, eyes behind the face mask gleaming with triumph at the chirp, buzz, or robot voice announcing a find.

Head and shoulders leaning out over the edge of the jetty, perilously close to overbalancing, I reached down into water to take a closer look. An inch or two more… my fingers touched, not the expected plastic wrapping, but cloth. I pulled the heavy half-submerged package towards me.

And stared down at a man's face, white in contrast with the sluggish black water. A man in overalls. If this was – had been – Jim Baxter, he wouldn't be responding to my shout.

Or anyone's.

CHAPTER SIX

Baxter's death – accident or murder? With sinking heart I reluctantly came to the conclusion that a fatal accident to yet another HMRC agent was too much of a coincidence. I had to treat his death as murder. Not, of course, that I conveyed the slightest hint of this to the policeman taking my statement.

I recounted in detail how I had slipped on that patch of oil. 'I might very well have ended up like him,' I added tremulously.

What I didn't mention, of course, was that the body had been concealed under the staging, not floating in full view as it had been when the police arrived on the scene.

Daylight was fading fast by the time they had finished examining the boathouse for anything that might suggest that this was anything other than an unfortunate accident. I noted that they seemed to be paying a lot of attention to that smear of oil on the jetty. One police officer went off to interview the returning residents to establish the last sighting of Baxter; another produced a notebook to take down my statement in frustratingly slow longhand.

It was getting dark by the time they'd finished with me. Back at the yurt I lit the oil lamp, my thoughts sombre. It wasn't the shock of discovering a dead body – I'd seen many in my line of work – but the realisation that I'd arrived too late. My mission had been to prevent the death of the agent-in-place, so in a way the mission had already failed. DJ Smith was now the agent-in-place. There was nobody to protect *me*, or to contact Gerry to pull me off the mission. That was what I had to concentrate on. I had to be very careful.

Tonight's shared meal in the farmhouse would enable me to study the reactions of my fellow artists and the Pear Tree Farm management to Baxter's death and pick up on any undercurrents while the news still had its shock value.

Safety first. Before hurrying off, I put out the oil lamp, then locked the door, leaving G engaged in an energetic wash and brush-up – no light needed for that – and switched on the torch provided courtesy of Pear Tree Farm Enterprises.

In the faint light still lingering in the sky, the waters of the lake glimmered, a pale patch on my left. The black yurts to my right were barely visible, indistinct shapes in the dark. I made my way over the hill, picked my way along the stony path that wound down among the pale trunks of the birches, and passing by the darkened studios, headed towards squares of warm light spilling from the un-curtained windows at the rear of farmhouse.

The back door stood open. Spaghetti with a meaty sauce was apparently on the menu tonight. A murmur of voices came from behind a door at the far end. I never pass by an opportunity to eavesdrop, so I didn't immediately announce my arrival, but slipped inside. Careful to make no betraying sound, I hung my jacket among the coats hanging on pegs on both sides of the narrow hall.

A man's voice rose above the murmur of conversation in the kitchen. 'Before Vic reveals what he has cooked for us tonight, may I have your attention for a moment. I'm afraid I've bad news.'

I had come at exactly the right time to judge reactions.

'Very bad news, I'm afraid.' The chatter stopped abruptly. 'I'm sorry to have to tell you that Jim Baxter died in a tragic accident at the boathouse this afternoon.'

The announcement was greeted with gasps, exclamations of 'How awful!' and 'What happened?'

'Drowned, it seems. That's all I can tell you. The only other information I have is that he was found by Tamsin Kennedy, who has just signed up for a residency here. She'll be joining us for the meal tonight, and will perhaps be able to give us more details.'

Cue to make an entrance, but I couldn't let them suspect I'd been standing outside the kitchen door listening. Again, careful to make no sound, I retreated down the hall to close the back door with a bang. To get the timing right, I mimed putting my coat on the peg, then advanced along the hall, opened the kitchen door and paused, framed in the doorway. The faces turned towards me exhibited a range of reactions to the news of Baxter's death, ranging from avid curiosity to barely concealed indifference.

A middle-aged man in tweed jacket, the very image of a dapper 1940s film star with his neatly trimmed moustache, slicked-back unnaturally black hair, and red cravat at throat, was on his feet to address the group round the table.

He turned towards me. 'Ah, Tamsin, I presume. There you are. I'm Pembrose McClusky, Course Director. Everyone knows me as PM. I was just informing them that you were the first on the scene of poor Jim's demise. A *most* unfortunate start to your stay with us.' Relishing that he was still the centre of attention, he adjusted the cravat at his throat and looked solemnly round the table.

Why did I get the impression that the death of Baxter meant little more to McClusky than the inconvenience of finding a new maintenance man?

If Jim Baxter's killer *was* one of those seated at the table, his – or her – main concern would be to find out if I shared the police view that Baxter's death was an accident, hoping that it had not crossed my mind that his death could have been anything other than that. But whoever was responsible for the murder had taken care to hide the body under the staging. Would he – or she –accept that the constant movement of the water must have moved the position of the body into full view?

'It was an awful shock when I found him,' I said, allowing a tremor to creep into my voice. 'I'd gone looking for him in the boathouse to ask him how to light the stove. After the bright light outside, the boathouse was dark so I didn't notice the smear of oil on the jetty till I slipped on it. That's what must have happened to Mr Baxter, he must have been knocked out and then fallen into the water.'

Expression is not a reliable guide as to what is going on in the mind, but body language can reveal a lot. Was that a flash of relief in the eyes of the grey-haired man sitting to my right? An infinitesimal lessening of tension in the shoulders of that bearded young man with retro tortoiseshell-framed glasses? A relaxation of the tense face muscles of the woman next to him? An unclenching of Bev's exquisitely manicured hands? Was that the whisper of pent-up breaths released? I couldn't be sure.

McClusky measured out a sigh to the appropriate length for the occasion. 'A dreadful happening, dreadful, *dreadful*! Poor Jim will be sorely missed. One minute here, and the next gone! Who can foretell the day the Grim Reaper will tap one on the shoulder?' He directed his gaze up at the raftered ceiling as if expecting a summons from On High. No answer being forthcoming that revealed an imminent visit from the Grim Reaper, he heaved a heavy sigh. 'But in this, the darkest of events, there's a ray of light. There will not be any further disruption to the creative activity of Pear Tree Farm. The police have thoroughly investigated, and have informed me that, though there will have to be a post-mortem, in their opinion Jim Baxter's death was a very tragic accident.'

Of one thing I was sure, the post-mortem would find no suspicious injuries, they'd have made sure of that.

McClusky pulled out the vacant chair beside him. 'Sit down, Tamsin. Of course you've already met our lovely secretary Bev, and round the table we have the artists who beaver away in their respective studios to come up with the *avant-garde* art for which Pear Tree farm is so justly renowned. It's first names here, no standing on ceremony. Allow me to make the introductions – on second thoughts, you'll get a better idea if they introduce themselves. You first, Carol. Tamsin will be sharing the ceramic studio with you.'

The woman half-rose, what could have been a pretty face instantly set in a belligerent scowl of discontent, hands pressing on the table to emphasise the strength of her opposition. 'First *I've* heard about sharing my studio with someone, PM.' She stared at me with narrowed eyes. 'Look here, Tamsin. I'll not hide from you the fact that I don't want to share with someone who might steal my creative ideas and pass them off as her own. Is that clear?'

My heart sank. Working in the same studio with someone like that wasn't going to be easy. Never-the-less, allowing her to dictate how we worked together would be a big mistake.

I stared coolly back. 'My work is experimental, decidedly *avant-garde* in its field, and publicly acclaimed. *Nobody* could mistake your work for mine.' Hanging in the air was, 'Your work is rubbish in comparison with mine.'

Wrong-footed by my unexpected counter-attack, and unable to come up with a cutting reply, she rose from her seat with a scornful, 'Hmph!' and stalked slowly towards the door, ensuring that her exit would be the target of all eyes.

In an attempt to soothe, McClusky called after her retreating back, 'I'm quite *sure* that copying your work won't be an issue, my dear Carol. Your work is quite distinctive, instantly recognisable. Any such attempt would be easily detected. And of course, an artist guilty of this practice would be required to leave Pear Tree Farm without refund of fees. What we aim for here at Pear Tree Farm is friendly rivalry, competition, a sparking-off of creative talent, so–'

The kitchen door slammed in unmistakable answer, followed two seconds later by the back door in audible reinforcement.

'Well… er… must make allowance for artistic temperament.' McClusky moved smoothly into gear again, waving a hand towards a woman with high cheekbones, sallow complexion, her black hair drawn tightly back from her face. 'And this is Dolores, our artist in oils and acrylics.'

She smiled a welcome. 'My de-a-h, I'm very pleased to meet with you.' Long-drawn-out vowels of Southern Counties England overlaid with the trace of a foreign accent.

McClusky indicated those sitting on the other side of the table. 'Over there are our three sculptors. They work in different media – Neil in stone, Stu in wood, and Madge in sugarcraft. Her work, of course, is just as… er… er… sculptural in its way as carving in wood and stone.'

Stu grinned. 'But a lot less permanent! Mice aren't going to eat *our* work, are they! Her Edinburgh Castle looked like it had taken a bombardment by cannonballs!'

Tears glistened in Madge's eyes. Her hands clenched. 'It was the best piece of work I've–' Voice trembling, she jumped up and ran from the room.

Anguish or rage? Understandable her distress over a piece of work ruined, understandable too, her anger at an unfeeling remark, but what interested me was why Stu had deliberately made a remark he knew would upset her. We heard her footsteps running along the hall followed by the click of the back door closing.

Dolores leapt to Madge's defence. '*You*'d be upset too, Stu, if some idiot made a joke about you discovering woodworm in one of the blocks you'd spent hours working on. So if you aren't a heartless bastard, go after her and make it up.'

'Women! Can't take a joke.' He ran his hand through his hair, scraped back his chair and stomped out of the room slamming the kitchen door with such force that the crockery on the dresser rattled.

She sighed. 'So childish! In that mood he'll only make matters worse.' She looked round the table. 'Go and make sure she's all right, Beverley.'

'It's *Bev*, not Beverley! How often do I have to tell you? Anyway, why *me*?' A disgruntled pout.

'A woman needs a woman's support, my dear Beverley. That's why. Off you go!'

Bev made no move to comply, instead spread her fingers to study each nail in a search of imperfections, then after a long moment, conscious of Dolores' steely gaze, lost her nerve, rose from the table, and flounced off. For a third time the kitchen door slammed, again the crockery rattled and danced.

I sat down at the table having noted the clash of personalities and the underlying tensions, but it was only later that I realised that Stu's unkind remark had been cleverly stage-managed for a purpose.

McClusky broke the awkward silence. 'Mustn't keep the cook waiting! Five servings will be enough, Vic.'

'Ok, grub's up!' The young man who had been stirring a large pot on the stove began ladling out spaghetti Bolognese onto a line of plates on the worktop.

McClusky turned to me. 'I omitted to introduce Vic, did I not? His artistic expertise is in the creation of amazing Wall Art from everyday objects. We have a resident chef, of course, but on Sundays the artists take it in turn to cook the evening meal. It nourishes the family atmosphere we pride ourselves in having created at Pear Tree Farm.' Then recalling the far from happy family atmosphere of the past few minutes, he shook his head sorrowfully and added, 'Unfortunately, as in any family, these little hiccups of Artistic Temperament occasionally erupt.'

While we ate, my companions' attention was on questioning me about my artistic background and experience. That posed no problem. I was confident that my cover story was foolproof. Gerry Burnside's setting-up of my new identity had been painstakingly thorough.

* * *

A shadowy figure slid the master key into the yurt's door. After the tip-off from Tenerife to the Farm two months ago warning of HMRC's interest in Pear Tree Farm Enterprises, steps had been taken to increase security, set traps for newcomers. It was standard security now to vet all new arrivals, the slightest suspicion enough.

Tamsin Kennedy had to be checked out while she was safely out of the way in the supper room, eating with the others and regaling them with her highly embroidered account of how she'd found Baxter's body. Baxter was the latest of three infiltrators, possibly HMRC agents, to have been uncovered. How many times had the silly sod been told to wipe up spills of engine oil lying on the jetty! That had provided the perfect means to kill him, make it look as if he'd been the victim of his own carelessness. Fortunate that Kennedy came along and slipped on the oil making an accident only to be expected. Certainly the police seemed satisfied that there were no suspicious circumstances. The downside was that Baxter's necessary death had drawn unwelcome attention to Pear Tree Farm.

At the sound of the key in the yurt lock, Gorgonzola's ears twitched. One eye opened, then the other. Warily she watched the dark shape of an intruder move about the yurt. Her eyes half-closed. Unnoticed, she uncurled from her snug nest in the folds of the duvet, slunk across the floor, nudged the door open a fraction and slipped out into the night, a shadow merging with the shadows.

Careful to leave no trace, the intruder searched through Kennedy's belongings. She appeared to be exactly what she said she was. Photo driving licence, Pottery Users' card for South Bridge Centre Edinburgh, bag of pottery tools, plastic apron, ring-binder with photographs of ceramic art, wooden rolling pin carefully bubble-wrapped for protection. And a small holdall of food tins for the cat. No sign, however, of the creature. Kennedy must have let out it out when she left for the meal.

The intruder's eyes roamed round the yurt for a final time. There was nothing out of the usual here, but that was only to be expected if Kennedy was, in fact, an HMRC agent. It would pay to keep tabs on the newcomer.

* * *

I looked round the kitchen table at the others. As if to make conversation, I said idly, 'Madge, Stu and Bev, haven't returned. Thought they'd be starving by now.'

My comment was met with unconcerned shrugs. Outbursts of highly-strung artistic temperament, it seemed, were only to be expected at Pear Tree Farm. A promising lead, however, was Dolores. Judging by the way she had skilfully taken control of the volatile situation, she was the one most likely to have a management role in the drug organisation here. I put her at the top of my list.

At nine o'clock, pleading the need to settle myself in, and declining an invitation to spend the rest of the evening with the others in a nearby village, I made my way back to the yurt pondering the significance of the evening's events. Those demonstrations of volatile artistic temperament had its pluses and minuses. They could be exploited for my own ends, but they had a downside too. Carol's aggressive attitude to sharing a studio with me, for instance. I'd have to be careful. She'd keep me under surveillance, eager to find fault with anything I said and did, an undercover agent's nightmare.

As I left behind the birch trees and topped the rise in the ground, I caught my breath. A huge orange-tinged Hunter's Moon had risen, poised low in the sky, as if finely balanced on the jet-black waters of the lake. For the moment all thoughts of temperamental artists, difficulties and dangers ahead shelved, I sat on a rock, mesmerised.

After a time I noticed that the perfect orange circle had developed a tiny black notch in the lower edge. It was as if I was witnessing a lunar eclipse. As I stared, the notch elongated, and I realised what I was seeing was the silhouette of a small boat coming from the direction of the island and moving slowly and silently towards a promontory further up the lake. That there was no sound of engine or paddles puzzled me at first, until I recalled the hand-winched cables used in remote parts of the world to transport goods over canyons and rivers. Was such a device in use now? It made sense. There'd be no engine or oars to draw unwelcome attention.

I took out my phone, set it at maximum magnification and captured the image. Too risky to investigate tonight while the boat operation was in progress. Careful planning was needed. I'd wander along the banks of the lake with G sometime during the day and see what traces I could find.

Elated that I'd made a possible breakthrough in my first few hours at Pear Tree Farm, I hurried back to the yurt. I'd left Gorgonzola contentedly engaged in a wash and brush-up, but after she'd been left so long in a strange place, what kind of welcome would I get? No welcome at all, as it turned out. I unlocked the door and with the aid of my torch located the oil lamp and lit it.

'Here I am, G,' I called.

In the yellow glow cast by oil lamp, nothing moved. I knew exactly where she'd be, on the bed, snuggled into the duvet. Wrong. There was a cat-shaped hollow, but no cat. She'd be hiding, one of her tactics when displeased. Wrong again. It took only a couple of minutes to search the limited furnishings of the yurt. No sign of her.

I stood for a moment, thinking it over. She hadn't rushed out, brushing against my legs as I opened the door, so there had to be a hole in the yurt wall somewhere. I made a circuit of the interior directing my torch low down on the walls. And there was indeed a small cat-sized gap where the wooden doorframe joined the fabric of the yurt. Mystery solved, I gave it no further thought. When she was ready, she'd come back by the way she'd got out.

It had been a long day, and I was ready for bed, even if G wasn't. Finding Baxter's body and fielding the questions at the evening meal had taken its toll, and I'd need to be up well before the 8 a.m. breakfast to prepare for my first session in the ceramic studio – ready for skirmishes, if not open warfare, with the disgruntled Carol.

Unfortunately sleep didn't come. My brain was too active, Baxter's death foremost in my mind. I acknowledged the fact that when agents take on an assignment, they accept the risk of injury or even death. Yet I felt guilty that my main emotion was relief that the drug and tobacco organisation had uncovered and eliminated Baxter. It lessened the danger to me.

Some time in the night, a tentative scratch at the door and a quiet *miaow* signalled the return of Gorgonzola. 'Surely you can come in by the way you got out, G,' I muttered, desperate for sleep. I pulled the duvet closer round me and made no move to let her in.

A short time later I was aware of a thump on the bed, followed by paws trampling on the duvet. At last I drifted off to sleep, safe in the thought that they certainly wouldn't expect another agent to be already in place at Pear Tree Farm.

CHAPTER SEVEN

My first full day as ceramic sculptor started off badly and continued on a steeply downward path. When I woke, opening a bleary eye, it took a few moments to realise that the bright rays seeping through the thin curtain covering the acrylic window were considerably stronger than the feeble grey light to be expected at the time I'd set on the alarm. I pulled the clock towards me. I'd overslept by an hour. So much for my plan to be at work in the ceramic studio before Carol put in an appearance. The first rule of undercover work is to appear to be no threat at all, not draw attention to oneself in any way. Up till now the studio had been Carol's domain with no one to oppose her slightest wish – and judging by the brief contact I'd had with her last night, there wasn't likely to be a U-turn in her attitude. I'd intended to be rolling out my clay when she arrived, sure that she would insist on taking more than her fair share of the worktable. I'd raise no objection though the restricted space would make it more difficult for me to work my clay. By giving in meekly, she'd think I was easily dominated.

Late as it was now, there was still a chance I'd arrive at the studio before Carol. I flung aside the duvet, tipping Gorgonzola without warning onto the floor. And that put two of us in a bad mood, so though I was prepared to skip breakfast, *she* was not, making that clear with plaintive yowls, and deliberately hindering my every movement by twining herself round my legs. I rummaged in the holdall for a tin of cat food and gave an impatient yank at the ring-pull. It snapped off in my hand leaving the lid raised by a useless centimetre. To jemmy it fully open with the handle of a spoon took more precious minutes. I scooped the contents onto G's dish, grabbed up the holdall of pottery kit, and while she was crouched over the dish, rushed out, locking the door. In my haste completely forgetting about the small exit-entry hole in the yurt wall.

By the time I reached the grove of birches I regretted not having taken the time to put on a thick jacket. In the cold northerly wind the thin branches shook as if they too were shivering, their yellow leaves drifting down to carpet the ground. It would take only ten minutes to go back, but in that ten minutes Carol could well have taken possession of the studio and arranged the workspace to her advantage. Decision made. Shivering was a small price to pay if I could arrive first, stake a claim to a fair share of the worktable, then allow her to commandeer most of it. Ignoring pangs of hunger, I reluctantly bypassed the farmhouse kitchen with its waiting breakfast.

Despite this sacrifice, my day continued on its downward path. Twenty yards from Studio D, the loud regular *thump thump thump* of clay thrown down on a board to expel air told me I was too late. Carol had beaten me to it and was already at work conditioning clay for her next sculpture.

As I stepped through the door, I switched to Plan B. From my arsenal of expressions, I selected 'friendly smile', designed to disarm her last night's hostile 'don't want to share', 'steal my creative ideas and pass them off as your own'. She looked up and thumped the clay down with vicious force, her scowl colliding head-on with my 'friendly smile'. For a moment we sized each other up. I dropped my gaze.

Walk-over detected, with a triumphant smirk she pushed several lumps of prepared white clay onto the already inadequate area of worktable she had allocated to me, positioning herself over four-fifths of the area. Her selfish worktop grab had taken possession of the territorial high ground, leaving barely a foot of work-surface for me.

'But–' I stuttered as an indication that I didn't dare protest, then forced a smile. 'Do you think you'd have time to show me round the studio?'

She pursed her lips as if considering. 'No. To somebody who *claims* to have knowledge of pottery, the equipment needs no explanation.' *Thump.* Another wodge of clay hit the board.

'You're right,' I said, and she was. It was an odd request for a supposedly experienced potter to have made. In an effort to cover up my mistake, I said the first thing that came into my mind. 'It's just that I'm used to more up-to-date equipment.' Frowning, I looked round the studio. 'Something less primitive, for instance, than that cheese-wire with toggle handles you've been using to cut these lumps from the bag of clay.'

I delved into the holdall and with the flourish of a magician producing a rabbit from a hat, produced an impressively large bow-shaped pottery saw. Alas, Carol's flushed face told me that I'd made matters worse, much worse, by implying that it was not professional to be satisfied with cheap and obsolete equipment.

On the fraction of work-surface left for me, I dumped my

holdall, zipped it open, and placed alongside the pottery saw, the rolling pin in its protective sleeve, the plastic apron, and an assortment of tools.

In a hasty effort to re-establish my role of easily pushed-about doormat, I gave her another chance to boss me. 'I wonder, Carol, would it be possible to move your clay, just a fraction, to give me space for what I've got in mind?'

I was relying on the fact that she definitely wouldn't agree, and I was right. No reply. As far as she was concerned, there was to be no ceding of territory. *Thump*. Another wodge of clay hit the board, invading even more of my allotted space while her other lumps of clay stayed exactly where they were. Just as I'd foreseen.

'Of course, I was wrong to ask,' I said meekly. 'I see you need all the space you've got. Well, I suppose I could change my project to something with a small footprint.' I had in fact, nothing in mind, nothing in mind at all.

In search of inspiration, I sauntered over to the rectangular blocks of bagged clay stacked several layers high against the back wall and read the labels. *Raku... Porcelain... Stoneware... White Earthenware... Terracotta.* Which of these would it be best to use with my very basic sculpture skills? Something easy enough for me to handle, something that didn't need any additional colour or glaze for the finished statue. In a word, something that wouldn't betray how much of a novice I was. It had to be the red terracotta – cheap, cheerful, fired to a thousand degrees, less likely to have problems in the kiln, no further finishing required.

I heaved the bag of terracotta clay onto the worktop, transferred everything except the bowsaw, coiling tool, and the plastic apron back into the holdall, and placed it on the floor. 'That's it! I'm off for breakfast now.' Pretending not to see Carol's triumphant smile, I headed for the farmhouse kitchen in search of breakfast and inspiration.

While I ate, I feverishly tried to think of the Work of Art that would convince everyone at Pear Tree Farm that I was a genuine sculptor. Something modern would do the trick. Something modern with tactile curves not too difficult for my unskilled hands to create. I'd pass off any infelicities as creative inspiration. Who dares to point a scornful finger at a Picasso, a Hepworth, or a Henry Moore?

Under the impression that my day had taken a turn for the better, I returned to the studio to start work on Earth Mother – a bosomy Sitting Figure with massive thighs. I'd told Carol that I'd be working on something with a small footprint, but a massive bum-print was what I now had in mind.

Her mood had not improved in my absence. Sweat-stained t-shirt and moist brow were evidence of energy expended in strenuous physical activity with a rolling pin to convert the lumps of clay on the worktop to centimetre-thick, perfectly smooth white sheets.

I chose the path of appeasement by resisting the temptation to remark on the lack of a labour-saving rolling machine. Too provocative, most importantly, counter-productive for Operation Smokescreen, and only a temporary satisfaction. Once a confirmed enemy, she would make it her business to catch me out, putting my cover at risk.

'My, you *have* been busy!' I cried in fake admiration. 'Wish I could accomplish as much in so short a time.' I slit open the bag of red clay.

My conciliatory remark fell on stony ground. 'I'm off for breakfast. Just watch what you do with that red clay, Tamsin. Even a single spot will ruin *all* my work!' She stomped off leaving her eight clay sheets to harden.

I set to work. Not for me the energetic kneading and rolling that had taken so much effort out of Carol. I'd build up Earth Mother from coils. With the saw I sliced the terracotta block in half to check for air pockets and applied the coiling tool in a sweeping movement to produce a neat sausage of clay.

It was more than a trifle unfortunate that the sweeping motion was a tad too sweeping, for the upward flick of the tool sent a fragment of red clay flying with deadly accuracy to target Carol's nearest rolled out white sheet.

Panic-stricken, I stared at the vile red splodge embedded in the pristine white clay. She'd think I'd done it deliberately! I stared in horror at the incriminating red mark. She'd be a dangerous enemy if she saw what I'd done.

A few calming deep breaths later, I found a solution. The terracotta fragment had landed close to the edge of one of her sheets. If I were, oh so carefully, to cut a tiny bit off its edge… Of course, I wouldn't make the mistake of doctoring only that one sheet. All of them would have to be the same size. With the aid of a paper template, ten minutes was all it took. I surveyed my work: eight white clay sheets now the same size, red mark eliminated, incriminating cut-offs discarded in the used-clay bin, contaminated piece washed away down the sink. Placidly, I resumed work on the construction of Earth Mother's massive thighs.

* * *

Gorgonzola's day, too, began badly and continued on its downward path. One moment, she was snoozing gently on the soft duvet. The next, she was sailing through the air to land with a thud on the hard wooden floor of the yurt. No apologies given, breakfast frustratingly delayed by that bungled attempt to open her food tin... All that was bad enough, but then to be sneakily abandoned, shut in the yurt while head in bowl, deprived of her early morning toilet-cum-hunting expeditions in the Great Outdoors, and expected to use that unsavoury litter tray! Enough was enough. With a sinuous wiggle she slipped out through the small gap in the fabric of the yurt, and tracking DJ's scent, headed up the hill.

* * *

The massive thighs had gained an impressive circumference by the time the rattle of the door handle alerted me to Carol's return. Without taking time to close the door against the cold wind, she rushed in. For a heart-stopping moment, she stood, head on one side, inspecting her clay sheets for contamination by red clay. She pursed her lips. Would she notice the sheets were that teeny bit smaller than she'd left them? Clay shrinks slightly as it dries. I held my breath.

'Needs to harden a bit more.' She plugged in a hairdryer and directed the warm air in wide sweeping motions over the clay.

I'd got away with it! After that bad start, it seemed that my day was at last taking a turn for the better.

She switched off the hairdryer and came over to cast a critical eye over my work. 'Coils, eh?' A disparaging sniff. 'You're taking the easy way, I see, by not carving your... er... whatever it is directly from the original block.' She wandered off in the direction of the tubs of coloured underglazes.

My day was about to hit rock bottom.

Miaow.

I looked down to see Gorgonzola crouched to leap up onto the worktable.

'No!' Dropping the coiling tool, I jumped to my feet.

'No-o-o-o!' Carol rushed across the room, hands outstretched to protect the work on which she had laboured so long.

Too late, much too late. My frantic grab for G failed to intercept her perfect four-paw touchdown on the worktable – or to be horribly precise – on one of Carol's pristine clay sheets.

Sensing retaliation, Gorgonzola made a swift getaway across the remaining sheets and was gone.

'*Ruined*! All ruined!'

Carol and I gazed in mutual horror at the perfect imprints of feline paws on the soft white clay.

CHAPTER EIGHT

So much for this morning's plan to ingratiate myself with Carol by doing nothing to offend her. It had all gone spectacularly wrong.

I let out a genuinely anguished cry of, 'Is there *anything* I can do?' If I had judged her character correctly, abject apologies would give her the opportunity to take revenge. I was right.

A vicious hissed, 'You can indeed!' Dumping the spoiled clay sheets into the recycle bin, she snarled, 'Bring over the two bags over there.' Arms folded she watched me struggle to drag the heavy bags across the floor and heave them up onto the work surface. 'Now, cut them up into eight equal pieces with that fancy saw of yours and–' She stopped, a slow, mean smile flitted across her face. 'No, just to let you understand how *much* effort I put into it this morning, all *wasted* thanks to you, instead of your fancy saw, use the cheese-wire, 'primitive' I think you called it. Next task, condition the clay – and don't imagine you can get away with skimping on that. I'll watch to ensure you use enough force to expel *all* the air so that nothing explodes in the kiln. If it does, you'll have to do *everything* all over again.'

I recalled her sweat-stained t-shirt, face red and perspiring from thumping down the clay while I was at breakfast. That was one demand too far. At first I had no intention of obeying. Potters usually regard accidental damage to their pottery by other users as unintentional, are annoyed, but not vindictive. But the mission took priority. With an effort I hid my resentment, bit back my angry retort, and meekly set to work with the cheese-wire to cut out blocks of clay.

The long hour of hard labour that followed established me in her eyes as a pushover, a doormat, and therefore no threat. Carol stood there, arms folded, snapping, 'Harder! Harder!' when she considered I wasn't thumping down the wodges of clay on the board with enough force.

The silver lining of the whole disastrous incident was that from now on I should be able to poke about the pottery studio without her paying much attention. Definitely worth a few aching muscles to be considered a person of no account, to be out-of-mind if not out of sight!

That afternoon I sat in the doorway of the yurt, arm muscles aching, coming to the conclusion that the residential courses here *must* be a key part of the contraband operation. How many of the artists were knowingly involved? All, some, or merely one? Try as I might, I couldn't yet understand why all the creative artists, with the exception of Dolores, were sculptors in one form or another. I hoped to find the answer by paying a visit to the studios to study their work in progress. Now was not the moment, however, as artists engrossed in their work do not welcome interruptions. I'd mosey along in another couple of hours when they might welcome an offer of help with the time-consuming business of tidying up.

The nearby lake and the island were likely to be a drugs or tobacco cache for distribution throughout Scotland. I shifted my gaze to the distant promontory, the destination of the little boat I'd seen last night gliding silently from the island. A wander along the lakeside to the promontory might uncover a pulley mechanism or storage for cargo. Of course, I'd need a reason for being there. After a moment's thought, I had it. By now Carol would have made a point of telling everyone in lurid detail about this morning's disaster and of how she'd chased the brute Picassa from the pottery. It was only to be expected that I'd be searching everywhere for a lost cat who had run off in a panic. In actual fact, of course, G was neither frightened nor lost. I knew exactly where she was. She was lying on my bed congratulating herself on the slickness of her getaway.

But I couldn't risk another incident like that. There'd be no more wandering without permission. On my release from durance vile in Carol's pottery studio, the first thing I'd done was to call in at the farmhouse, borrow a staple gun from Bev and close up the gap at the door frame of the yurt. There'd be no more Houdini escapes for G.

With cat lead dangling ostentatiously from my hand, I set off along the banks of the lake. The short grass in the vicinity of the yurts soon gave way to knee-high grass, scrub, and a scattering of juniper bushes. Stopping at intervals to shout, 'Come here, Picassa!' or 'Picassa, where are you?' I walked some distance past the promontory. In case binoculars might be trained on me, I made a detour inland as if it was of no interest to me whatsoever, then stood for a moment looking around, hands on hips, compressed lips expressing irritation. Hoping I'd done enough to allay suspicion from watching eyes, I turned back, this time heading towards the edge of the lake and the promontory.

Five minutes later, I stood on the edge of a steep bank, looking down on a tall cylindrical water tank open to the sky, its surface rippled by the wind. A narrow pipe ran across the strip of pebbles to supply it with water from the lake. Beside the tank was a small hut, its flat roof camouflaged by turf. Mere coincidence that the hut was so conveniently screened from the distant yurts by the stand of slender-trunked birches on the promontory? I'm not a believer in coincidence.

'Is that you hiding down there, Picassa?' I scrambled down the steep banking and slithered to a halt on the pebbly foreshore. No boat tied up here, it was probably moored on the far side of the island or hidden among reeds as the hut was not big enough to hold it. The door's large heavy-duty padlock supported my theory that the hut was the storage point for smuggled goods. I'd sneak back later with G and let her nose tell me if I was right.

This decided, I turned my attention to the thought that the hut had another purpose. There'd been no engine noise as the mysterious boat had crossed from the island to this point, raising the possibility that the boat was cable-drawn, powered from a winch sited in the hut. If so, the cable essential to provide underwater traction for the boat would stretch across the pebbles into the lake at this point. No sign of it, no sign at all. Was I building up a theory that had no substance? Just wishful thinking? Could it be that there *was* no link between hut and boat.

In frustration I kicked at the pebbles, picked one up and threw it into the lake. It sank with a rather satisfying *splash*. I bent to pick up another. That long shallow groove at the water's edge… Could it have been made by the keel of a boat? Thoughtfully, I traced along the shallow gouge with my finger.

Behind me, 'Looking for something are you?' A man's voice, heavy with suspicion.

I had a split second to decide how to react: a startled cry could indicate someone caught where they knew they shouldn't be. So I didn't turn round, just a laugh as if I wasn't at all alarmed that someone had found me here. 'Looking for a flat stone to skim across the lake. Watch this!'

I selected a suitable one, held it at what I judged to be the correct angle, and sent it hopping *plop…plop…plop* across the water leaving a neat line of concentric rings marking its passage. Only then did I turn round. Standing looking down at me from the top of the banking was the tall figure of the wood sculptor, Stu. Turning up here at the same time as myself was worrying. If he *had* followed me here, someone had seen through my pretence of searching for my cat, and I'd aroused further suspicion by entering a 'red' zone.

'Impressive!' Stu smiled and nodded his head in seeming appreciation of my stone-skimming skill. The glint from the round lenses of his glasses hid whether the smile reached his eyes. He scrambled down the slope to join me on the pebble beach. 'Thought you'd be hard at work in the studio?'

'Oh well.' I shrugged. 'Couldn't face Carol so soon after this morning's disaster. You'll have heard about it?'

He nodded. 'Who hasn't!' A slight upward turn of his mouth indicated amusement.

'You asked me if I was looking for something, and yes, I am.'

Definitely not the sort of admission a snooper would make.

How would he react?

No narrowing of eyes indicating suspicion confirmed, merely eyebrows raised in polite enquiry.

'My cat ran off when Carol threw the rolling pin at her.' Only a slight embroidery of the truth – Carol certainly would have done so, if there'd been time. 'Poor Picassa will be cowering somewhere, afraid to come out. I'm so *worried*. You haven't seen her, have you?'

'Nope. My eyes were on the ground on the lookout for driftwood or old juniper bushes for my next project.' He looked up and down the shoreline. This is a good spot. Wind and current usually bring in something, you know, but no luck today here either.'

Was this friendly ease of manner as much an act as mine? There was no soil or mud on his hands, but there wouldn't be if he hadn't found anything to pick up and examine.

With no convincing reason for lingering here to examine that groove on the beach more closely, and wade into the shallow water in search of a submerged chain, I turned to make my way up the bank. 'Well, I'm heading back to the yurt. I'll just have to hope my cat will be sitting there waiting for me.'

He didn't offer to accompany me. When I looked back he was following slowly some distance behind. Was he keeping tabs on me, making sure I really intended doing what I'd said?

Stu, someone to beware of? I couldn't decide.

CHAPTER NINE

As I approached the yurt, Gorgonzola was not outside waiting for me. She'd still be snoozing on the duvet. Locked in the yurt she was safely out of sight, but when she sensed my presence, there would undoubtedly be very audible mews from inside which would expose my 'lost cat' story as a complete fabrication to Stu a mere two hundred yards behind me. For a moment I stood, hands on hips as if in exasperation that the cat hadn't turned up, then without a backward glance set off at a brisk pace up the gentle hill towards the studios, hoping I'd fooled Stu into thinking that I had no idea of her whereabouts.

Now to put into operation the second part of today's plan. I'd offer other artists help in tidying up for the day, giving me the opportunity to find out more about them and poke about their studios. The last person I wanted to meet was Carol, and to my relief, the door of Studio D pottery was closed. I scurried past and moved on to Madge's Studio C. I had a hunch that there was more involved in the destruction of the cake sculpture than damage by mice. Why had she been so *very* upset last night about her wrecked sugar-icing sculpture? Providing a sympathetic ear might throw light on the undercurrents at the dinner table.

I poked my head round the door. Madge in regulation kitchen-wear white trousers and jacket, hair now tidily confined in a net, was standing with her back towards me at the sink stacking dishes on the draining board.

'Need a hand to clear up?' I called out.

She didn't reply or turn round to see who her visitor was, but continued lifting dishes from the water. The fast-running water drumming on stainless steel and the clatter of dishes had masked the sound of my voice. I crossed the room and touched her lightly on the shoulder.

'Oh!' She spun round. A china bowl fell from her grasp and shattered on the stone floor. Her hand flew to her mouth. Wide, frightened eyes stared at me in a mystifying over-reaction.

'So sorry! I didn't mean to startle you.' I bent down to pick up the pieces.

She didn't move to help me, just stood there, trembling.

I looked for a bin. 'What will I do with these?'

With a visible effort she pulled herself together and pointed with shaking hand to a cupboard under the sink.

With a casual, 'Were you expecting someone else, Madge?' I dropped the pieces in the bin.

A vehement shake of her head. 'No! Just for a moment I thought–' Colour was seeping back into her face. She forced an unconvincing smile. Wearily she wiped a hand across a cheek, transferring a smear of green fondant icing. 'Silly me! I'm just a bag of nerves after... after...' She turned back to the sink without completing the sentence.

Mouse damage to her sugar craft castle wouldn't have reduced her to a bundle of nerves like this. I was more certain than ever that something more serious lay behind it, and I'd probably never have a better chance to bring up the subject, catch her while her defences were down.

A glance round the studio gave me an opening. The ruined sculpture hadn't been disposed of. It stood on a turntable on a worktop in front of shelves of neatly stacked packets of fondant icing, foil-wrapped blocks of marzipan, and dark bottles of food colouring.

'I'm at a loose end. I'll dry while you wash.' I grabbed a dishtowel. 'Carol was in a terrible temper this morning and I daren't go back to the studio till she cools down a bit.' I rattled on, aiming to steer the conversation round to her problems, not my own. 'All that effort to get her work exactly right! Of course, I can quite understand how she felt after seeing paw prints on her clay sheets.'

A covert glance showed me Madge was a lot calmer, perhaps more ready to open up. I seized a pile of dried plates and carried them over to a glass-fronted cupboard positioned conveniently close to the sugar craft castle and stowed them inside. Turning away, I pretended to notice the castle sculpture for the first time.

'Oh! What's happened here?'

Madge came over to join me. She gazed down sadly at the broken battlements. 'That's the first large cake-and-icing sculpture I've tried. Took me a whole week to complete.'

I rotated the turntable slowly with one finger. A large part of the side wall of the castle had crumbled as if it had indeed, in Stu's heartless words, received a direct hit from a cannonball. The rock face below had not escaped either, for a tunnel had been gnawed into the heart of the sculpture.

'All that work, what a shame! Do you think you'll be able to repair it?'

'Don't know,' she said listlessly. 'Not much point is there?'

'Of course you must try!' I cried. 'It's a work of art. Such detail – the tiny windows, the One o'Clock Gun, the ledges on the Castle Rock, even the Scottish flag on its pole! You *certainly* can't risk this happening again. If you think mousetraps won't be enough protection, a visit from my cat Picassa should do the trick.'

She shook her head. 'Won't work.'

'It's worth a try,' I encouraged. 'I'll bring her round on a lead to wander round. Picassa won't even have to spend the night here as mice will detect that a cat has been prowling around. You'll see, they won't come back.'

Her shoulders slumped. Then, so softly that I only just caught the words, 'It wasn't mice. There was a footprint.'

Had I heard correctly? 'You mean… you think one of the other artists… *deliberately*–?'

She nodded. A tear rolled slowly down her cheek and plopped onto the castle rampart.

I got nothing more out of her in spite of making clear my shock and disbelief that someone at the Farm could have stooped so low as to deliberately ruin another artist's work. Though I urged her to say who she suspected, I was met with a stony face and a blank wall of silence. She subsided onto a stool, head in hands, straggly hair hanging in a curtain over her face.

As I turned to go, I heard her mumble, 'There's nothing you can do. Don't tell anyone, *please* don't tell anyone. I shouldn't have said anyth–'

Lost in thought, I stood outside the studio. The motive for

the vandalism of Madge's sugar craft sculpture was perhaps nothing more sinister than spiteful jealousy, unfortunately an all too common reaction from a less successful rival sharing a studio. But there *was* no sugar craft rival here and nobody shared the studio. So what was the motive? What could timid Madge have done to provoke such revenge?

What if she had seen or heard something she shouldn't, something that endangered the drug organisation? Had the cake been vandalised to drive her away from Pear Tree Farm?

Was there a link between the damage to the cake and the drug operation I'd been sent to investigate?

CHAPTER TEN

The last rays of the setting sun were by now gently fingering the bare twigs of the birch trees, touching them with gold; the only sound the harsh cries of geese on the other side of the hill as they circled before settling on the lake for the night. In half an hour I'd be joining the others for the evening meal in the farmhouse kitchen – not an inviting prospect in itself with Carol glowering and making snippy remarks. But it was of the utmost importance for me to keep a low profile. If I didn't turn up, my absence would be the subject of speculation. *Any* undue interest in me was an unwelcome interest. Decision made. Though it would be a race against time to get back to the yurt, feed Gorgonzola and make myself presentable, there was no getting out of that farmhouse meal.

Neil's studio was in complete darkness as I passed, definitely no one at work in there. That made me change my mind. Why waste time going over the hill to feed G when I could do a quick snoop here at a short distance from the farmhouse and still be in time for the meal? Picklock in hand, I paused. There was the chance that Neil might set off early from his yurt on his way to the farmhouse meal. Even so, I'd have a useful eight minutes before suppertime to discover if he and his studio merited any further investigation.

The lock presented no obstacle to my picklock. I closed the door behind me. A torch beam moving in the darkened studio would definitely signal 'Snooper at Work'. I switched on the fluorescent lights, confident that anyone passing by would assume Neil was tidying up after a day's creativity.

Little in the studio had changed since I'd glanced in yesterday except that Neil had finished chiselling the surface of the large block of green slate into an intertwined Celtic design. Highly polished, it stood on the nearest heavy-duty table ready for tomorrow's exhibition. Something was bothering me, though I couldn't at first figure out what it was… That was it! A thick layer of powdery grey-green grit now lay on the surface of the table, and a closer inspection of the sculpture itself revealed traces of grit in some of the grooves and on the shiny surface, indicating that Neil had done more work on the sculpture after he had polished it. Possibly a last minute change of design, but it was unlikely he would have left disfiguring grit on the surface of his Art Work. Could he have been working on the base? I stared at the heavy block. Would I be able to lay it on its side without it crashing down onto the table? Should I risk it? Any damage to the artwork would be a giveaway, but curiosity, at times my downfall, won over caution.

I took a deep breath and tensed my muscles to take the weight of the stone. To my astonishment, it was not nearly as heavy as I'd feared. And when I laid it on its side, the reason was clear. The inside had been almost completely hollowed out. Barely an inch of thickness of slate remained at top and sides. From my experience of working on clay sculpture, laughably limited as that was, I had learned the hard way that clay statues need to be hollowed out or they would explode in the kiln. No kiln treatment needed for slate, of course, so why had Neil spent time chipping away at its interior?

That was something to think about, but it would be unwise to linger here any longer. I took care to replace the sculpture exactly as I'd found it, finally blowing grit right up to the base to hide any evidence that it had been moved. I switched off the light and eased open the door to peer out. No one coming down the hill path. Safe to leave. I locked the door and strolled off towards the farmhouse.

The clatter of dishes and an appetising aroma of garlic roast chicken met me as I hung up my jacket in the hall and pushed open the kitchen door.

Dolores was standing in front of the oven, dishtowel in hand. 'Ah, Tamsin! Just in time to set the table. Madge was *supposed* to be here to help me. She's not reliable at all now. Quite gone to pieces since that cake sculpture of hers was nibbled by mice. Silly girl should have known something like that might happen. We *are* on a farm, after all. What she needs is a good shake.' She seized a pan off the stove and emptied its contents into a colander. 'The cutlery is in that drawer there and the wine glasses in the cabinet.'

'Wine? Last night we had tea and coffee with our meal. Who gets to decide if there's wine?'

'Special occasion. When you arrived yesterday, you'd have heard that all of us – except Madge, of course – had our current projects selected for exhibition and, hopefully sale, in the St Andrew Blackadder Church Hall, North Berwick. But in view of poor Jim Baxter's fatal accident, it wouldn't have felt right to have our celebration last night, would it?'

I gathered up a handful of cutlery. 'Anyone not coming?'

'Everyone except Neil will be here. My cooking and the wine will make sure of *that*.'

I started laying out knives and forks. 'Left it to the very last minute to work on his exhibit, hasn't he?' That would explain the hollowed-out block.

What I'd thought to be a promising lead might very well turn out to be merely a last-minute design change by the sculptor. Nevertheless, I wasn't entirely dismissing the idea that it had been hollowed out to hold drugs.

Dolores stooped to open the oven door. 'Oh no, he's away to the Lake District to get more slate. He finished off his exhibit last night, ready to go off with the other artworks early tomorrow morning.' She gave a quick stir to the casserole. 'Just pour an equal amount of wine into each glass, then nobody can glug down more than their fair share. One thing I've learned here is that creative artists can be very self-centred.'

I was only half-listening, mind busy. What she'd just said didn't fit with what I'd seen in the studio. That sculpture was definitely not ready to be taken to the exhibition tomorrow, as it was unlikely he would have left that disfiguring grit on the surface of his Art Work knowing he would be away when it was taken off for exhibition.

A sharp, 'Mind on the job, Tamsin!' from Dolores. 'Too much wine in that glass!' Then, an apologetic, 'Sorry, that's me in teacher-mode. One of my vices, I'm afraid. It's a hard habit to break.'

I focused on something more pressing than thinking about Neil's sculpture. 'What time does the exhibition open? Can't wait to see my fellow artists' work and find out what standard I'll have to achieve to be chosen for the next one.' My interest and trepidation was genuine. What if the best I could do fell far short of what was required and exposed me as the fraud I was?

'Public admitted at 2 p.m.' She lowered her voice. 'Confidentially, by the end of the week when it closes, I expect *all* my pictures will have sold. Of course, a percentage is deducted towards insurance and the hire of the hall, but I'll still have a nice little sum to put in the bank to spend on canvases and frames.' Then raising her voice to normal level, 'I'm *very* particular in my choice of frames. They must be chosen to enhance the picture so a lot of thought goes into choosing the frame.' She glanced at the kitchen clock. 'The others'll be here any minute. You could put these plates in the oven to heat.'

An order rather than a request, by someone used to giving commands and having them obeyed. Mentally I moved her higher up on the list of those who would be of interest to Operation Smokescreen.

Footsteps hurried along the hall and Madge burst into the kitchen. 'Late! Sorry... sorry!' her words gasped out.

Something had made her late, but whatever it was, judging by the trace of green fondant paste still on her cheek and the cursory attempt to tame her hair with a ribbon, it certainly hadn't been sprucing herself up for dinner. Suddenly aware of my somewhat scruffy jersey and mud-spattered jeans reflected in the dark glass of the un-curtained window, I was not in a position to criticise. What pre-dinner preparation had Tamsin Kennedy made, after all?

If Madge hoped Dolores would welcome her belated appearance with relief, she was mistaken.

'Late, I should think so! Too damn late to be of any help! It's just not good enough, Madge! Lack of organisation, that's the trouble with you. What's the excuse this time?'

The noisy arrival of Stu and Vic diverted Dolores' attention, their flushed faces and beery breath making it clear how they had spent the afternoon.

'It's obvious where *you*'ve been, boys.' Her tone frosty.

They grinned. 'What's not to celebrate! We're in the cash now, aren't we!'

She frowned. 'Taking things a bit for granted, aren't you, celebrating sales before the exhibition has even opened?'

The effect on the men was surprising. No cheery banter brushing off the waspish rebuke. Instead, they glanced at each other and fell silent.

If someone behaves out of character, I've found that it is usually worth following up, letting the problem niggle away till I find an explanation, so I busied myself picking up the pile of plates and putting them in the upper oven to warm. That interaction between Dolores and the two men was something else to think about in bed tonight.

McClusky arrived precisely on time. 'Aah!' An appreciative sniff. 'An ambrosial bouquet, indeed! Our kitchen goddess is at work once more.' He sat down at the head of the table, tucked a paper napkin over his cravat and picked up knife and fork. 'Ready when you are, Dolores!'

Clack clack clack in the hall announced the arrival of Bev teetering on impossibly high-heeled shoes, quite impractical for use outdoors, and unsafe indoors, especially when descending the stairs from her room to the hall. Tonight, skimpy vest and denim shorts had been cast aside in favour of tight leopard-skin trousers, an off-one-shoulder white top, and another application of spray tan. Huge hoop earrings, curling eyelash extensions, and bright red lipstick expertly applied, completed the outfit. One green-shadowed eye peeked out from beneath the cascade of hair to gauge spectator reaction.

A slow wolf whistle from Vic. 'New togs again, Bev! Like 'em!'

From Stu, 'Look who's now in the cash! Been shopping at Harvey Nick's, eh?'

Dolores' hard stare swept over all three of them. 'Harvey Nick, indeed! She bought them at Primark, fashionable but cheap! It's obvious that you boys know nothing about clothes! I suggest you keep quiet till you sober up.'

Bev's mouth fell open in surprise. Then after a long pause, 'Oh…oh, yes, Primark! Fooled you, boys!' Faced flushed, she pulled out a chair and sat down.

That quite unnecessary humiliating put-down of Bev surprised me too. Was Dolores irritated because the late arrival of diners was in danger of spoiling her carefully prepared food, timed to the minute? Or was it something else? Even more intriguing was the rudeness of the snapped, 'Suggest you keep quiet till you sober up'. She had been quick, too quick, to rubbish any suggestion that Bev's clothes had been purchased from a pricey Edinburgh store. Could she be sending a veiled warning to Stu and Vic that they were saying too much, were in danger of revealing to me, a stranger, that the craft activities at Pear Tree Farm generated a suspiciously large amount of money? Or was I just reading too much into these exchanges in my desperation to open up a lead?

McClusky broke the awkward silence. 'Don't take it to

heart, Bev! Dolores is a bit stressed, that's all. Everything you wear looks like a fashion statement so it's not surprising the boys thought you'd been patronising an upmarket department store.' He cleared his throat and looked ostentatiously at his watch. 'Dolores, ready to serve?'

A snapped, 'More than ready! The food's spoiling. I'm not waiting any longer for Carol. Now that you're here at last, Madge, make yourself useful.'

For a celebratory meal, the ensuing conversation round the table was somewhat sporadic. McClusky concentrated on eating, Bev sulked, Stu and Vic were uncharacteristically subdued and monosyllabic. This suited me fine, giving me time to ponder what lay behind that strained exchange over the cost of Bev's clothes. I was a bit on edge myself. If it came up that I'd been poking around near the water tank, my 'looking for lost cat' story would ring alarm bells with the drug organisation.

All at once I became aware that McClusky was looking at me enquiringly, expecting a reaction to something he'd said.

'Um…' Totally at a loss, I steered a piece of chicken slowly round the plate as if debating my answer.

'Well, what do you feel about that, Tamsin? *Do* say yes. We'd all like you to agree, wouldn't we?' Dolores glanced round the table at the others.

Nods and smiles.

It's never a good idea to agree to something when you don't have the slightest notion as to what is involved. I was already in Carol's bad books. Could I afford to have the others turn against me too?

What else to do but smile and say, 'Of course! Whatever you think best, that's fine by me!'

'Settled then. Since much of the minibus seating is required to lay out the artworks for transport to the venue, there won't be room for all of us, and it's only fair to give priority to those who have items in the exhibition.' He looked from Madge to me. 'Disappointing, I know, for you both, but the plus side is that staying behind will enable you to forge ahead with your work and get it ready for the next exhibition.' McClusky raised his glass. 'Success tomorrow, everyone! May your talents b- '

The kitchen door crashed back against the wall. Flakes of white plaster drifted to the floor, dishes rattled on the dresser as Neil hurtled into the room, face flushed, grey hair dishevelled, fists clenched. McClusky's arm jerked, sending drops of wine leaping from his glass to bloody his immaculate shirtfront as if he'd been the target of a gangland killing.

Neil spluttered, his words barely comprehensible. 'Who was it? Wait till I get my hands on the bastard!'

'What the-?'

'Did *what*?'

'Cool it!'

'What's got into you, man?'

Dolores' voice, calmly authoritative, rose above the clamour. 'Sit down, Neil. We thought you were miles away in the Lake District collecting more of that special green slate you've been working on.' As if nothing untoward had taken place, she pulled out a vacant chair. 'You're just in time. There's not much of my special garlic chicken left, but enough, I think.' She reached over to the dresser for a plate, ran a serving spoon round the casserole and slid the plate in front of him. 'Now, not another word till you've got some of this inside you, and then you can tell us what's happened to upset you like this.'

The efficiency with which she had dealt with and defused that tricky situation definitely showed someone well-used to taking command. Should I move Dolores to the top of my Operation Smokescreen suspicious persons list?

Neil's sudden switch of mood left me with another question mark. The fight out of him, he hesitated, then slumped onto the chair. Eyes downcast, he stuck his fork into a piece of chicken and ate slowly with no enjoyment, the simmering anger within betrayed only by vicious stabs of the fork.

Frustratingly, since I was as impatient as the rest, perhaps more so, to find out the reason for Neil's outburst, any immediate attempt by the others to challenge him over his accusation was quelled by Dolores' stern glance and sharp, 'He can't talk and eat at the same time. Let him finish!'

Keeping my head down and appearing to concentrate on the food on my plate, I studied under lowered lids the range of expressions round the table. There was no evidence that anyone knew what lay behind his outburst. On all faces merely curiosity, puzzlement, and in the case of McClusky, irritation as he examined the wine stains on his shirt. Was somebody at the table responsible for whatever disaster had occurred? Neil certainly thought so.

When at last he laid down his fork, Dolores poured half her wine into an empty glass and pushed it across the table towards him. 'Now, take a deep breath and tell us what's upset you.'

Alas, her attempt to calm him down had merely postponed another outburst, for Neil gulped down the wine in his glass, and jumped to his feet. '*Somebody* here was responsible. And I demand to know who it was!' He stared at us one by one, glaring from face to face. 'Come on, admit it!'

'Responsible for *what*? Spit it out or shut up, for God's sake!' Stu's long, yawn was clearly intended to provoke. 'This is a celebration dinner, not the Spanish Inquisition. Come on, grandpa, lighten up. Making a mountain out of a molehill is your speciality. Whatever *mini*-disaster's happened to your work, it isn't the end of the world.'

'Really, Stu, that's not–' McClusky half-rose to his feet. 'Remember, here at Pear Tree Farm we're one big family. A trouble shared, is a trouble er…er…' He searched for a word that indicated 'shared by the seven of us present', failed, and reached over to pat Neil's shoulder.

I judged rightly that this would have as much effect as placing a restraining hand on the muzzle of a charging bull.

Neil leaned across the table and seized Stu by his shirtfront. 'Knowing that I would be away in the Lake District, your crackpot idea of a joke, I suppose, vandalising my exhibition-ready work!'

A sharp intake of breath round the table. Even I appreciated what a nightmare that would be for any artist.

Stu shook off Neil's hand and squared up to him with clenched fists. 'Bloody maniac! What exactly am I *supposed* to have done to it, old timer?' A sneer in every word.

'Gentlemen! Gentlemen!' McClusky collapsed onto his chair. 'My dear Neil, surely you must be mistaken? Interfering with another artist's work? Unheard of!'

'You…you…*rat*!' Neil looked wildly round the table, picked up the nearest wine glass – which happened to be mine – and slowly and deliberately poured the contents over Stu's head.

Not waiting for reprisals, he strode from the room, slamming the door behind him. A second snowstorm of plaster drifted down. A plate on the dresser trembled for a moment then toppled off and smashed on the stone floor.

There was a moment's stunned silence, all eyes on the red wine trickling down Stu's forehead and drip drip dripping from his glasses to form a spreading stain on the tablecloth.

'Really, that was quite uncalled for, no matter how provoked he was by finding his work vandalised.' Dolores handed over a wad of paper towels from the kitchen dispenser.

What could be behind the deliberate targeting, first of Madge, now of Neil? To establish that I'd never paid a visit to studio B, I asked, 'What was he working on?'

'The oaf was hacking lumps out of a massive block of green slate.' Stu gave a final mop to his face and pitched the wad of paper towels into the bin.

'Vandalised! Vandalised in what way?' McClusky pursed his lips. 'Daubed with graffiti? Chunks knocked off? Scratched?'

'No use sitting here speculating.' Dolores pushed back her chair and rose to her feet. 'Of course, it may be a *brouhaha* about nothing. I've noticed that he *does* tend to be a little melodramatic at times of stress. I suggest we make our way to the studio to find out.'

McClusky seized a powerful torch from the table in the hall. 'We'll need this. No moon tonight.'

He set off at a fast pace, Dolores close behind. The pool of yellow light danced ahead, highlighting hazards, only for them, that is. The rest of us had to take our chance. Much stumbling and the occasional muttered oath marked our progress.

No rays of light struggled through the thick layer of dust that coated the window of Studio B, Neil having presumably stormed off to brood in his yurt. Fumbling with a bunch of keys, McClusky opened the door and switched on the light. We crowded in after him. In the hour since my illicit visit to the studio, a hand had been at work decorating the austerely elegant dark green surface of the block of slate with swirls of gold and silver paint. The effect was gaudy, cheap, tasteless – a view, from their comments, not shared by my companions.

'Vandalised? What the hell was he raving about?'

'Nothing wrong with this! Definitely an improvement.'

'Pretty stylish, sure to sell tomorrow! No doubt about it now!'

McClusky turned on his heel. 'Chap over-reacted. Well, that's that. Dessert awaits. I'll have a word with him later tonight. Sort things out then. Puzzling, puzzling…'

Puzzling indeed, I thought. An artwork is precious to the creator, no matter how crude in the eyes of others. The other artists and McClusky, the director of a 'renowned Creative Art Centre', must know that *any* unauthorised alteration to an artwork would definitely provoke justifiable anger and distress. Equally puzzling was their lack of surprise that someone had sneaked into the studio to interfere with Neil's work just before it was due to be exhibited. Had they, in fact, *known* it was going to happen? On my way back to the yurt I tried to work out just why it had been necessary to alter the sculpture's appearance.

Forgetful that G would be furious after her long imprisonment inside, I opened the door of the yurt. A snarling mew, a soft brush of fur against my legs, a ginger streak shot past me and disappeared into the night. The last I saw of her was an insolent twitch of her moth-eaten tail.

Damn! She'd only return when she calculated that I'd realised how inconsiderate I'd been. My plan was to investigate the artists' exhibits in the transit van while it was still dark and everyone was asleep. Now that I was convinced Neil's slate sculpture had been hollowed out to conceal drugs, all the other artworks could be used the same way. I needed G's nose to confirm my suspicions, and if she wasn't back by the time I was ready to go, I'd summon her with the ultrasonic whistle, confident that training would win.

I locked the yurt door behind me and lit the oil lamp. Only then was it clear that G had worked out her frustration by rucking up the sheepskin rug into a series of folds like breakers pounding a rocky shore, and by snoozing on my pillow (strictly forbidden), leaving a cat-shaped depression and a telltale red hair. Her *pièce de resistance* had been to scatter the granules from her hated litter tray across the floor, clearly the feline equivalent of a rude two-finger salute, a not too subtle signal to bring to my attention the lack of consideration for her needs.

Brushing all the scattered granules into the tiny dustpan seemed to take forever, so I wasn't in the best of moods by the time I pulled the duvet over me. Sleep didn't come. I tossed and turned, thoughts busy. Why had Dolores been so very quick to scorn Stu's remark that Bev had been 'splashing the cash' at a very expensive shop? Why had Bev agreed that her outfit had been bought in Primark, to me an obvious lie?

Why had it been so necessary to alter the slate sculpture's appearance? And who of the others would have had the opportunity? When I had left the studio the slate sculpture had been undecorated.

There had been only half an hour's window of opportunity for the vandalism before Neil had burst in. Any one of those who had arrived for dinner could have done it. Madge? Late for her kitchen duties, but the elaborate paint decoration would have taken longer than ten minutes, so that ruled her out. For the same reason I eliminated Stu and Vic. That left as possibles, Bev and McClusky, and Carol, of course, who hadn't appeared at all. I gave some thought to that. Had not Dolores said everyone except Neil would be there? Yet neither she nor anyone else had commented on Carol's absence.

Carol? Opportunity (tick), artistic ability (tick), lack of comment on her absence by the others (tick). The more I thought about it, the more convinced I became that Carol was responsible. Ticks three, crosses none. Motive? From personal experience, I knew she was a bully who got a kick out of upsetting others. I could certainly imagine Neil exploding with some angry retort over some action of hers that had left him seething. So possibly the vandalism was merely her payback to Neil.

One thirty a.m. and still sleep refused to come. Perhaps… perhaps… Sighing, I turned onto my back and stared up at the patch of night sky visible through the little window in the yurt. Suddenly I was wide awake. Got it! What was important was not who did it, but *why*. Neil had arrived back unexpectedly. Could the vandalism, therefore, have been a clever attempt to prevent him finding out that the sculpture had been hollowed out? With a temper like his, when he saw the paint makeover, they'd know he'd freak out and rush off to find the perpetrator without taking a closer look.

My eyelids grew heavy and closed.

CHAPTER ELEVEN

02:00 hours.

No moon, heavy cloud, as one by one at prearranged intervals stealthy figures slipped from their yurts and made their way to the farmhouse. A blustery wind rattled the kitchen windows, and after a check that there was no gap in the heavy curtains to allow prying eyes to look in, the emergency discussion began…

02:30 hours.

Plan in place, rendezvous at the transit van set for four hours ahead, the farmhouse door opened and closed as they left one by one at short intervals. Loud in the silence of the deserted kitchen, the wooden clock on the wall ticked softly on.

* * *

05:30 hours.

Buzzzzzz. I woke with a start from a deep slumber and drew the alarm clock towards me. The night sky visible through the window was the faded black of an old washed-out t-shirt. I was already regretting my decision to get up before dawn to examine the artworks in the minibus before it drove off to the exhibition. Why bother? Intent on snatching another two hours precious sleep, I turned over, pulled the duvet over my head and drifted off…

Buzzz. The alarm's snooze function jerked me awake. I flung back the duvet, thwarted from giving in to self and snuggling down into the comfort of a warm bed. Ahead lay the prospect of a cold, dark trek across to the farmhouse.

I dressed in black sweater and trousers, and as an afterthought pulled on a tight-fitting balaclava before picking up my torch and slipping out of the yurt. I'd hoped that Gorgonzola would have got over her outburst and be sitting outside waiting, but there was no sign of her. I fumbled in my pocket and blew the ultrasonic whistle, confident that she would appear out of the darkness. After a couple of minutes I blew again. No mew of greeting, no G. I'd only myself to blame.

05:40 hours.
I made my way to top of the low rise, making use of the torch only where necessary. Below me the faint glimmer of the lake marked the position of the dark shape of the yurts with no sign that anyone was awake to see the shielded beam of my torch. Another blow of the whistle in the copse of birch trees brought only a faint rustling in the undergrowth, too insubstantial to be made by a cat. As I approached the studios I had no more success with the whistle.

The farmhouse itself was in darkness, the hush of pre-dawn broken by a man's rhythmic snores floating through a half-open window on the upper floor. McClusky's room, the adjoining room with the chintzy curtains would be Bev's. I shoved the torch into my trouser pocket. Too much of a risk to use it so near the windows of the house.

Cursing the absence of G, I picked my way towards the ancient pear tree and the dark shape of the minibus parked under it, easy to distinguish by its height from the other cars. A sharp *ping* frighteningly loud in the silence as gravel shot from under my boot and hit a metal wheel trim. I froze, heart thumping. The snores from the room above faltered, then resumed with increased volume. After a moment I crept on.

One turn of my picklock and the driver's door slid back, bringing on the interior light. I flicked it off, but I'd seen enough. I'd assumed there'd be only five artworks going to the exhibition, Neil's plus one submitted by each of the four other participating artists. Wrong! There must have been at least twenty wrapped packages of different sizes and shapes wedged for safe transport between and on the seats. I'd also assumed that though the artworks would be protected with blankets and cushions, they'd be easily identifiable for me to investigate without anyone being any the wiser. Another wrong assumption, another miscalculation, for they were all wrapped in black plastic and securely taped up. Impossible to see what they were, let alone examine them without it being obvious that someone had tampered with the packaging.

Controller Tyler's criticism rang in my ears, 'Assumption, I'm afraid, is one of your flaws, Smith.' I had to admit he had been right. This might be the only opportunity to test my theory that artworks were hollowed out to carry drugs – and I'd blown it.

Disappointment and exasperation boiled up into a quite unwarranted irritation with the missing Gorgonzola. 'Disobedient brute!' I hissed. 'I bet you're enjoying yourself stalking rodents! Bloody well *answer* this, will you!' I put the whistle to my lips and blew with the full force of my lungs. If the blast had been audible to human ears, I'd have deafened myself, jolted awake the sleepers in the farmhouse, and even roused the artists cosy under their duvets in the distant yurts.

Hrwoooooo G's drug-detecting croon, very close, seemed to come from above my head. I peered up into the pear tree. High on one of the ancient crooked limbs was a dark bulge, a huge gall-like growth. Had it been there two days ago when G had dangled Bev's expensive headphones from her paw like some exotic fruit? I stared at it. Was that a movement? Yes, the bulge had definitely shifted position. The next moment, another *hrwoooooo*, a self-satisfied *miaow*, a scrape of claws on bark. *Thump*. G made an expert four-point landing at my feet and twined herself triumphantly round my leg. An extra long *hrwooooooooooo* emphasised just how well she'd done by detecting drugs without even the need to go into the van.

My theory had proved correct. I let out my breath in a sigh of relief, picked her up and whispered in her ear. 'You heard the whistle each time I blew it, but you'd already found and staked out the big reward, hadn't you? So no need to for *you* to move, was there? You let *me* come to you.'

As if she had read my thoughts, G leapt from my arms onto the top of the van. HRWOOOOOO.

The chintz-curtained window flew up. Bev's head poked out. '*Shurrup*, mog!'

I pressed myself against the side of the minibus, discovery prevented only by its bulk, parked windscreen towards the farmhouse, concealing both me and the telltale open door from her view.

Hrwooooooooooooooooooooooo

Bev's head shot inside and a moment later her hand appeared holding a jug. Water hurled from the jug hit the ground. *SPLAT.*

With a yowl of indignation at the uncalled-for reaction to her success, G leapt into the van and crouched on top of the nearest package. After a cursory sniff, the crooning resumed. *Hrwooooo.*

'Now bugger off!' *Clang.* Bev's hairbrush bounced off the roof of the van. The window slammed shut.

I grabbed G and held her to me to silence her. Just in time.

McClusky's sleepy voice drifted down from above. 'What's going on out there?' A pause. 'Who's–?'

From my extensive repertoire for emergencies, I summoned up an impressive plaintive *miaaoooow* made even more convincing when G responded with a most satisfactory competitive *yaowooowl.*

'Bloody cats!' His window closed with a bang.

I glanced at my watch. 6:15 a.m. As at least one of these exhibits was being used to conceal drugs, there was no doubt now that Neil's block had been hollowed out for the same reason. No need to investigate further. I never believe in pushing my luck when I've got what I want. Time to beat a strategic retreat to my cosy duvet, sure that it would be 7:30 a.m. before the sleepers in the yurts were awake, and even later before anyone thought about making their way up to the farmhouse for breakfast. Plenty of time.

By 6:25 a.m. G and I had reached the first of the birch trees, my thoughts flying ahead once more to the cosy bed awaiting me in the yurt. No need now for the balaclava. I stuffed it in my pocket. Judging by the pull on the lead, G too was concentrating on getting there as quickly as possible, in happy anticipation of her well-earned fishy reward.

The murmur didn't at first register. It was only when G stopped suddenly, ears pricked, front leg poised in mid-air, that I heard what she'd heard – hushed voices approaching from the far end of the clump of birches. I'd assumed that no one would be leaving their yurt for at least another hour. Assumption! Something I'd vowed never to be guilty of again. Although the incriminatingly suspicious balaclava was safely stuffed in my pocket, they would definitely find it suspicious to see me dressed in black and there was no way I could produce a convincing explanation of why I was here.

The fact that some of my fellow artists were out and about when it was scarcely light with the minibus already packed for the exhibition meant that it must be leaving well before the scheduled time. Why?

The voices were closer now, the light of a torch bobbing and flickering through the trees. The slender birches provided no cover. I took three or four quick strides away from the path, then holding firmly onto G's lead and ignoring every instinct urging speed, with face averted, hugging a trunk, I slid slowly, slowly, down to lie flat, telltale pale blob of face pressed into the yellow carpet of damp leaves.

At this critical moment a sharp tug on the lead indicated that G was seizing the opportunity to go on the hunt, signalled by a *rustle, rustle, RUSTLE* that would undoubtedly attract the attention of those coming along the path. I flicked the catch on the retractable lead, reeled her sharply in, and unclipped the hook from her collar to set her free. Seizing this rare opportunity of a little nocturnal stalking and pouncing as merely her due reward for services rendered, with a gleeful bound she was gone.

Hurrying footsteps, a muttered curse as someone stumbled. I was aware of dark trunks paling to grey as torch lights approached and came level with where I lay. I held my breath... The footsteps passed on. I let out a long sigh of relief. A mistake. Micro-organisms stirred up from the leaf mould tickled my nose and brought on an irresistible need to sneeze. *Shmnff*.

The passing footsteps stopped abruptly. 'What was that?' Sharp and anxious.

A few yards from where I lay, torchlight played across grass and fallen leaves. Closer... closer... dangerously close. I tensed myself for the cry of discovery. Farfetched excuses raced through my mind, only to be discarded. Not even a child would believe I was lying on the ground looking for mushrooms or examining ants' nests or recovering after hitting my head on a low branch. My black outfit would make it clear to the drug organisation that I was a danger that must be eliminated.

Chook chook chook. Off to my left, the sudden alarm call of a startled bird.

'Something moving... Over there!' Definitely Stu's voice.

The trunks of the nearby birches switched from grey to black as the beam of the torch swung away from me.

'There it is! It's that brute of Tamsin's. Chuck something at it!' Carol, typically callous.

Seconds later, the soft *thunk* of a heavy stone sinking into earth or, heart-stopping thought, a furry side. A moment of dread, then the relief of hearing G's cheeky *yah-missed-me* yowl, followed by the rustle of long grass and the crackle of twigs marking the progress of an unhurried strategic withdrawal.

'Lets go. No more time to waste!' A whisper so low that I couldn't determine if the voice was male or female.

The footsteps resumed… faded over the rise. Only then did I stir. A blast on the ultrasonic whistle brought G back to me, and ten minutes later we were back in the yurt. Snuggled under the duvet, I drifted off to sleep to the sound of G's contented purring, her stomach full of the promised reward.

CHAPTER TWELVE

'Everybody away to the exhibition, then?' I directed my question to Madge, the only other occupant of the kitchen.

She looked up from half-heartedly wiping a dish mop over an egg-stained plate, one of the pile of breakfast dishes in the sink. 'Suppose so.' A scowl. 'The whole lot left early and didn't bother to wash their dishes. So who *was* going to do it, then?' The brandished dish mop sent greasy droplets flying round the kitchen. She mimicked McClusky's plummy voice to a T, "Staying behind will enable you both to forge ahead getting your work ready for the next exhibition." Another brandish of the dish mop. 'Huh! Fat chance!'

'Tell you what,' I said. 'I'll finish the washing up and let *you* get on.' My offer with an ulterior motive: with her off to work in her studio, with McClusky and Bev away with the others to the exhibition, the coast would be clear for me to snoop around the farmhouse.

No smile of gratitude, no half-hearted, 'Well, if you're sure...' She flung down the dish mop, untied her apron, and was gone.

For a moment I contemplated the half-submerged pile of

greasy dishes, then leaned over, pulled out the plug, and watched with satisfaction the water swirl down the drain. Those artists, lazy slobs, hadn't bothered to wash their breakfast dishes, taking for granted that Madge or I would do them. Hadn't Mr Stuffed Shirt, McClusky, told me that the compensation for being left behind would be that I could spend valuable time on my work? Well, was not my work to investigate the goings-on at Pear Tree Farm? And that was what I was about to do. But first I'd check that everybody had indeed gone to the exhibition. I stood in the hall, listening. Upstairs, no footsteps, no movement, no creaking of old floorboards. No sound at all apart from the *tick tick* of the clock in the kitchen. The coast was clear to snoop.

From outside, a screech of brakes followed by an aggressive *TO-O-OT*. A minute later someone beat a tattoo with the fox-head knocker on the front door. I hesitated, my foot on the first tread of the stairs to the bedrooms. At that very moment, from above came the muffled sound of a door opening. Footsteps hurried towards the top of the stairs.

'Coming! Coming!' McClusky's voice.

Prevented in the nick of time from making a disastrous mistake. Heart beating fast, in a flash I was back at the sink running hot water over the dishes and busily wielding the dish mop. I had been so very close to blowing the mission. It would have been packed bags for G and me, and a hasty departure from Pear Tree Farm, Controller Gerry's meticulous planning all for nothing.

Before McClusky was halfway down the stairs, the visitor beat another frenzied tattoo with the knocker. *TAP TAP, TAP TAP TAP*.

He reached the door and flung it open with a somewhat

breathless, 'Ah, you'll be the prospective recruit to our artistic community. I'm Pembrose McClusky, director of Pear Tree Farm Enterprises. Welcome, Mrs...er...Miss...'

'Sapphire McGurk. And it's Ms!'

I gasped. I couldn't believe the bad timing of the arrival here of Sapphire McGurk, my unscrupulous fellow exhibitor at last year's Pittenweem Art Festival. Someone who knew me not as Tamsin Kennedy, but as Kirsty Gordon. Someone who bore me a grudge. Into my mind flashed her plump figure as I'd last seen her – shoulder length henna-dyed hair, short sturdy legs clad in black fishnet tights, waving her fists in impotent rage at the getaway van as I sped off with my White Lady sculpture rescued from her clutches. Would my changed appearance, blue-streaked spiky hair and heavily blue-eye-shadowed eyes, fool her? No, they would not. I'd made an enemy for life. There'd be no chance of talking my way out of *this*.

But perhaps... I allowed the plate I was holding to slip from my grasp and shatter on the stone floor. I knelt, head down, slowly picking up the pieces in the slender hope that McClusky would merely glance in, and with a reproving, 'Tut! Tut!' bustle off with the latest would-be recruit in tow.

From the hall, 'What on earth!' McClusky was standing in the kitchen doorway with Sapphire trying to peer over his shoulder. 'Tut! Tut! Don't bother with that, Tamsin! I want to introduce you to Ms McGurk. She's considering enrolling with us.'

'Just a moment, Mr McClusky. I'd better sweep this up first. Health and Safety!' Head now in the cupboard under the sink, I scrabbled for longer than was necessary for dustpan and brush, muttering to myself, 'Bugger off, damn you.'

In vain.

'Do hurry up, Tamsin. You're keeping Ms McGurk waiting.'

I couldn't put off the moment any longer. A cursory sweep of the china pieces into the dustpan and I turned to face them with a weak attempt at a welcoming smile. 'Hi there!'

For a long, long, moment Sapphire stared at me. Then her eyes narrowed in dawning recognition. 'Tams-in?'

McClusky waved a plump hand in my direction. 'Tamsin's ceramic sculpture has won awards. She joined us recently to take advantage of our world-class facilities.'

Sapphire's heart-shaped mouth slowly formed the word, 'Sculp-t-u-ure,' then firmed into a line, and I knew she had in mind that daring rescue of my White Lady after her brazen attempt to flog it on e-bay.

Oblivious to the tense atmosphere, McClusky turned to go. 'Now,' a professional smile, 'I've things to attend to, so I'll leave you two to get acquainted. Once Tamsin has given you a tour of the studios, drop in to my office here, Ms McGurk. Places are much sought after, only one left. I'll need your decision today. When it's gone, it's gone.' With this persuasive gambit, he turned on his heel and hurried off, leaving us staring at each other in silence.

Surprisingly, she had not taken the chance to denounce me, no doubt calculating how she could turn the situation to her own advantage.

After a moment her lips spread in a sly smile. 'Pear Tree Farm will be the ideal place for me to continue my latest experiments in natural dyes sourced from India. I've made my decision. I'm staying. Yes, I'm *definitely* staying, Kirsty Gordon – or whatever you call yourself now.' I recognised this for an exploratory thrust, an attempt to unsettle me, a probe for a vulnerability that could be exploited.

'Oh, my change of name? That!' A carefree toss of my spiky blue coiffure. A toss of flowing tresses would have been more emphatic, but *faute de mieux*... 'Just a re-branding! You see, Tamsin has a more *je ne sais quoi* ring to it now that I'm concentrating on selling my chubby sculptures to the French market.'

She frowned, unsure whether or not to accept my explanation. There was definitely a trace of disappointment that I hadn't shown any sign of being flustered by her challenge.

I congratulated myself on having selected just the right choice of words to confirm that there was nothing suspicious about me now calling myself Tamsin Kennedy, and therefore nothing for her to use as blackmail.

Quite carried away by my own cleverness, I added, 'The French do so *love* the plumply-rounded female figure.' Laughing, I made exaggerated rounded shapes with both hands.

Her expression changed. '*Plumply-rounded female figure*! You're poking fun at me!' She flushed, her face only a tone or two lighter than her hennaed hair. 'An insult direct!' She drew herself up to her full five foot two inches. 'Well, let me tell you, you've chosen the wrong woman. Oh yes, I'm staying. I know your devious ways, and I'll take care to find out what you're up to, madam! I haven't forgotten – how *could* I forget – that you cheated me out of the sculpture you left in my possession. *No one* gets the better of Sapphire McGurk, you can be sure of that!'

CHAPTER THIRTEEN

My flustered attempts to explain that she had quite misunderstood my reference to a plumply-rounded figure fell on deaf ears.

A glare. The short sturdy legs stomped off in the direction of McClusky's office. 'I'm off to enrol right now. *Pembrose* will show me to my studio!'

Biting my lip, I surveyed Sapphire's receding back and fought down rising panic. This time she had definitely scored a hit, dealt me a blow with her, 'I'll find out what you're up to, madam, you can be sure of that!' Think positive. In a crisis keep cool. Worse case scenario she'd vent her anger in the next few minutes by warning him that I was up to no good, hoping that I would be told to leave. She'd certainly get a *lot* of satisfaction from that.

But I took heart. That worst case scenario wouldn't happen, at least not yet. I'd got to know her well enough to predict that what counted most with Sapphire was *cash*. She was totally unscrupulous in her pursuit of money. Blackmail, therefore, was more likely to be her choice of weapon. Furthermore, the accusation that I had stolen a sculpture from her would be a matter of indifference to the bosses of a drug organisation. My cover was watertight, so to blackmail me she'd first have to catch me out. But that was something to be dealt with in the future.

What I had to deal with at the present moment was how to get to the exhibition hall. My discovery that the artworks in the transit van concealed drugs had put a new slant on McClusky's reason for leaving Madge and myself behind. His explanation had been that there would be no room for us in the minibus. But thinking back, there'd been more than a hint of tension as he waited for my answer. Perhaps he was worried that I'd turn up at the exhibition and might respond with a chirpy, 'That's ok. I'll take my car.' I'd played right into his hands, of course, by rashly agreeing to stay at the Farm when I hadn't even heard the question. Dolores had expertly steered me to the desired response with her, '*Do* say yes. We'd all appreciate it, wouldn't we?' Dolores, whom I'd already mentally moved to the top of my suspicious persons list. Yes, the more I thought about it, the exhibition hall was where I was going to head right now. Their reaction to my arrival would certainly be interesting.

Putting Sapphire and the threat she posed to the back of my mind, I tossed the dish mop into the sink, abandoned any temptation of remaining in my studio to enhance the voluptuous curves of Earth Mother, and headed for the car park, determined to arrive in North Berwick while the setting-up of the exhibits was still in progress.

The artists' cars were parked in the courtyard along with a dusty dark-blue mini-van cosied up uncomfortably close to my multi-coloured old banger, now disfigured by a vertical dent and an ugly scrape across my carefully executed self-designed artwork when that careless fool of a driver had flung open his door. Well, that just added to Old Banger's disguise, nothing to get upset about.

I turned the ignition. *Click click.* I waited a moment… tried again… and again. Frowning, I climbed out, suddenly uneasy. If I'd made it clear that I was determined to go to the exhibition, a convenient breakdown was exactly what they'd have arranged. I lifted the bonnet. As was to be expected of a decrepit car like mine, the engine compartment was dirty and oily, expertly disguising the fact that HMRC mechanics had serviced the engine to peak condition before handing it over to me, so not at all likely for a mechanical fault to develop so soon.

My gaze swept over the engine. To the eye, all leads seemed secure, but nevertheless… I gave various wires a gentle tug. Ah, movement on a connection. Closer inspection revealed that one of the leads to the ignition had been imperceptibly dislodged from making full electrical contact. I left it as I'd found it. Foolish to let them realise I knew someone had tampered with the car.

How was I to get to the exhibition now? Footsteps crunched on the gravel and I turned to see Neil running towards me.

He stared wildly round the car park. 'Where's the transit van? Where's the bloody van?'

'Something wrong, Neil?'

'My exhibit's gone from the studio, that's what's bloody well wrong! Wait till I get hold of that bastard McClusky!'

I pointed to the iridescent patch of oil where the Farm's transit van had stood. 'You're too late. McClusky and the others have already left to set up the exhibition.'

A frantic, disbelieving, 'They *can't* have left already! How could any of them *imagine* I'd allow that apology of an artwork... that *travesty* to be exhibited under my name?' A spluttered, 'Well, they're bloody well not going to put it on sale without my permission.' He squeezed through the narrow gap between our vehicles and wrenched open the driver's door, in the process redesigning the bodywork of my car with another dent, another scrape. 'Just wait till I get to the hall and I'll–'

'How about giving me a lift? ' I cried. 'My car's broken down.'

A grunted, 'Hop in. Hurry up.' He pulled the ignition key out of his pocket.

Problem solved. I buckled my seat belt and sat back. Not be long till I'd be walking through the door of the exhibition hall with the satisfactorily credible excuse of being eager to help with the setting up of exhibits.

Neil rammed the key into the ignition. After the third attempt to start the engine, he reached down, pulled the lever to release the bonnet and flung open his door. *Thunk.* Another dent in my car. I kept quiet. I wasn't going to jeopardise my lift by bawling him out.

Together we stood looking into an engine compartment in the same oily and dirty state as mine.

'Don't know much about what goes on in there.' He poked tentatively at a few leads, then stood up scratching his head. 'How about you?'

'Not a thing.' I adopted a helpless woman expression, a tactic that has often stood me in good stead. 'In an emergency I wait for a man to come to the rescue.' A silly giggle.

He let the bonnet fall back into place. 'Leave it to me. No mobile signal here. I'll phone for a taxi from the farmhouse landline.' He set off at a run.

I watched him go. The same sabotaging hand had obviously been at work on Neil's mini-van. It can't have been coincidence that these two vehicles had failed to start. I could understand why the gang would take steps to prevent *him* being present at the setting up of the exhibits, as he'd probably discover that his slate sculpture was now hollow. Very worrying, however, that they did not want *me* there. That they'd tampered with my car was proof they hadn't believed I was searching for my lost cat near the water tank.

CHAPTER FOURTEEN

Neil came back five minutes later. Before he spoke I could tell from his face that that his attempt to phone a taxi had been unsuccessful.

'No luck. Damn, damn, *damn*.' He drummed his fingers on the roof of the transit. 'All booked, or off on the airport run, a hundred miles round trip. Nothing available for a couple of hours, and even then half an hour more to North Berwick.' He ran a hand through his hair in a gesture of despair. 'Too *late!*'

'Cheer up. We'd still arrive well before the exhibition opens to the public.'

'You don't understand, Tamsin! Once set up, it's too late to withdraw an exhibit.' He sagged against the van.

I shared his frustration. This was a setback for my plans too. I stared at my immobilised car. I could suggest to Neil that damp on the electrics might be the cause, let him wield the can of WD40 to spray all likely components, then when he turned to go back into the van to try the engine, I could surreptitiously push in the loose starter lead. That would fool him – but not the gang. I mustn't allow suspicion to harden into certainty. Once they were aware that they were under surveillance by HMRC, my usefulness to Operation Smokescreen would be at an end, Operation Smokescreen shut down.

But time was running out. I was already under suspicion. I *had* to get to that exhibition. Drugs hidden in artworks and then moved from Pear Tree Farm to an exhibition was only one piece of the jigsaw. Today might be my only chance to discover the next stage in distribution round the UK.

Dilemma. Blow my cover by fixing car or van – or miss a golden opportunity?

I was still trying to come to a decision when Neil straightened up. 'Got it! Easy enough to thumb a lift in a rural area like this where there's two hours between buses.'

Five minutes later we were standing on the grassy verge of the country road listening for the sound of an approaching car. The first flashed by, leaving us gazing dispiritedly after it, but the second driver slowed, stopped, and lowered the window.

'Going anywhere near North Berwick?'

'Aye, Dirleton. That near enough?'

While Neil in the front passenger seat engaged in animated football talk with the driver, I sat in the back rehearsing how I was going to handle my unexpected and definitely unwelcome arrival at the exhibition hall.

The road ahead twisted and turned, just one of a network of narrow roads threading through a rolling landscape of honey-gold stubble fields and isolated clusters of cottages with red-pantiled roofs and walls of dark-red stone hacked more than a hundred years ago from the Law, the volcanic plug that dominates the small town of North Berwick. On my right, the low mass of the distant Lammermuir hills, on my left a hazy blue line marking the Firth of Forth and beyond, the hills of

Fife.

A sudden thought. What if I was making exactly the wrong move by turning up at the exhibition hall? What if that *heightened* their suspicion, made uncertainty certain? Yes, it would be foolhardy to accompany Neil into the exhibition hall. Plan A shelved. Trouble was, there *wasn't* a plan B. Foolishly, I hadn't thought it necessary. A moment of panic, then relief. I wouldn't have to explain my change of mind to Neil as all I had asked him for was a lift. I hadn't given a reason, not even mentioned the exhibition. A woman's love of shopping is no secret, so all I had to say to him was that I'd heard one of the great attractions of North Berwick was the fantastic variety of shops in the High Street, and that's why I was heading there.

'Here we are then. Direlton.' The car drew up at a bus stop beside the village green. 'This is as far as I go, but East Coast buses come along every half hour.' He drove off with a cheery *toot toot*.

Neil peered anxiously at the timetable fixed to the bus stop and ran his finger down the list of times. 'We're in luck, only a ten minute wait, unless it's running late.' He joined me on the nearby seat and following my gaze, pointed across the road to where the walls of the ruined castle kept watch over the village. 'One of the many castles Cromwell redesigned! Lovely garden, I hear. Dolores goes painting there every Wednesday, even when it's raining.'

'Out in all weathers, eh? Shows she's the dedicated artist. Hope she uses oil paints! Unless of course she's into watercolour wet-on-wet technique.' I laughed, and quickly changed the subject. I was very interested indeed in Dolores' weekly visits to Dirleton Castle gardens.

After that, conversation lapsed. He spent the time gazing into space, interspersed with impatient glances at his watch. Any attempt to get him to talk about sculpture in general, or to comment specifically on the vandalised sculpture, met only with monosyllabic replies or grunts.

The bus, ten minutes late, hurtled along the straight stretch of road between Dirleton and North Berwick in an effort to make up lost time. More than fast enough for me, but not fast enough for Neil, judging by the way he leant forward gripping the back of the seat in front as if that could somehow get him to the exhibition hall sooner. Then we were driving past imposing Victorian villas... braking reluctantly to an abrupt halt at traffic lights... sweeping downhill... Ahead, an expanse of putting green bordered by sea, and across the curve of the bay a line of pantiled cottages perched on a red-stone harbour wall, behind them the squat shape of the distant Bass Rock.

'We're here!' Neil reached for the bell as the bus turned sharply right. He leapt from his seat before the bus had come to a halt and stood impatiently waiting for the door to open.

Definitely too risky for me to go into the exhibition hall during the setting up, the very time they had taken such trouble to ensure I wouldn't be present. Obviously, anything illegal would be well and truly concealed by 2 p.m. when it opened to the public. It would be much less suspicious for an enthusiastic fellow artist to turn up in the afternoon.

I put part one of Plan B into operation: to make Neil believe that I had come to North Berwick only for the shops.

I called after his rapidly disappearing figure as he pushed his way along the crowded pavement towards St Andrew Blackadder Church, 'Don't wait for me, Neil. I'm going to hit the shops.'

With a wave of acknowledgement he hurried on, only one thing on his mind. There was a chance, of course, that he might not mention he had given me a lift – but if he happened to bring it up, the reference to shopping just might satisfy the gang that I had no interest at all in the setting-up phase of the exhibition.

Turning left along the High St, I browsed the shop windows in search of inexpensive purchases to produce as evidence of a self-indulgent spending spree. First stop the charity shops, a treasure trove of quality items at very reasonable prices. I purchased a large multi-coloured 'Visit North Berwick' shopping bag, a multi-coloured t-shirt in keeping with my image, a pair of red sandals, and an interactive cat toy for G. Other High Street tourist shops were just as rewarding, yielding up dangly earrings, a couple of china mugs showing a beach scene, and a paper bag of to-die-for cardamon buns from Bostok Bakery. I finished off the morning at the Seabird Centre with a snack of tea and toastie looking across to the Bass Rock while I mulled over the details of Plan C.

I'd visit the hall this afternoon, list the exhibits on display, and make a rough sketch of the layout of the building with particular regard to exits. The drugs hidden in the artistic works wouldn't remain there for long, they'd be moved on as soon as possible. From what my fellow artists had let slip, the exhibition was going to be a sell-out, no item returned to Pear Tree Farm unsold. So my Plan C would be an after-hours stake-out of the building to spot comings and goings. The buyer of the 'sold' artworks with their hidden cargo would need some form of transport and I was hopeful I'd be able to note the registration plate as an artwork was loaded into van or car.

At three o'clock I made my way along the High Street to St Andrew Blackadder Church. On the front steps a large poster directed the public to the exhibition entrance at the rear. Dolores was the first to catch sight of me amongst the encouraging number of visitors. She looked up from studying a list of names and addresses in a notebook.

'Well, Tamsin, didn't expect to see you here.' Her only reaction, eyebrows raised in mild surprise as she unconcernedly added to the list in the book with no attempt to hide the name. Damn! I'd been so sure I'd be able to detect signs of alarm when I turned up in spite of the clever steps they had taken to prevent that very thing. But at least I'd keep her guessing as to how I'd got here with my car out of action.

'Shopping!' I said brightly, giving a hitch to the multi-coloured shopping bag on my shoulder to draw attention to it. 'And, of course, while I was here, I just had to come and see how your sales were going.' I looked round the stand. 'I must say, there are an *impressive* number of sold stickers.'

Her eyes narrowed. She thought I was implying the sales were too good to be true. I had indeed provoked a reaction, but not one that I wanted.

In an attempt to cover up my blunder, I added, 'Congratulations! I do hope my stay at Pear Tree Farm will bring *my* work up to that standard.'

Had I done enough? My eyes rested for an instant on the red sticker attached to Neil's vilely-decorated slate sculpture. This morning he'd been adamant that he would not allow the sale because his name would be linked to what in his opinion and mine, was now a very inferior piece of work. My feelings exactly if horror of horrors, some vandal were to 'improve' the rounded hips of Earth Mother by adding a skimpy polka-dot bikini.

Now his sculpture was *sold*! What could have happened to make him change his mind? Something fishy about that. Even if he had been offered a huge sum of money for it, could I envisage him accepting? No, I could not.

Nothing made sense – unless the slate sculpture had not in fact been sold. If the red sale sticker on Neil's work was fake, what if all the rest of the sold stickers were too? What if the method of distribution was for 'buyers' to turn up and carry off their 'purchase' to other parts of the UK? If so, it had been a bad move indeed for me to have brought up the subject of sale stickers with Dolores.

'Oh dear!' I sighed, trying again to undo the damage done by my comment on the large number of sold stickers. 'Such quality of workmanship makes me realise the standard I'll have to meet to be confident of selling.'

Completely ignoring my remark, she embarked on an offensive of her own with a series of cunningly-worded questions, a clever way to find out what she had wanted to know in the first place.

'That shopping bag of yours *does* look heavy. Hope it's not too much of a slog to where you parked your car? On a busy day like this, you've more chance of winning the Lottery than of finding a parking place in the High Street!'

My instinct not to fix the fault had been right. There was little doubt now that she was one of the brains behind the drug organisation at Pear Tree Farm.

'Oh, no parking problem.' An airy wave of my hand. 'My car wouldn't start, it's still at the Farm. Don't know what's wrong. I'll phone a garage tonight and get someone to come and investigate. They'll soon pinpoint the fault.'

Foiled, her pen hesitated for a moment as she added a name to the list in her book. Then, 'Well, how *did* you get here?'

I'd have to answer with care. If Neil had told them we'd hitched a lift together, she'd be keen to know if I thought it strange that *both* our cars had broken down on the morning of the exhibition.

I shrugged. 'Managed to hitch a lift. That's the trouble with cars and computers, I don't know much about either. Fine if they work, but when they breakdown…' That should satisfy her that I had no suspicions.

To reinforce the idea that I'd already dismissed this morning's events from my mind, I peered closely at one of her pictures that didn't bear a red sticker. 'Those dew drops hanging on the leaves! So realistic! You must have had to work fast with your paints to capture the play of light on them before they disappeared.' Dolores was undoubtedly a gifted artist.

The tactic worked. Successfully diverted from asking further awkward questions, she waxed eloquent for some time about the necessary skills involved in *plein-air* painting.

A cough from a well-dressed man wearing a camel-hair coat and highly polished leather brogues attracted Dolores attention.

'Excuse me? Are you in charge of sales? I've come to collect that wooden sculpture.' He indicated Stu's two foot high carving of a seabird perched on a heavy piece of driftwood bearing the telltale red sticker.

So, no sticker on artworks to sell to genuine members of the public, red sticker on those artworks concealing drugs? A simple means to prevent drugs falling into the wrong hands.

For a moment Dolores seemed unexpectedly flustered. 'I'm afraid that won't be possible, Mr...er...?'

'The name's Phillington Carruthers.' Posh name to go with posh plummy voice. 'I think you'll find my name on that list of yours.'

Dolores ran a finger down the names in her notebook, then looked up. 'Ah, yes, but...er... Unfortunately, Mr Carruthers, the exhibition doesn't close till six o'clock. We have a duty to the public to display all artworks till then. Half-empty shelves leave a bad impression, you see. Wouldn't do!'

'I think,' Carruthers persisted, 'that if you check with a Mr McClusky, that a special arrangement has been made for me to take it this afternoon. Cash discount as agreed.'

I moved away, pausing to examine one of Carol's ceramics, while studying Carruthers out of the corner of my eye. The second piece of the jigsaw had fallen neatly into place. This respectable-looking man was a courier picking up a drug consignment.

'Er... Mr McLusky's not here at the moment...' Definitely a warning in the look she cast at him. 'but...' She tapped in a number on her mobile, obviously discomfited that I was still within earshot.

I'd heard and seen enough. Too risky to loiter here. I turned away to wander past the shelves of exhibits, stopping to make admiring comments to Carol, Stu, and Vic. After congratulating each of my fellow artists, I made an unhurried exit from the exhibition and took up position in a shop doorway on the other side of the street, ready to follow Carruthers when he left with his package.

* * *

Dolores' eyes followed DJ's progress past the shelves of exhibits and through the swing doors of the hall. Frowning, she reached for her mobile. 'Trouble… Kennedy turned up here and witnessed the handover to Carruthers… Yes, too much of a coincidence. Can't take a chance. Listen carefully, what I want you to do is…'

CHAPTER FIFTEEN

Luckily the seabird driftwood sculpture was large and heavy. Carruthers could hardly walk away with it under his arm, so some means of transporting it would not be far away. Phillington Carruthers, or whoever was controlling him, would have made sure of that. I'd follow him and note the make and registration of his vehicle. The perfect spot to keep watch was from among the rows of cars in the busy car park opposite the rear of the church. As cars arrived and left, plenty of people were around, good enough cover. I wouldn't stand out as a lone figure. With a clear view of the hall's exit door, all I had to do was wait…

…I glanced at my watch. Twenty minutes had passed, more than enough time for the sculpture to be wrapped and handed over. Still no sign of Carruthers. Foolish to think it would be so easy. He must have slipped away with his 'purchase' via another exit at the side, or out the front door of the church. Something I should have foreseen. Damn, damn, and more damn! I had to accept that the most promising lead to date had petered out.

Dispirited, I left the car park and took the shortcut to the High Street in search of a taxi. The face of the man just coming out of the front door of the church was hidden by the tall cardboard box he was carrying clasped to his chest, but the camel-hair coat was unmistakable. Feet obscured by the bulky package, he was feeling his way down the steps one by one, giving me time to dash across the road. I darted into a charity shop and kept watch on him through the window while pretending to study some items. On reaching the bottom of the steps, he turned right, tilting the box to avoid collisions on the narrow crowded pavement. I left the shop and sauntered along some distance behind on the opposite side of the road.

The gang had not left it to chance to find a parking place near the exhibition hall, for after only a couple of minutes Carruthers stopped beside a mud-bespattered Mercedes, its raised bonnet and flashing hazard lights advertising to all and sundry that it had broken down. The type of vehicle one would expect to be driven by a man wearing such an expensive coat and shoes. The number plate was partially obscured, caked in dried iron-red East Lothian mud.

I walked on slowly, as if searching for something in my North Berwick shopping bag, but keeping him in view as he lowered the package to the ground, opened the passenger door and shoved the box inside. When I was twenty yards past his car, I turned phone in hand to record the car and number plate. Foiled. A Belhaven brewery lorry came to a halt in the slow queue of traffic, blocking my view. By the time it moved on, the Mercedes was gone. That lead had petered out, nevertheless my discovery of Pear Tree Farm's clever method to distribute their drugs was definitely a breakthrough.

In case I was under surveillance myself, I spent more time browsing shops in North Berwick looking for something I could use to placate Sapphire for the offence caused by my 'plumply-rounded female figure' remark. A bottle of Bombay Sapphire Gin from Lockett's Wine Shop would do the trick.

I called a taxi to take me back to Pear Tree Farm. Tempting as it was, it would have been too risky to pay another visit to the exhibition hall.

As we wound our way along the twisting country roads, I spent the journey puzzling over Neil's slate sculpture. A couple of things didn't add up. He had left me with the definite intention of snatching back his work of art, would have stormed into the exhibition hall, but no mention had been made of that. The other odd thing was that he would never have agreed to let it go on sale, his artistic reputation being more important to him than money, yet there it was, not only up for sale, but sold!

When the taxi drew up outside the farmhouse, to my surprise Neil's broken-down van was no longer parked in the courtyard. How would *I* have reacted when they refused to take the sculpture off sale? I'd have taken a taxi from North Berwick to the Farm, phoned a garage, and once the van was fixed, driven back to the exhibition hall to carry off my property. That's what he must have done. The others, however, would have pointed to the sold sticker and refused to let him remove the sculpture. What then? He'd hide in the church building, wait till late in the evening when there wouldn't be many people about, then let himself out, making sure the door was ajar for his return with a trolley and hoist. I'd know from their reaction if Neil had been successful when McClusky and the others went back to the hall tomorrow to clear the hall of 'sold' and unsold items.

The only other vehicles at the Farm, apart from my own, were Madge's green mini and Sapphire McGurk's flashy car, abandoned a couple of yards from the Farm House front door where she'd carelessly left it on her arrival. No sign of McGurk herself, thank goodness.

I hurried past studios A and B, anxious to let Gorgonzola out of the yurt where she'd been cooped up so long. She'd be demanding attention and compensation in the form of one of her favourite foods, and plenty of it. I quickened my pace as I approached Madge's studio. How would timid mouse Madge be coping there under the thumb of such a domineering and selfish woman as Sapphire McGurk?

I slowed at the unexpected sight of the studio, window frame and glass artistically decorated since this morning with trailing strands of Sapphire's yellow, scarlet, orange, blue and green wools. These vibrant colours were presumably the natural dyes she had 'sourced from India' and come to experiment with at Pear Tree Farm, strikingly different from the muted greens, ochres and dark reds of the plant and vegetable dyes she had exhibited at the Pittenweem Art Festival. Much as I disliked her, I had to concede that in the few hours since her arrival she had established her artistic image.

Not content with a window advert for her wools, she'd then wound strands of burnt-orange wool round the trunk of a small tree on the other side of the path. This must have meant mounting a stepladder to lead one orange woollen streak high up the trunk, the end secured in a bunch of twigs on a leafless branch. Intrigued, I stood and gazed in admiration at her handiwork, in its way a minor version of Nature Art at its best, as seen in Antony Gormley's early work. I had to admit that this effort to raise her profile with her fellow artists had certainly succeeded.

I whirled round as the studio door burst open with a

deafening crash. Sapphire stood framed in the doorway, face flushed and contorted with rage. 'You set this up on purpose, you cow, didn't you?' she screeched. 'Come to gloat, have you at all that expensive wool of mine *ruined!*'

Behind her, I glimpsed Madge, white-faced, eyes wide, hand over mouth.

Sapphire rushed towards me intent on inflicting grievous bodily harm with the heavy ladle used for stirring a vat of dye. Had the woman gone mad? I could only come to the conclusion that she was still brooding over the fact that I'd liberated, or in her eyes stolen, my White Lady Sculpture from her studio in Pittenweem and this had unhinged her mind, already a little unbalanced.

Two seconds to decide what do. Bravely stand my ground and calmly ask her what was wrong? Or beat a hasty, ignominious retreat, leaving her heated accusations and my denials for another occasion when she'd calmed down and was in a more receptive frame of mind? One glance at her face, at the ladle brandished like a mediaeval mace. I fled.

At the copse of birches I slowed and glanced back towards the studios. She'd given up pursuit. Her heavy body and stumpy legs had been no match for my long legs and physical fitness. I hoped she'd now be taking out her anger on the wool, savagely scouring it to remove grease and oils, or dunking hanks in buckets of dye with unnecessary force, while Madge nervously kept the lowest of profiles.

Just my luck that her dislike had made her pick on *me* as the perpetrator of the ghastly deed. Anyone else would see the wool decorating the tree as an unusual work of art and be of the opinion that the creator was to be congratulated.

Seething, I continued towards the yurt. Soon the slender grey birch trunks and the carpet of gold leaves worked their magic and by the time I'd reached the top of the rise, my mind had veered onto another tack. I hadn't draped the wool round the tree, so who *was* the inspired artist? With nearly everyone away at the exhibition, who else could it be but Pembrose McClusky? Or Madge? Must have been Madge. McClusky lacked the creative imagination, and the physical ability to climb a tree. Madge shared the studio with Sapphire, had the opportunity to get her hands on the wool and the artistic temperament to create Nature Art. The evidence stacked up against Madge. One niggling doubt. The Unwritten Law in an artistic community is *never* to touch another artist's work or materials without permission. I couldn't envisage timid Madge even contemplating breaking that taboo. I sighed. Whoever was guilty would lie low, only too happy for me to take the blame.

I'd something more important to consider. At supper tonight Sapphire would renew her attack on me. This time her assault would be verbal, not physical. All she really knew about me was that I had changed my name. I thought my explanation of the name change being a new branding for my work was credible, but my worry was that she would twist the truth about my time in Pittenweem, implying I was someone to be watched. And for the rest of the time I was at Pear Tree Farm, she'd lie inventively to get me into trouble. Result, I'd be asked to leave. Or worse, be considered a threat to the drug organisation, my life in danger.

Below me now were the rounded shapes of the yurts and the waters of the lake, sullen grey under the rain-bearing clouds massing overhead. I increased my pace, anxious to get under cover before I was drenched. The first heavy drops spattered the ground as I fitted the key in the lock. I eased open the door, blocking the widening gap with my leg to forestall the anticipated dash of G to the freedom of the Great Outdoors. But no gingery body rushed towards me. I wasn't really surprised. Even she wouldn't want to be out in weather like this!

'Sorry to be so long, G,' I called out ingratiatingly in the most placatory of tones.

No answering angry *miaow* of protest, no sound at all but the hollow drum of rain on the roof of the yurt. I sighed, again not too surprised. She'd opted for the Search and Find fun-game. For her, the fun was from her hiding place *not* being easily discovered, a hiding place from which she could smugly view my efforts. Places to hide in the yurt were low down and laughably few: settee, bed, table, chest of drawers. Not having the see-in-the-dark powers of a cat, I lit the oil lamp, the subdued lighting adding deep shadows to the places for me to pretend to search.

I looked first in the least likely places, no giveaways to ignore such as exposed paw, ear, or tail. Settee cushions were lifted and replaced, sheepskin rug ditto, drawers opened and shut, shadows peered into... A suitable time having passed, I stood hands on hips, shoulders drooping in simulated defeat, then advanced slowly on the most obvious hiding place and knelt to peer under the bed. No cat. G had obviously spent a considerable time fashioning cosy caves under the duvet, but I left the duvet bumps till last, before with a theatrical flourish whipping the duvet aside.

'Found you, G, at la–!'

No cat there either. The duvet dropped from my hand.

A rumpled sheet and a couple of red hairs, the only evidence she had been there. This time my slumped shoulders of defeat were genuine. She must have got out of the yurt, but how? After her escape from the yurt a couple of days ago, leading to the disastrous red clay incident in Carol's studio, I'd made a careful inspection of the yurt wall till I'd found the hole and stapled it securely, so she must have clawed at it and opened it up again.

But she hadn't. The repair was just as I'd left it without even the smallest tear in the felt wall at that place, or any other. The only possible explanation was that someone had used a master key to get into the yurt. I reconstructed what must have happened… Sound of key turning in the lock… door opening… G dashing out, not believing her luck.

With a growing sense of unease I sank down on the bed. Despite my efforts, I had somehow aroused suspicion. The evidence pointing that way was clear. First, the engineered breakdown of my car this morning, now the search of the yurt.

Where had I slipped up? I stared up at the ceiling. As an undercover agent I'd made errors of judgement in the past, but this time the stakes were higher than they had ever been. I was close to letting down my controller, Gerry Burnside.

What had blown my cover? Was it that decision of mine to investigate the promontory, the destination of the little boat I'd seen gliding silently from the island? I cross-examined myself as Gerry would at a debriefing. 'Let me get this clear, Deborah. You went there in daylight, didn't you? In *daylight*. And *knowing* there was a risk you'd be seen there?' No getting away from it, I had to face the truth. Stu hadn't been there by chance. Either he'd followed me or he'd been there on guard. Black Mark, DJ.

Worse still, my breakthrough, the discovery of their use of

artworks to distribute drugs from the Farm, had been put at risk by me turning up at the exhibition. Not only had I attended the opening when the gang had made it clear that they hadn't wanted me to be there, but already a suspect, I'd witnessed the crucial moment, the handover of drugs. Black mark after black mark.

And that must have had led Dolores to phone Pear Tree Farm to ask one of the two people back at the Farm to search my yurt. Who? Madge or McClusky? Not Madge. The damage to her cake and her reaction to it counted against her being one of the gang. The yurt had to have been searched by McClusky. Sunk in gloom I stared into space.

What makes Gerry one of the most respected controllers is that he reminds his operatives, 'When things are going badly, don't lose heart. There's always at least one silver lining.' What was it in this case? Well, McClusky wouldn't have found anything incriminating among my possessions, I'd made sure of that. And the gang members couldn't have been *sure* that I posed a threat or I would by now be a lifeless body floating in the lake. Taking all that into consideration, not one but *two* silver linings!

I'd been subconsciously aware of rain drumming on the roof, and I'd totally forgotten that G was out in that downpour, soaked and shivering. I leapt to my feet, rushed to the door and flung it open. In the light spilling from the doorway were stair-rods of rain pooling on the saturated ground. I peered out into the darkness. If G had found cover nearby, she'd answer to the whistle. I blew loud and long. A faint *me-ew* came from the boathouse, a dark shape through the driving rain. Another blast on the whistle, another answering *me-ew*. A come-and-get-me mew. The meaning clear: someone was going to get wet, and it wasn't going to be G.

Exasperated, but relieved that she was safe, I shrugged on my raincoat, grabbed my torch, and splashed over the soggy ground trying to ignore the discomfort of wet trouser legs and socks. A sweep of the torch beam over the platform round the boathouse revealed the glint of a cat's eyes in the foundation space beneath. Tucking her under my raincoat, I dashed back to the shelter of the yurt. Ten seconds later, G was lying cosily in front of the stove. My sodden shoes kicked off, dripping raincoat dropped on floor, I sank onto the settee, legs outstretched towards the welcome heat of the stove and contemplated the steam rising gently from wet material. Time to relax and work out the best line to take in the unavoidable confrontation with Sapphire at supper tonight.

G had other ideas. The first tendrils of steam had hardly risen from my trousers when an impatient paw tapped my leg and she sprang onto my lap. I ran my hand over her coat, slightly damp but a good deal drier than me.

I reached for her towel. It was when I was drying her feet that I noticed, caught in a claw, a strand of bright orange wool, muddied but unmistakably the same wool I'd seen twined artistically round the tree. I stared at it in disbelief, then at G.

I was indeed responsible, albeit indirectly, for the misuse of her expensive wool! Sapphire had been right.

That would put me in the weakest of weak positions at the evening meal when faced with Sapphire's broadsides. Nothing would persuade her that I hadn't deliberately sent my cat to create havoc in her studio. Profuse apologies would be taken only as clear admission of guilt.

My remaining days at Pear Tree Farm were definitely numbered. G's little bit of mischief had further stacked the odds against Operation Smokescreen. The gang were already suspicious, so McClusky would be looking for any excuse to get rid of me. And both Sapphire and Carol would gladly provide him with the evidence.

CHAPTER SIXTEEN

Dolores closed the notebook with some satisfaction. There'd been four handovers this afternoon, £100,000 in cash. Tomorrow the other transfers at arranged intervals would double that. However, all her customers, aware of the value of the merchandise hidden in artworks marked by the red stickers, might very well be tempted to make a pre-emptive grab overnight. Why pay when you could take?

Well, she'd left nothing to chance. The church authorities had been quite amenable when she suggested she'd bring in a security firm to guard the premises overnight. She'd stressed the value of the gallery art, one-off pieces that could never be a hundred per cent replicated even by the creator. What they didn't know, of course, was that it wasn't a genuine security firm. She had arranged to call on a strong-arm team from the Organisation to deal suitably with any opportunistic rival gang, any violence discreetly handled and covered-up.

* * *

Neil's dusty dark blue transit van swung into the parking space at the rear of Turnbulls Home Hardware shop, now closed for the day. Only a couple of hundred yards from the back door of St

Andrew Blackadder church and the entrance to the exhibition hall, yet conveniently out of sight round a corner, so no chance of that bitch Dolores and her pals spotting him if they'd stayed around tidying up after the exhibition. He scowled. They'd promised to take his slate sculpture off-sale and bring it back tomorrow after the exhibition! Thought he was a fool, did they? The lying bastards. They'd pull a fast one – sell it by 'mistake', hand him some cash, think he'd be satisfied. All *they* thought about was cash. Some things were more important.

He had carefully planned the rescue of his work of art. The last of the public had been ushered out an hour ago, the exhibition hall and the outer doors locked. But that notice about the special service being held in the church upstairs at seven-thirty this evening had given him an idea. The front entrance would be open. Once inside the building he'd mingle with the congregation and afterwards lie concealed between one of the rows of seats until everybody had left the building. Then he'd go downstairs, unsnib the Yale latch on the back door, drive his van into position and jemmy the lock of the exhibition hall to gain entrance. The bastards had transported his slate stone even using *his* porter's trolley so it would be here to load his heavy artwork into the van – no sweat! And he might just give them a touch of their own medicine before he left, 'improve' some of *their* artworks with spray paint. 'An improvement', that's how they'd described the vandalism on his stone, hadn't they? What he'd give to see their faces when they turned up tomorrow to find his stone vanished and their artwork redesigned!

Time to go. He got out of the van, grinding out his cigarette stub under his heel.

* * *

Bong...bong...bong... Nine loud chimes from the clock tower died away. Streetlights filtering through the glass doors lit up the front vestibule of St Andrew Blackadder church. One of four heavily-built men opened the corridor door leading to the back entrance of the church.

'Keep this open so we'll hear the rival gang if they interfere with the back door. Check your taser batteries are fully charged, that way, no shots, no knives, no noise. Boss's orders, any trouble didn't happen, Joe Public to be none the wiser, understood? Targets to be immobilised, thrown into the van. Give 'em a few swigs of alcohol and dump them over the harbour wall. Up to them if they sink or swim, either way, nobody'll be complaining to the police.

He switched on the television-sized monitor mounted on the wall, set up to show services and other events in the church. 'And with this we can keep a check on upstairs.' The blank screen changed to a view of banks of seats barely visible in the darkened upper church. Eyes on the screen, professionals in their field, they sat in silence, arms folded, ears alert for sounds.

Ten minutes passed... Movement in the upper room. The watching men tensed, leaned forward. On the right of the screen a head raised cautiously above the line of seats. The head turned slowly left, slowly right. A crouching figure rose and slid out of the row. Silhouetted against the huge stained-glass window, the man moved quickly to the front of the church and disappeared through a door.

A whisper. 'He's coming down. Making for the back entrance.'

Backs pressed against the wall, soundlessly the watchers moved as one along the unlit corridor, tasers at the ready.

Neil slid a hand down the banister rail, foot groping for the next step. Wouldn't do to fall down the stairs in the dark, sprain an ankle, break a leg, when everything was going according to plan, but with windows giving onto the street, crazy to risk using his torch. All he had to do now was fetch the van, break into the exhibition hall, and load his sculpture. Twenty minutes should do it. He stretched out a hand to locate the snib of the Yale lock.

50,000 volts from a taser surged through his body. He collapsed on the wooden floor, body convulsing.

Outside, a stray dog twitched an ear at the faint sounds within and slunk on.

CHAPTER SEVENTEEN

6 a.m.

For more than an hour Dolores had been tossing and turning, mind busy thinking what to do about that other problem, Neil. There'd been no sign of him or his van by midnight last night, but one thing was sure, he would definitely cause trouble when he did return today. She stretched out an arm to put off the alarm clock, congratulating herself on her foresight in taking precautions to thwart a rival gang from stealing the drugs at the exhibition hall. She'd text the others for ideas.

Dolores to All : *Need plan to deal with Neil. He'll turn up today looking for his precious sculpture.*

Stu: *Unpredictable when he finds artwork gone. Big problem.*

Vic: *Might claim we've stolen it and go to the police.*

Carol: *Don't want police poking noses in here.*

Dolores Text to All: *Can't take chances. Imperative Neil is disposed of. Agreed?*

Reply from All: *Agreed.*

Dolores: *Suggestions?*

McClusky: *Fatal traffic accident?*

Carol: *Accident in his workshop?*

McClusky: *Give the Removal Men his van's registration number. Force him off the road.*

Dolores : *Good idea but must be no link to us. Imperative to organise the accident far from Pear Tree. If Neil turns up today, we'll send him to a fake address to collect his artwork. The Removal Men will take care of everything.*

She placed the mobile on the bedside table, and lay back against the pillow, satisfied. After she'd got in touch with the Removal Men there'd be no unwelcome police attention as happened after that staged handyman's fatal accident in the boathouse. She dozed off...

...A text whistled its arrival. She groped for the mobile and peered at the screen. A message from the Removal Men. *Overnight intruder to exhibition...* Her heart beat faster. She opened up the message. *Overnight intruder to exhibition dealt with. Steps taken to ensure no return.* Underneath was a photo of the intruder. Neil.

Steps taken to ensure no return. No need to worry about him any more, then. Whatever method they'd used to get rid of him, there was now no possibility of him going to the police or anyone else to create a fuss. Problem dealt with. Expensive, yes, but worth every penny.

The moment of satisfaction faded... Hollowing out works of art to hold drugs had been a brilliant idea that had gone undetected for more than a year, but she had to concede it would be only a matter of time before a rival gang discovered Pear Tree Farm's clever method of drug distribution. Up till now she'd had no worries about leaving the artworks overnight in the Farm's car park, overlooked as it was by Bev and McClusky's bedroom windows. It would have been impossible for an intruder to drive off the van without detection.

But drugs stored overnight in an exhibition hall, she now realised had been a much greater risk. She thought about it for some time... *Inside* information was their Achilles Heel. Information leaked by someone at Pear Tree Farm would alert a rival gang. There had been no problem with previous exhibitions, but last night had been a wake-up call. Anyone who joined the course in future, or indeed had joined recently, could very well be a spy from a rival gang. Madge, Tamsin, and the McGurk woman? Madge's seeming timidity could very well be only pretence. Just *too* shy, lacked the social confidence of other artists who had come to the Farm. For some time they'd had reservations about her, had decided to get rid of her by messing up that prized sugar craft castle of hers. That had deeply upset her. So why was she still here?

And as for the other new-on-the-scene, Tamsin Kennedy. She could be a mole who would leak the information to a rival gang. It was more than slightly suspicious that she had been found near the water tank *and* turned up at the exhibition at the very moment a drug transfer was being arranged. No hard evidence against her yet, but the fact that she and the McGurk woman knew each other would be worth digging into... Could the ill-feeling between them be feigned to hide the fact that the two of them were working together?

She came to a decision. To ignore misgivings was always a mistake. And she wasn't intending to make one now. All three women would have to be dealt with. She'd speak to Carol at breakfast, take her off the packing-up at the exhibition hall this morning, and instruct her to suss out the three suspects.

CHAPTER EIGHTEEN

I counted off the days to the next exhibition. Only seventeen till another batch of artworks would be chosen. And if by that time I hadn't finished sculpting Earth Mother, I might very well be asked to leave, having failed to provide even one artwork suitable as a hiding place for drugs. An early start working on Earth Mother was called for.

The dew was still on the grass and the sun barely up when I slunk past Sapphire's studio with a sulky G safely imprisoned in the cat carrier. I wasn't going to chance any repeat of yesterday's incident. Though the loops of brightly coloured wool were gone from the studio windows, accusing burnt-orange strands were still in evidence on the small tree. But I needn't have worried. No irate face was pressing against the window. Thankful that the studio door remained firmly closed, I quickened my pace.

I was looking forward to having the studio to myself, as Carol would be away in North Berwick with the others packing up the exhibition. An added bonus was that she had cleared away all her clay sheets, so I was able to spread out my tools, brushes, pot of water, and a bag of clay just as I wanted. I set down the carrier. Taking this as a possible sign of release, G thrust her face against the bars with a piteous *miaow* cunningly calculated to pull at the heartstrings. A limp paw, claws sheathed, implied virtuous and innocent thoughts. I wasn't fooled. Best behaviour wouldn't be guaranteed, but if I told her she was on duty, she'd prowl round the studio looking for drugs. That would keep her interested and out of mischief.

I looked around assessing the surroundings. There had been a big delivery of clay in the last couple of days. The wall of bags was now four feet high, six long, and three rows deep. Carol must have several super-sized projects in mind.

'Ok, G, search!' I said, and let her out, first having made sure the outer door was closed with no possibility of escape from the studio.

With a 'you're looking at a sniffer pro' twitch of her moth-eaten tail, she sashayed towards the five-litre plastic tubs of glazes and underglazes lined up on a bench. Confident that she would have nothing on her mind but professional duty, I removed the protective covering from Earth Mother. The clay was in perfect condition for adding more to build up the body, and I lost count of time as I worked happily away in a world of my own, forming coils, joining with slip, smoothing, shaping… Satisfied with progress, I replaced the plastic covering on the sculpture to retain the right amount of moisture in the clay until I was ready to attach the breasts.

I set about forming the first voluptuous bosom. Without having to bother about Carol's malevolent presence, I was making good time, looking forward to soon completing Earth Mother, perhaps make a start on another sculpture, even manage to finish it before the deadline. I hummed as I moulded and fashioned a ball of red clay into the perfect rounded breast.

A final smoothing and–

A loud CR-O-O-O-N reverberated from the dark corner where the wall of clay bags were stored. Startled, my hands clenched with disastrous effect. To my consternation, the shape of the perfect breast transformed in a moment from youthful round to old-hag pendulous. I flung down the misshapen lump of clay and hurried over to investigate.

'Found something have you, G?'

From behind the bags, another CROOON telling me she had homed in on a consignment of drugs ready for concealment in the next batch of artworks. The sound appeared to be coming from somewhere in the middle of the stack. I stared at the tightly-packed bags. How could she have managed to squeeze between them? I tried to insert my fingers into the minute gap at each side of a bag in the centre of the front row, but it was too tightly packed, too heavy, the plastic wrapping too slippery. I tried again. Same result, again leaving smears of red where my clay-covered fingers had scrabbled for purchase. On closer inspection there did seem to be a gap between the bags in the back row and the wall, just wide enough to give G access.

'Thought I'd find you here, Tasmin.'

I whirled round. Carol was standing in the doorway.

Her eyes narrowed. 'Oh!' She stared at the telltale smears of red clay my hands had left at various places on the stacked bags and rushed forward. 'What are you *doing*?' clearly agitated that she'd found me poking among the bags of clay.

If drugs were indeed stashed there, I'd only seconds to come up with a credible explanation that would disarm suspicion.

'I'm so glad you've come, Carol!' Relief, not alarm in my voice. 'Picassa's got herself stuck behind the bags but they're too heavy for me to shift. Can you help me move some of them to let her out?'

A direct request with a win-win outcome for me. I was confident that she would refuse to help. She certainly didn't want the bags moved as she knew drugs were hidden behind them. I'd take refusal to help as being her revenge for the damage G had inflicted on her sheets of clay. And it would be only natural for me, a pet-owner in distress, to have pulled at the bags in a fit of desperation. But I hadn't counted on her being as quick-thinking as myself.

'*One* person must *not* attempt to lift a sack by themselves. Risk of back injury, you know. Mr McClusky has laid down *strict* health and safety rules.' With the skill of a politician pressed to answer a tricky question, she'd dodged a direct answer to my request for help.

Full marks to her. I would have been taken in, believing that McClusky had indeed issued that sensible health and safety edict. Except for the fact that my arms were still aching from my efforts only two days ago, when Carol herself had ordered me to drag not one but two heavy bags of clay across the studio floor in complete disregard of that very health and safety rule. She had just stood there, hands on hips watching me, making no attempt whatsoever to help heave them up onto the work surface.

A most inopportune crooon from behind the bags. How could I explain that away? Inspiration.

'Oh dear, I think Picassa's found a mouse.'

Another CROOOOOOOOON, loud, extended, signifying an impatient, 'What's taking you so long to come? Where's my reward?'

I'm quite inventive in a crisis. 'Oh!' I cried, 'it must be a *very* large mouse. Or a rat! Cats do like to play with anything they catch, then allow it to escape so they can chase it. What will we *do*?' My voice rose in feigned panic.

'A *mouse*! Don't know what you're going to do. I'm getting out of here fast.' She backed hurriedly away. 'As for that cat of yours, it can come out the same way it got in. I'm going nowhere near any *mouse*!' Left hanging in the air was, 'If the brute's stuck in there and never gets out, tough!'

A louder, more exasperated CROOON.

She beckoned me across to the door. 'Can't stand that frightful din. I've something to ask you. Let's go outside.'

The door safely shut against the escape of rodent, she draped an arm round my shoulders. Six marks out of ten for the accompanying attempt at a friendly smile. What was she up to?

Looking around as if there were eavesdroppers lurking behind nearby bushes, she murmured, 'I'll let you into a secret, Tamsin. I hope to put on an exhibition of my ceramics at the Pittenweem Festival. That event is on your CV isn't it? So I'm counting on you to give me some tips. I want the low-down from a fellow-worker with clay.' She was obviously fishing for information.

'Oh,' I said, unwittingly laying a trap for myself, 'only too happy to help but I don't have any tips. I've only exhibited there once, you see, sharing a studio with Sapphire.'

A smile played on Carol's lips as she turned to go. 'You're right. Should have thought of that. Sapphire's the one to ask. She'll be able to tell me *all* that goes on at the Pittenweem Festival.'

Mention of Sapphire had been a big mistake.

CHAPTER NINETEEN

Carol's parting words, "...able to tell me *all* that went on at the Pittenweem Festival". Her stress on 'all' indicated that she suspected something had happened there that I didn't want her to know about, something that Sapphire could tell her. Should I be worried? After all, Sapphire knew nothing about my Revenue & Customs undercover role in Pittenweem. As far as she was concerned, I was merely a clay sculptor trying to make my name at the Pittenweem Festival. She had known me as Kirsty Gordon, but on her arrival here at the Farm I had given a convincing reason for my change of name, I was sure of that. So all she could say about me to Carol was that I had been a very unreliable helper.

Of course, there was nothing I could do about her resentment at my snatched repossession of the White Lady, a grudge unfortunately reinforced by G's woollen Work of Art on the tree. Hopefully my abject apologies and the large bottle of her favourite drink, Bombay Sapphire Gin, purchased in North Berwick would smooth over relations between us. I'd visit her in her yurt tonight, clutching the bottle.

However, first things first. Earth Mother's breasts couldn't wait, they'd have to be shaped and left to firm up before being hollowed out and attached to the torso. I set to work. G still hadn't emerged from behind the wall of bags, but I knew how her mind worked. First puzzled, then aggrieved that I'd not reacted in the expected way to her drugs-find croon, she'd have resorted to a mega sulk. Tough. I concentrated on shaping two perfectly formed breasts, and satisfied, placed them side by side on the wooden board. A burst of warm air from the old hairdryer on the shelf firmed up the clay surface. Perfect. By tomorrow they would be ready to hollow out and attach.

From the direction of the bags of clay, a squeak, a scutter... something small raced across the floor towards me. A scratch of claws on plastic, a blur of movement, as Gorgonzola intent on slaughter, burst from a gap low down behind the wall of bags. The mouse scurried up the leg of the workbench and disappeared behind the ample hips of Earth Mother. No time to intervene before G gathered herself to spring and launched herself in a flying leap.

'No-o-o-o!' I cried.

Too late. In a blink of an eye, with guided-missile precision two large paws reconfigured the two perfectly rounded breasts into two flat rounds bearing a marked resemblance to cowpats, each feline pad and claw clearly stamped onto the soft surface. Earth Mother trembled, threatening to topple under the impact of G's questing paw. I lunged forward and grabbed G. Unbalanced, together we toppled to the floor.

A cry from me, a yowl from G, a squeak from the mouse as it abandoned its refuge behind Earth Mother, scampered down the leg of the bench, squeezed a getaway through an impossibly narrow gap under the studio door and disappeared.

Mutual recriminations: my yells, G's yowls, mutual sulks. Tail ramrod straight, moth-eaten tip twitching angrily, G stalked off, heading for the spot where drugs must lie concealed behind the wall of bags. I waited for the croon. No croon. Payback time. The silence lengthened.

That did it. 'Look what you've done!' I shrieked, eyeballing the cowpat breasts. 'All that work wasted! *Wasted*, I say, completely *wasted!*'

From behind the clay bags drifted an unrepentant *his-s-ss*.

With gritted teeth I scraped up the now useless clay and hurled it into the bin. I didn't have the heart to start again. For the moment, Earth Mother would have to be content only with her massive thighs.

I flung off my apron and stomped out of the studio. 'That's *me* away, G!' I called over my shoulder and didn't look back.

Why waste time on a miffed, huffy cat, when I could work on building a rapport with a miffed, huffy, dyer of wools! I'd collect that bottle of Bombay Gin from my yurt and seek her out. Abject apology and bribery, a winning combination!

A rapport with devious, unscrupulous Sapphire McGurk would be mere pretence. On both sides, of course.

For seven hours now, there'd been no sign of Gorgonzola. When there's been a serious falling-out, both sides are reluctant to take the first step towards reconciliation. But as the hours passed, my anger had given way to annoyance, dwindled to exasperation, been replaced by guilt. She would not have known why I was angry. The more I thought about my conduct, the guiltier I felt. After all, it's only instinct for a cat to hunt and chase. Had not G many times made me a present of a dead mouse, loving gifts to the human in her life?

As the figures on my digital watch changed from 19:59 to 20:00, a timid *miaow* and a wary tap on the wooden door signalled Gorgonzola's cautious return to the yurt for her supper. I leapt up from the settee where I had been brooding about my behaviour to her, and mulling over that abortive meeting a couple of hours ago with Sapphire McGurk.

Gorgonzola made no attempt to come in, just crouched down, unsure of her welcome. Contrite, I gathered her up and carried her off to the settee, murmuring endearments and stroking her until her rhythmic purring and the lick of a rough tongue indicated that she knew whatever it was she'd done wrong had been forgiven and all was well between us.

I'd had one of her favourite fish dinners ready for her, and while she nibbled daintily, one morsel after another, I eyed the rejected, still unopened, bottle of gin lying on the sheepskin rug where I'd abandoned it after stomping back from Sapphire's yurt. Frustration at all the setbacks of the last few hours could be contained no longer.

'See this bottle, G!' I picked it up and brandished it. 'All the trouble I went to! And all for nothing! Far from looking upon it as a peace offering, that woman spurned it!'

I pictured again the faint curl of Sapphire's lip and the dismissive wave of her hand as she drawled, each word enunciated slowly and clearly for maximum effect, '*If* you'd bothered to ask me, I'd have informed you that I've transferred my allegiance to award-winning North Berwick gin, selected, I'm told, for events attended by the Queen herself. Bring me a bottle of that and then we can talk.' As I'd turned away, I'd been all too aware of her lips shaping the word 'maybe.'

'Might as well not have bothered to try to mend relations,' I groaned. I had to face the fact that G and I had made an implacable enemy in Sapphire, an enemy whose spite might very well force me to leave Pear Tree Farm and abandon the mission. And I'd actually encouraged Carol to seek her out, thereby handing both of them a golden opportunity to make mischief! That smile of Carol's as she'd hurried off indicated that she'd be on the lookout for anything she could use against me. At best, I'd be asked to leave Pear Tree Farm as someone undesirable for the course. At worst, be killed as a threat to their operation, under suspicion as a member of a rival gang, or as a mole infiltrated by Revenue & Customs. The danger of staying on at the Farm was clear, but there was still much to find out. Gerry was relying on me. I slumped back on the settee.

Startled, G paused in mid-nibble, sensed my dejection and leapt onto my lap. A comforting paw reached up to pat at my cheek.

CHAPTER TWENTY

Dolores laid aside her paint brush and turned her attention to the assessments she'd asked Carol to make on McGurk, Kennedy, and Tiverton.

<u>Sapphire McGurk</u>: Self-centred, unscrupulous, no moral principles.

<u>Tamsin Kennedy</u>: Devious, double-dealing, a liar, according to McGurk.

<u>Madge Tiverton</u>: Nervous, agitated, frightened of her own shadow.

Dolores frowned. It was worse than she'd thought. All three posed a problem for the Organisation. So… prioritise which of them to neutralise first.

If the woman McGurk discovered what was going on at the Farm, she'd definitely be quick to resort to blackmail, threatening to sell the info to a rival gang. There'd be no phone call from her to the police. But no threats from her so far. Sapphire McGurk could safely be attended to later. Action not urgent.

Kennedy, now. She'd had her doubts about Tamsin Kennedy for some time, since that more than suspicious turning-up at the exhibition to coincide with the arrival of the drug courier.

Worth investigation? Definitely. But not just yet.

When it came to Madge Tiverton, however, definitely a red alert, there. Her agitated behaviour ever since the damage to her sugar craft sculpture indicated she knew about the drugs hidden in the hollowed out art pieces. Obviously terrified that we'd find out that she knew.

Yes, a threat like Tiverton's had to be dealt with *immediately*. Counteraction couldn't be postponed. First, set up a meeting in the grounds of Direlton Castle with the strong-arm team, or as she preferred to call them, the Removal Men. Have to be tomorrow. Tuesday was not her usual day to go there, but when needs must. Visitors entering the grounds with their eyes fixed on the colourful herbaceous borders of the main garden often walked towards the castle without noticing the Formal Garden with its sheltered seat on the far side of the thick yew hedge. That seat would be ideal for a private meeting.

Decision made, she dropped Carol's notes into the stove and picked up the phone. 'Emergency meeting tomorrow, Tuesday. 10 a.m. Dirleton Castle.' Annoying to have to make that extra trip to Dirleton but the Removal Men's rule was payment before a job. She'd give them Madge's photo and arrange for her to be in position near the Seabird Centre on Tuesday night. They'd know what to do.

CHAPTER TWENTY-ONE

Early on Tuesday the risk to the mission presented by Sapphire McGurk's spite was confirmed. I had decided to turn up at the Farmhouse at seven-thirty, make myself a quick tea and toast and be gone long before the others appeared. No opportunity then for Carol to confront me with information spurious or otherwise that Sapphire might have provided. Breakfast didn't officially start till eight o'clock so I was surprised to find the back door of the farmhouse ajar. I was not the first to arrive after all, it seemed. Perhaps I should forget about breakfast, just slip away to the studio and get started on Earth Mother. Even though protected by plastic wrapping, the clay would slowly but inexorably be hardening beyond the stage when those mighty breasts could be successfully attached.

I'd turned to go, when loud and clear from the kitchen, 'So you see, Carol, you can't trust that Tamsin woman an inch. Would you believe it, she's using a false name! What does that tell you?' Sapphire was already drip-feeding poison.

'Is that so-o-o?' Carol, slow and thoughtful. 'We'll have to find out what she's up to, won't we? See what you can do, Sapphire.'

I crept away, all idea of breakfast forgotten. Closing the door of the studio behind me, I sat at the bench staring at the plastic-shrouded figure of Earth Mother. Sapphire would report to Carol *anything* I did as being a suspicious activity worthy of investigation. After that, the gang wouldn't need proof. They'd act. How much longer would it be safe to stay? No question of leaving now, however. I'd made some progress, though not quite enough. I'd just have to be very careful.

With my mind on personal security, needless to say my attempt to recreate those perfect boobs was half-hearted and soon abandoned. I stared at them critically – much too large, not the right shape. I left them unattached, covered them and Earth Mother with the plastic sheet, and headed back to the yurt where G was stretched out on the soft sheepskin rug in front of the still warm stove, no anxieties on *her* mind.

I settled back on the settee with a mug of coffee. Lying on the small table was the as yet unread *East Lothian Courier*, bought in North Berwick when I visited the exhibition. I picked it up and glanced through it.

Could the pet in your life be our Pet Idol? Fancy £300? Send in a picture of your cute pet to win the star prize.

I contemplated the mound of ginger fur gently rising and falling in untroubled slumber. Moth-eaten tail and scruffy coat... As a Pet Idol, *nul points*. As an Undercover Agent, five stars. Sensing my scrutiny, one ear swivelled, one eye opened. And closed again. The message was clear, Do Not Disturb.

I flung down the newspaper, still no decision made about the date of my departure from Pear Tree Farm. I'd learned how drugs were concealed, how they were distributed through art exhibitions, but there was much I still needed to find out.

Dolores might be the boss of the gang's operation here, but who was higher up in the chain of command? What was the purpose of her weekly visits to Dirleton castle? Was it to pick up drugs for distribution via Pear Tree Farm? Best way to find out would be to go there and take Gorgonzola with me. No problem, accustomed as she was to travelling inconspicuously on missions. In fact, she actually liked the dark comfort of the rucksack with the prospect of search and due reward to follow. If, as sometimes happened, she grew restless and drew attention to herself, I'd remark that a visit to the vet had upset her.

That decided, when should I suss out the castle and its grounds? Dolores' visits took place every Wednesday, rain or shine. Quite safe, then, for me to go on any other day, so why not today, Tuesday? The quiet little village of Dirleton was only half an hour's drive away. Yes, that's what I'd do. No time like the present. Unwise, however, as an undercover agent to take my eye-catching old car with its paintwork of random streaks and splashes of bright colour. I'd drive as far as North Berwick and after a bacon roll and coffee in one of the many cafès there, continue by bus.

'Fancy a trip to a ruined castle, G?' I held the rucksack invitingly open.

No need for the me to trot out the vet story, Gorgonzola snoozed in the rucksack all the way to Dirleton. Or as she would prefer to put it, getting herself Mission Ready. Fuelled by bacon roll and coffee, I too was mission ready. Not that you could term a stroll round the Castle Gardens and a poke inside the Castle as anything more than a *possibly* useful reconnoitre.

From the bus stop beside the village green, only the merest hint of the battered mediaeval castle was visible peeping warily from behind the tall trees inside the surrounding high wall as if fearful that twenty-first century English invaders might be preparing to launch a surprise attack.

To get my bearings I bought a guidebook from the kiosk, and with no set plan in mind wandered down the garden between the long herbaceous borders. In summer they would have been a blaze of colour. At this time of year, traces of this glory lingered on: faded gold and brown foliage, yucca leaves outlined against the blue sky like dark swords, red rose petals like drops of blood, white gold feathery pampas grasses and tall purple buddleia.

The normal rule for surveillance is to take up position an hour or more in advance of the target's arrival. Today was a trial run to plan where best to place myself. As the grounds didn't open till ten o'clock, the time Dolores normally arrived, tomorrow I'd wait unobtrusively at the far side of the village green until I saw her go in, otherwise our arrivals might coincide. Since the windows of the entrance kiosk had a good view of most of the garden, I'd buy a coffee and sip it while looking to see if she had set up her easel on the grass to paint the flower borders. If so, I could still keep out of sight by taking that little path behind the tall yew hedge at the entrance.

An impatient squeak from the rucksack reminded me that I had a partner looking forward to her reward for a search. A partner who had waited too long be let out.

'Patience, G. You'll soon get your chance to investigate.'

Ignoring the grumble of protest, I picked up the rucksack and set off up a grassy slope towards the domed sixteenth century dovecot to house pigeons, once an important food source for the castle. I ducked under the low lintel of the grey stone building. Sunlight streaming down through the large circular hole in the ceiling high above dramatically lit the dark squares of nest holes spiralling upwards in ever decreasing concentric circles. A small package of drugs could be thrust deep into any of the recesses above eye level, be invisible to the casual visitor, its position conveyed for pickup by means of a simple code, such as 10x25R or 10x25L, meaning count ten rows up, 25 boxes right or left from the door.

Perhaps I was onto something. Encouraged, I unzipped the rucksack to put G to work. She leapt out and gazed up, her eyes narrowing as she calculated the reward for the search of what must be close to a thousand apertures. Unfortunately, those inward-sloping stone walls would offer no purchase even for G's sharp claws.

A moment's thought and problem solved. If I walked slowly round the interior, holding the rucksack up with her head sticking out at the height anyone could reach without a ladder, there was a chance she'd pick up a scent. I patted the bag invitingly and looked at G. She looked at me, her strident *miaow* evidence of what was in her mind, 'You can't be *serious*! If you think I'm going back into that rucksack right now, think again! A cat needs to stretch her legs. A cat needs to *roam!*' With that, she was gone.

Oh well… if I really needed her, I'd summon her with the cat whistle. No use wasting time looking in the lower holes, anything there would be too easily spotted by one of the many visitors to the Gardens. I stood on tiptoe and shone my flashlight into one nesting hole after another. Nothing, all empty. That didn't mean, of course, that one of them hadn't been used in the past, or wouldn't be in the future, perhaps tomorrow when

Dolores made her usual visit. Damn! I'd have known for sure if drugs had recently been stored in the dovecot if Gorgonzola hadn't had her Diva moment. That's one of the downsides of a cat as a colleague.

On the lookout for other places Dolores might think suitable for a rendezvous, I picked up the rucksack and took the path towards the castle itself. A long flight of shallow steps wound up the lichen-covered rock on which the castle had been built. At the top of the steps a gravelled courtyard offered glimpses down into the shadowy space of vaulted cellars. A wander through these proved them all to be unsuitable for a secret assignation, would definitely be rejected as a meeting place by security conscious Dolores. Talk would easily be overheard through the gaping holes in the interior walls. And conversation drifting down from the upper floors showed they too would be unsuitable for a clandestine meeting.

The bus back to North Berwick would be due soon, so time to track G down. I retraced my steps to the Dovecot. No Gorgonzola there. She'd be at large somewhere among the impressive borders of the flower garden. I made my way towards the entrance kiosk, admiring the brilliant blue agapanthus and jewel-like red flowers of fuchsias, excellent subjects for Dolores' paintings.

I was feeling in my pocket for the cat whistle when the sudden *tchook tchook tchook* of a blackbird's alarm call told me that G was in stalking mode somewhere nearby. She always ignored any bird too easy to catch, so I'd no real fears for the blackbird. The challenge of the hunt was what seemed important to G. She never tired of the sport of creeping up within springing distance of crows and seagulls, despite the frustration of them flying off with raucous mocking cackles. Ever the optimist, she looked forward to her revenge if they miscalculated.

A path on the left offered me a glimpse of a parallel garden, very different from the exuberant herbaceous borders on this side of the high yew hedge. Not much of it was visible from where I was standing, but those colourful formal flowerbeds set in a manicured lawn would definitely be attractive to an artist. Its position on the far side of the hedge made it more secluded and suitable for a private tête-à-tête. I hesitated… but no time to explore it now. I'd leave it for another day. The bus was due in three minutes.

I blew the ultrasonic whistle. Waiting impatiently for G to respond, I heard from the entrance kiosk a *ting ting* signalling the arrival of visitors, and from the other side of the thick yew hedge a murmur of voices. From the mass of dead leaves trapped at its base a *rustle rustle*. G's gingery face peered out. I scooped her into the rucksack and with a cheery 'Bye!' to the custodian in the kiosk, set off at a run.

The app on my mobile told me I was too late. The bus I'd hoped to catch was now well on its way to North Berwick. Should I go back into the Castle grounds to take a look at the formal garden behind the yew hedge instead? With G quietly asleep in the rucksack after her investigation of the gardens, I relaxed with a carefully timed coffee at the Open Arms Hotel.

Half an hour later as the North Berwick bus drew away from the bus stop, I gazed despondently out of the window at the gazebo-tower built into the outer wall of the Castle grounds. From start to finish this morning's visit to Dirleton Castle had definitely been unsatisfactory. With time running out for me to be safe at the Farm, nothing much had been achieved. Thanks to G's uncharacteristic lack of interest in any sniffing search, evidence was inconclusive that drugs were being left in the Castle buildings or grounds for Dolores to collect. I'd been so very confident that Dolores was making use of the castle ruins for a clandestine weekly meeting with a courier. Today's visit, however, proved that Dolores' meetings probably took place in the grounds rather than the castle.

Damn it! There'd been no need to hurry away. I'd prioritised catching the bus over the investigation of a more promising part of the grounds. That had been a big mistake. I might have found somewhere to spy without being seen. Behind that tall yew hedge near the entrance, for instance.

Of the fatal mistake I'd made, I was completely unaware.

* * *

A couple of yards from the Castle kiosk, in the Formal Garden behind the tall yew hedge, Dolores handed Madge's photo to the Removal Men. 'I'll make sure the target will be waiting in her car outside the Seabird Centre tonight. You know what to—'

She broke off. It had suddenly registered that the ginger cat she'd seen a short time ago clawing its way carefully down the trunk of an old cedar tree in the Formal Garden had looked horribly like Tamsin Kennedy's scruffy creature. Yes, definitely… the same moth-eaten tail… There could be no mistake. She frowned. Why would it be slinking about the grounds of Dirleton Castle, so far from Pear Tree Farm?

Her eyes narrowed. Where the cat, there the *owner*! Kennedy had obviously known enough about the Wednesday Direlton Castle meetings for her to suss out the grounds today in preparation for spying on tomorrow's important meeting with the boss. Something would have to be done to prevent that.

What if... She stared thoughtfully at the cedar tree's fissured trunk, discarding one idea after another... Then inspiration! In the TV programme last week featuring Alnwick Castle and its Poison Garden, the gardener had said that cherry laurel released cyanide fumes identifiable by the characteristic almond smell when crushed in a wood chipper. She'd been particularly interested because a hedge of it grew near the lake. According to the programme there were instances of people feeling faint, even passing out in an enclosed space from breathing the almond scent of crushed cherry laurel.

Got it! Kennedy would need to sneak off early tomorrow morning to be in place here in the Castle Gardens as soon as the gate opened. If the Removal Men were to chop up some of the hedge this afternoon and leave the bag of chippings in the car park under the pear tree... Then all that was needed was for Bev to be on watch at her bedroom window overlooking the car park, intercept Kennedy and persuade her to carry off the bag in her car. Bev liked her lie-in in the morning and would be a bit stroppy, but orders are orders. In the confined space of the car, the cyanide fumes should cause Kennedy to pass out, lose control of the car, and crash. Injured or uninjured, she'd be delayed, and so unable to spy upon tomorrow's important meeting with the boss.

First things first. The danger from Madge took priority. Dolores turned back to the Removal Men. 'This is your target for tonight.' She tapped Madge's photo. 'And I'll have another job for you tomorrow.'

CHAPTER TWENTY-TWO

Tuesday night 7 p.m.
Though a whole hour had passed since Carol had come breezing into the studio, Madge's hand still shook as she fashioned the soft red fondant paste into the shape of a high-heeled shoe. The one and only reason for the visit seemed to have been to discuss what might have caused the damage to the ruined fondant castle, for that had been the only topic of conversation.

Finally Carol had asked, 'Are you sure *mice* were responsible? Have you ever considered that the damage might have been deliberate?'

The attempt to laugh off that last suggestion had been unconvincing even to her own ears. What *had* been behind Carol's persistence? And why had Carol looked at her in that calculating way? That's what was so worrying.

Perhaps it was time to leave Pear Tree Farm. In spite of the excellent facilities, she wasn't happy here, had hoped to make friends, had instead become the target of insensitive jokes. Worse than that, knowing how much it would upset her, *someone* – Stu? Vic? Neil? – had disliked her enough to destroy the fondant castle on which she'd spent so much time. She'd seen the impression of a footprint in the sugar fondant on the floor. But that was the sort of spiteful thing a *woman* would do. So… Bev? More likely to have been Carol herself. Yes, the reason for this visit, the reason behind all these questions must be that Carol wanted to find out if she herself was suspected of vandalising the castle.

But to leave Pear Tree Farm now would mean throwing away two months of already paid residency. There'd be no refund. After building up a photo portfolio of all the fondant sculptures made in the month she'd been here, where would she find a studio with even half the facilities of this one to finish the portfolio? She sighed. With a fondant smoother she began rolling out two slim cylinders to form stiletto heels for the fashion shoes.

It was when she went over to fetch the base of the shoe sculpture, a fondant-covered cake in the shape of a shoebox, that she saw a note had been pushed under the studio door. Curious, she stooped to pick it up.

Madge, I can't keep quiet about it any longer. You're being treated very shabbily. It wasn't mice that damaged your cake. I know who did it and why. And I've got the proof. I'll be in North Berwick tonight. Meet me 8 p.m. outside the Seabird Centre. We can buy fish and chips at The North Berwick Fry, so don't bother with supper at the Farm.

No signature.

'Oooh'. She stared down at the paper. Her hand shook, this time with excitement. At *last* she had a friend. Malicious damage to a fellow artist's work was an offence that was never tolerated in artistic circles. She could take the proof and the identity of the perpetrator to Mr McClusky for action and the person responsible would be expelled from the residential course. She did a little dance of joy. Now no need to leave, she could stay at the studio for another two months.

Before she rushed off to North Berwick there'd just be time to attach the fondant heels to the shoe with a spike of dried spaghetti and a dab of water. She carefully positioned the shoes on top of the shoebox, then stood back, hands on hips, to check the effect. Yes… possibly one of her best cake sculptures. Tomorrow when it had hardened she'd take the photo for the portfolio.

A glance at the studio clock told her the work on the fondant sculpture had taken much longer than she'd anticipated. Mustn't be late. She wasn't too familiar with North Berwick. What if she got lost? What if the writer of the note didn't wait? She grabbed her jacket from a hook, felt in a pocket for the keys of the mini, locked the studio door behind her and ran to the car park.

The light was already fading from the sky though a faint sunset flush lingered over the horizon to the north-west. Soon be dark. Driving on these narrow winding unfamiliar roads flicking between full and dipped beam made her edgy. She slipped a cd into the player and hummed along.

All my trials soon be over…

She repeated the words softly. *All my trials soon be…* A sudden thought struck her. Who *was* the well-wisher? How would she recognise him – or her? Obviously it must be one of her fellow artists, someone who knew about the damaged cake and had seen how upset she'd been. One of the men, ashamed of the way he'd treated her? Or, more probably, the newcomer, Tamsin Kennedy. Seemed a nice person.

A sigh of relief as she reached the main road on the outskirts of Dirleton. On her left the dark bulk of the ruined castle where Dolores set up her easel every week, never seeming to tire of painting the gardens and the ruins. At last a straight run, no more twisting and turning. Madge relaxed. In five minutes she'd be in North Berwick with its welcome street lighting.

Through the traffic lights… a downhill sweep past the white chains edging a putting green, and house lights next to the harbour across the bay. A new anxiety. Where *was* the Seabird Centre? With the streets deserted, there was no one to ask, but it must be beside the sea. Choice of roads… straight ahead then, ignoring any roads to the right, glimpses of the sea on the left. Crossroads, a sign *Scottish Seabird Centre,* pointing left down Victoria Street. At the end of the street, a low building beside the sea, its angular roof pointing at the sky. The Seabird Centre. She'd made it just in time for the rendezvous.

Parked cars lined the seafront. Nowhere to stop except bays marked *Disabled.* Unlikely that all of them would be needed at this late hour. She drew into the nearest, switched off the engine, lowered the window, and waited expectantly for someone to approach. No one about. The only sound, waves breaking on the rocks.

At last, five minutes after the rendezvous time, the soft *pad pad* of approaching footsteps. A man, someone she didn't recognise, was walking quickly towards the car. He spoke into his phone and with a glance in her direction, hurried past. Suddenly uneasy, she got out of the car and walked to where she could look up Victoria Street. Three rough-looking men were walking purposefully down the long narrow street.

A shout of, 'That's her!' They broke into a run.

A trap! Fired by a surge of adrenalin, she whirled round.

Half a dozen strides to the car, a desperate wrench at the door handle and she flung herself behind the wheel.

An angry shout. 'Grab her!' Close. Too close.

With shaking hands she twisted the key in the ignition. Two attempts to start the engine as a hand pulled at the door. Reverse gear, frantic stamp on the accelerator, and the mini shot backwards, door swinging open. A thump. A cry. Wrenching round the steering wheel she drove off, tyres screaming.

The road stretched ahead, on the left sand and sea, on the right, Victorian villas. A Give Way sign. Go straight ahead on alongside the beach, or curve off to the right? Which? *Which?* Decide! A quick glance in the rear-view mirror showed a car pulling out of the line of parked cars, the men scrambling into it. That made the decision for her. A quarter of a mile ahead, no houses, no street lighting, dark countryside where she could hide. Much better to head that way, rather than take a street leading back into town.

They weren't far behind. Their headlights on full beam illuminated the interior of the mini, their reflection in the rear-view mirror dazzling her. She tilted the mirror and concentrated on the way ahead, driving faster than was wise. Climbing. The road narrower now. A single track squeezed between a long drop to rocks and sea with high ground to the right.

At the top of the hill the tarmac road finished. No country road stretching ahead, merely a grassy track leading to the fairway of a golf course barred by a wooden gate. No time to stop. The crack of splintering wood. The mini jolted to a halt, front wing crumpled, steam hissing from the damaged radiator. She stood beside the car, looking round desperately. The short grass of clifftop and golf course offered nowhere to hide. On the road below, the pursuing car had come to a halt, had not yet started the ascent. Hope flared, but only for a moment. With sinking heart she knew the answer. They had no need to hurry. They knew she was trapped. As she watched, the car moved away from its position at the foot of the hill and began a slow climb.

The open ground of the golf course with its greens and fairways stretched into the distance. That way, no chance of escape. They'd run her down with the car within a few hundred yards. She swung round in panic. Over there, something she'd missed in the dark – a narrow path just below the top of the cliff and very close to the edge. Hazardous going even in daylight. But what choice did she have?

She set off at a run, eyes desperately searching the uneven surface of the damp earth for tangles of long grass and treacherous stones that might send her tumbling over the edge. Tripped, almost fell. Slow down, *slow down*. The slam of car doors signalled that her pursuers had arrived at the splintered gate and the wrecked mini. Any moment now she'd hear the thud of feet on the path behind, hear a triumphant shout, feel violent hands grab her. To her dismay, the path was narrowing to little more than a sheep track, making each step more hazardous. Sobbing, she stumbled to a halt, heart pounding, ears straining for sounds of pursuit. None. They'd given up, assumed she'd scrambled down to the beach or somehow made her escape across the golf course. She let out her breath in a long sigh of relief.

From the edge of the golf course a few feet above, a whispered, 'Hi there, Madge.' A chuckle.

Three dark shapes loomed above her. Startled, she leapt

back.

Beneath her feet, not solid earth, but insubstantial air.

CHAPTER TWENTY-THREE

Wednesday morning.

Drowsily I opened first one eye, then the other. Daylight shouldn't have been filtering through the yurt's small plastic window. How *could* I have been so careless about setting the alarm when it was so important to get up at six a.m. long before daybreak? I raised myself on one elbow, twisting over to look at the clock. *Seven* forty-five. I had intended to be in Dirleton to stake out the Castle entrance by nine o'clock. Damn, damn, *damn*. My plan to go into the Garden and take a photo of any visitor who approached Dolores at her easel had come to nothing, and *all* because I had inexcusably overslept.

Perhaps there was still a chance to get there by nine a.m. I leapt out of bed and dressed quickly. No need to rely on the bus. I could save a lot of time by taking my car. After all, the original decision to go to Dirleton by bus had been because my car's distinctive paintwork was too memorable. I'd leave the car, not in Dirleton itself, but at the nearby Archerfield Walled Garden from where a brisk twenty-minute walk would take me to a surveillance position on schedule. I'd have to go right away, no time for breakfast. I left Gorgonzola sleeping on the bed, locked the yurt and set off at a run.

I pounded up the hill towards the farmhouse, repeatedly glancing at my watch. There would be little chance of keeping to my plan unless I saved a few precious minutes by cutting away from the path winding its leisurely way through the birch trees. Risking a twisted ankle, I slithered and stumbled down the steep slope to the latched gate that marked the boundary between countryside and Pear Tree Farm. Not far to go to the car park now. I panted past the studios, closed and dark, except for the bulb shining palely above Madge's door. She must have been working late last night and forgotten to switch it off. Everyone would be at breakfast by now, nobody to ask me where I was going in such a hurry.

I rounded the side of the farmhouse, car park just ahead, pulled the remote out of my pocket, pressed the button, heard the *clunk* of the car door unlocking.

Tap tap tap. The sound of knuckles on glass. I turned round. Bev was signalling wildly from her upstairs bedroom window, her lips were moving but I couldn't make out what she was saying. Whatever she wanted, it would delay me. I gave a cheery wave and turning my back, walked quickly towards my car. The sash window slid up with a thud.

'Tamsin! W-a-i-t, *w-a-i-t!*'

I took another couple of steps towards the car. 'See you when I get back.' Nothing she was going to say could be more important than getting to Dirleton in time.

'No! No! Stop! It's *urgent*. It's... it's... about the cat!'

I whirled round. No one at the window now, only curtains billowing in the stiff breeze. I hesitated. Gorgonzola was snuggly snoozing in the yurt. Wasn't she? On the other hand,

G *had* managed once before to find a way out of the yurt, had followed me to the studio and messed up Carol's clay slabs.

I'd hesitated too long. The front door flew open. Bev came teetering out of the farmhouse on her high spiky heels, face flushed, lipstick half-applied.

My heart thumped. 'Urgent, you said? Something to do with my cat?'

The perfectly-shaped eyebrow rose sharply in surprise. 'Cat?' The plump lips pouted. 'Cat? Whatever do you mean? Oh, you thought I said cat? No, no. The *cast*... of the... of the... pear tree.' A long pause. 'Er... it's to be the new centrepiece for our exhibition stand. Yes, that's it. For our exhibition stand.'

'But why is it urgent? What's it to do with me?' I edged towards my car.

'You see, the *cast* is needed in a couple of days and Carol's going to be away. You're the only one who knows how to cast from a mould.'

I didn't. Never done it, never even seen it done. The beginners' pottery course I'd attended hadn't covered that sort of thing, whatever it was. But I was planning to leave the Farm in a couple of days, so could pretend I knew all about casting. I gave a confident nod. 'Ok. See you about it asap. Got to go now.'

'Oh, won't keep you then. Where are you off to so early?'

'Dunbar,' I said. Fake news. Exactly the opposite direction from my intended destination.

'Couldn't be more perfect!' she beamed. 'You see that bag of bark chippings under the pear tree? I'd asked Dunbar Garden Centre to send a bag of chippings for the top of our display stand to complement the pottery pear tree that you'll be casting. Silly me, didn't realise Mr McClusky meant *rubber* chippings. Won't take you too much out of your way to return the bag to Dunbar. That'll get Pear Tree Farm, and me, out of a hole. I'll help you lift the bag into the car.' Taking my consent for granted, she hurried over and flung open the boot.

Damn! I should have said Edinburgh. I'd have to go along with this to establish my destination was indeed Dunbar. Together we dragged the large bag of wood chippings over to my old banger of a car.

'It'll be too big to go into that small boot,' she said. 'We'll put it on the back seat.'

With a bit of a struggle, Bev pushing and me pulling, we wedged it into position behind the driver's seat.

I put my hand into the open bag and stirred the chips around. 'Mmm, nice scent of almond. That's unusual, must be pricey.'

'That's why they have to go back. We can't use them. I'd never have heard the end of it from Dolores. Thanks a million.' She closed the rear door. 'See you later, Tamsin.'

As I drove off, Bev gave a cheery wave.

CHAPTER TWENTY-FOUR

That awkward question of Bev's as to where I was going was just what I'd hoped to avoid. But no harm done. My hasty choice of Dunbar as my destination fitted in beautifully. I'd deliver the stuff to the Garden Centre *after* my visit to Dirleton, handily confirming that I hadn't been lying about where I was going. In the rear-view mirror I caught a glimpse of Bev staring after me, hands on hips, broad smile on her face now that she'd managed to cover up her mistake with the chippings.

I pressed my foot hard down on the accelerator, but my old banger was already rattling along at fifty miles an hour, as fast as it could go, much faster than was safe on the network of narrow winding roads, threading their way through the gently undulating landscape of stubbled fields dotted with bales of harvested crop. My nose twitched as a powerful scent of almonds wafted from the bag of chippings on the back seat. Very pleasant in the open air, rather too strong in the confines of the car.

Took that corner too fast. I'd lost concentration for a second. Slow down… In the distance the unmistakable green volcanic cone of The Law pinpointing the position of North Berwick.

The blare of an oncoming car's horn… Momentary view of the road hog of a driver mouthing a swear word. Oops, a bit too close, that! The road was busier now, better slow down. I eased my foot off the accelerator to allow for these inconsiderate drivers so intent on getting to their destination come hell or high water.

I stifled a yawn. Taken me ages to get to sleep last night mulling over yesterday's visit to Dirleton and planning for today's. No wonder I'd overslept this morning. Still tired, though. Another yawn sucked in a deep breath of almond-scented air. The smell from those chippings was *really* strong. Perhaps some fresh air… This old jalopy has its disadvantage, no press button to lower the glass. Taking one hand off the wheel, I fumbled for the window handle. Too stiff to move. I applied more pressure. Encouraged by signs of movement, I pushed harder. Something snapped as the handle came off in my hand. The window glass slid down into the door space. An instinctive wrench at the steering wheel sent the car swerving off the road to shoot across the soft verge and bury its nose in a hedge. Pressing against the windscreen was a tangle of prickly hawthorn.

Muttering and cursing, I flung the door open and swung my legs to the ground. Had to get the car back onto the road… Suddenly everything was too much effort. My legs gave way. Slumping onto the seat, I rested my head on the steering wheel, head muzzy. No chance of getting to Dirleton on time now…

'You all right there?' The man's voice seemed to come from a distance. A hand shook my shoulder.

Two concerned faces were peering down at me, lycra-clad cyclists, one holding two bicycles.

I sat up, dazed, and a bit shaky. 'I'm ok, thanks. My own stupid fault. When I opened the window, the handle came off in my hand. Sort of lost control.' Somewhat unsteadily, holding onto the door for support, I heaved myself out of the car.

Together they studied the deep grooves cut into the muddy ground by the tyres.

'*Might* be able to reverse out.'

'Worth a try.'

Doubt in both voices.

I slid into the driving seat and restarted the stalled engine, shoving the gear lever into reverse. The bonnet struggled out of the prickly embrace of the hedge, but my hopes were dashed as the car lurched to a halt, engine note rising to a whine.

The cyclists moved hastily aside, managing to dodge most of the mud spraying from the spinning wheels. They shook their heads. 'No use. Got a garage number?'

I nodded and took out my phone. With a car as old as this, that's an elementary precaution.

'They'll soon have you sorted.' With a cheery wave the couple cycled off.

I might have known it wouldn't be as easy as that. The breakdown truck was out on another call, waiting time at least an hour. The only consolation was that the sun had appeared from behind a bank of cloud so despite the cool breeze it felt quite warm. The downside was that the interior of the car was also heating up, intensifying the now unpleasantly strong scent of almonds drifting from the back seat.

I moved further away to sit on a roadside wall fretting over the missed opportunity to discover what Dolores was up to at her weekly meetings in Dirleton Castle grounds. And now I was lumbered with that load of bark chippings Bev had foisted on me. 'Won't take you too much out of your way,' she'd chirped breezily. It damned well would! I gave a vicious tweak at a weed lodged in the drystone wall.

Then relief. I didn't *have* to take the smelly stuff to Dunbar, did I? Just *announce* that I had. By the time Bev made enquiries about a replacement for the chippings, I'd have left Pear Tree Farm for good.

With a bit of a struggle I tugged the heavy bag to the tipping point at the edge of the seat, letting gravity spill half the contents onto the ground. Easy then to empty the rest of the bag, fold it up, and, with a twinge of environmental guilt, stuff it under the hedge.

By the time the breakdown truck had dragged the car back onto the road, enough time had passed to give Bev the impression I had in fact driven to Dunbar. Nevertheless, I went there anyway. When you're living a lie, you have to be very careful that every little detail corroborates the story you've spun. Not that she was likely to have noted my mileage when she loaded the chippings, but from bitter experience I've learned never to assume. So after a pleasant hour spent in Dunbar Garden Centre café, I bought a plant of pungent catmint as proof of my visit, guaranteed to delight G, before making a leisurely way back to Pear Tree Farm.

Bev seemed surprised to see me, probably thought I'd have taken a lot longer. After all, my car to all appearances was a decrepit old banger and she wasn't to know that the dirty oily engine compartment disguised an engine in peak condition.

To distract her from asking any awkward questions, I waved the smelly cat mint under her nose. 'Look what I bought for Picassa. Cats find this plant irresistible. Strange, isn't it?'

'Hmm,' she wasn't really listening, all her attention on the car. 'A bit cold to be driving with the window open, isn't it?'

I shrugged. 'You can say that again. Handle broke as I wound the window down to peer at a signpost. Next thing I knew, the glass had disappeared inside the door panel.' Better not to mention what I'd done about the chippings.

She bit her lip and muttered something I didn't catch, probably unsympathetic. Any moment now she would bring up the delicate subject of the delivery of the chippings.

I turned away. 'Got to rush. Picassa's been on her own too long. Better give her this peace offering.'

'W-a-a-i-t!' she called after me. 'What about the chippings?'

'Oh, them?' I hurried off, turning to give her a thumbs-up sign. 'The Garden Centre will be in touch.'

* * *

Dolores listened to Bev's phone call with pursed lips. So her plan to use the fumes of the cherry laurel to get rid of Kennedy had failed, and all because that wreck of a car was falling apart. She thumped the desk in frustration. Nothing for it but to meet with the Removal Men at Dirleton tomorrow. They were the experts. They'd come up with something that would leave *nothing* to chance.

CHAPTER TWENTY-FIVE

Next morning I was pushing back my chair to leave the breakfast table when the kitchen door opened and McClusky came in. He looked round the room. 'Dolores not here? I wanted a word with her.'

'Just missed her. Gone off to Dirleton.' Stu reached out for the marmalade and spread it on his toast. 'Ouch! Watch what you're doing with your feet, Carol. That hurt!'

McClusky frowned. 'Dolores was to meet me after breakfast to discuss the next exhibition, it was all arranged. She might have let me know she wouldn't be here. Not at *all* convenient.' He turned on his heel, closing the door with unnecessary force.

Careful not to show the slightest interest in that exchange, I carried my plates and cutlery to the dishwasher. 'The garage has fitted me in to fix the car window if I manage to get there before nine o'clock.' I glanced at my watch. 'Better be off.'

All lies. I just had to be at Dirleton to spy on Dolores. Her meeting must be *really* important for her to go there two days running. Also it was another opportunity to find out who else she was meeting, perhaps even to get a photograph of them together.

I'd just fitted the key in the lock and was opening the car door when a shout of, 'Hold on a mo', Tamsin!' made me turn. Carol was running towards me, red in the face, frantically waving a sheet of paper.

'Thank God I caught you,' she panted. 'I *so* need your help. I'm *so* excited! Yesterday afternoon I had a phone call from the BBC! They want me to come to Edinburgh this morning to finalise details for a short film on ceramics featuring *my* pots. It's to be shown on BBC 2. Need your help because–'

'So pleased for you, Carol. But I'm afraid I'll have to say no. Maybe this afternoon...' I slid behind the wheel and pulled at the door. 'Glad to assist with anything this afternoon, but just now I've got to–'

My second attempt to close the door was thwarted by Carol inserting an arm through the glassless driver's window and clutching at the steering wheel.

'You don't understand!' she wailed. 'It's absolutely *vital* that my pots are loaded into the kiln *this morning* because I've to take them to the photographic studio on Friday. It takes two days, first for the firing and then the cooling down.'

'Sorry, no can do. Ask Vic or Stu.' I turned the key in the ignition.

'Really, Tamsin,' her hand remained where it was. 'I don't need to tell *you* how so *very* fragile ceramics are at this stage. These two men don't have any experience in handling pottery. Some of my pots will definitely end up broken.'

Bound to happen, she was right. But I hardened my heart. The mission came first. I revved the engine ready to move off.

Carol played her ace, abandoning the velvet glove approach to show the iron fist. 'That...er...lovely sculpture of yours, the fat woman. Surely it won't be long before *it's* ready to be fired? If I asked Vic or Stu to put it in the kiln, just think what might happen...' Her eyes met mine. No mistaking the message.

Foiled! An agent should always prioritise a mission over anything else, but I'm ashamed to admit that the veiled threat to Earth Mother weakened my resolve to go to Dirleton. Perhaps it was not so *very* important that I go *today*. After all, there'd be another chance to go there next week. A couple of seconds thought convinced me that to agree to Carol's request was the right course of action. Pear Tree Farm seemed to favour hollowed-out art, so unlikely as it seemed, Carol's pots too *might* conceal a hollow section to conceal drugs. Today would be my one and only chance to make a proper examination of Carol's pots when she was safely out of the way.

I frowned, a petulant pout artfully designed to convey sulky submission. I switched off the engine and followed Carol to the studio. She'd given me the perfect opportunity. I couldn't believe my luck. But I should have been thinking: beware of something that seems too good to be true.

'There you are, then.' Carol threw open a cupboard door and waved an airy hand at the rows of squat thick-walled African cooking pots lining every shelf. They were nothing like the stylishly elegant, thinnest of thin-walled vases featured in the portfolio she'd thrust under my nose with the aim of intimidating me with her expertise when I'd first arrived.

My surprise must have shown for she said quickly, 'Ethnic Art is trending this year. Hence the interest from the BBC. My aim is to have a new range of these cooking pots in every expensive store.' She glanced at her watch. 'They're ready for loading into the kiln. Can't over-emphasise how *fragile*, so handle with extreme care. Every one of them is needed, *any* breakage would be a disaster!'

'About setting the kiln temperature... er... I'm not familiar with this type of kiln, so not quite sure.' In fact, I had not the faintest idea how to operate *any* kiln. In the one and only pottery class I'd attended, the teacher had carried off the beginners' masterpieces to the kiln room and produced them a week later like rabbits out of a hat.

'*Tsk!*' her curled lip indicated, 'Call yourself a potter!'

The sneer would have stung if I *had* been a potter. I adopted a suitably crestfallen expression.

'Just close the door and switch it on,' she snapped. 'Kiln's already programmed for firing. Got to dash now. I'll look in just before supper. Get on with it!' The studio door banged shut behind her. Left hanging in the air was, 'Or *else!*'

I surveyed the task ahead of me. These thick-walled pots weren't thin light pieces. 'Extremely fragile!' she'd said. I snorted. Each must weigh several kilos. By the time I'd lifted each one and carried it carefully across the room to the kiln, I'd be exhausted.

Better get started. Tensing my muscles to take the weight, I eased my hands under the curved belly of the nearest pot and lifted it slowly off the shelf, surprised to find it was not nearly as heavy as the thickness of the walls had led me to believe. Intrigued, I laid it down on the nearest bench to examine it. The bulbous outer shape had suggested that it would hold enough soup or stew to feed up to twenty people. But the actual interior volume was very small, about two litres. Perhaps the pot was an experimental type of slow cooker making use of the extremely thick clay walls to retain the heat and cook the food. But a slow cooker needs a lid and there wasn't one.

All the artefacts created at the Farm had a hidden built-in cavity for the storage of drugs. So why would this pot be an exception? I examined the pot again. Could it be two thin-walled pots looking as if it were one, a tall slim pot fitted inside a squat fat pot, creating an interior hidden space? If so, to prevent it cracking and exploding in the kiln, there would have to be a tiny hole allowing the heated air to escape, that much I knew. Was there a hole? I ran my fingers over the smooth exterior surface of the cooking pot, turning it round, changing the position of my hands each time so I could examine every area of the circumference. And there, under the rim, was the tiniest of holes.

Mustn't get too excited. Perhaps Carol had pricked the clay to measure the thickness of the pot wall. After all, I knew almost nothing about pottery, even less about pottery thrown on the wheel. How could I find out if there really was one pot inside another?

Maybe, just maybe... I got out my phone. Googling 'double pots' brought up 'Stainless steel cooking pots and bains-marie', but 'Double pots pottery' struck lucky. There was no doubt about it, it could be done. Several videos showed how to create a double-walled pot on the wheel by raising up first one pot, and then another outer one from the same mass of clay, then joining the rims seamlessly together. Seemed quite easy, but it obviously wasn't. I could visualise the mess I'd get into if I tried, even an expert potter like Carol might have a little difficulty.

I stared at the pot in front of me. Two pots or one? The temptation was strong to find out for sure by cutting the fragile pot in half with the pottery saw. A bad move to test my theory, conclusive proof to the gang that an undercover agent had discovered their secret. I didn't need more evidence for what was going on at the Farm. I'd already discovered their *modus operandi* was drugs hidden in the hollowed-out art objects about to be transported to an exhibition, and the fake 'sales' picked up by a courier.

Instinct told me it had become too dangerous to stay any longer. Important as it was to find out who Dolores was meeting at Dirleton, I didn't need to be staying at the Farm to spy on her.

Yes, best to leave *now* while I had the chance. I'd certainly not waste time loading the kiln. I heaved up the pot I'd placed on the bench and walked over with it to the cupboard. Relishing the prospect of Carol's rage when she returned to the studio to find kiln empty, cupboard full, I replaced the heavy pot on the high shelf, but a moment's lapse of concentration dislodged the neighbouring pot. It teetered for a nerve-racking instant on the edge of the shelf before crashing to the floor and breaking into three large pieces.

How *could* I have been so careless! It had been so important to slip away without it being obvious that I'd discovered the secret of the hollowed-out cooking pot. Like the fallen pot itself, my plan now lay in ruins. I fought down rising panic. Then training stepped in. Think! By taking away the pieces of ruined pot, loading the others into the kiln, and starting it up, I could buy myself some time. Carol wouldn't discover one pot was missing till tomorrow night when the kiln cooled. I wouldn't have to leave immediately. I'd creep away tonight after supper. That way no one would miss me for some time.

First things first. Remove the telltale evidence. I did a satisfying little dance on the broken pieces of pot. 'Take that,

Carol!' *Crunch...* 'And that!' *Crunch...* 'And *that!*' *Crunch...* Once the pieces had been reduced to unrecognisable fragments, I swept them up and deposited them in the bag of dry clay waiting to be recycled. Then I set about loading the kiln. Now that I was working not for Carol but for myself, what had seemed an onerous task, seemed much less of a burden. At last, kiln full, cupboard empty, I swung the kiln door shut and switched on the programme.

I had the rest of the afternoon to turn my attention to Earth Mother with her tiny head, shoulders only a *little* too broad, massive thighs, and large feet, and two large holes where the perfect boobs were still to be attached. I gazed at her fondly. No way was I going to leave her behind when I left the Farm. She'd been left sitting there not quite finished for so long that the clay had hardened despite the protective polythene bag.

The two abandoned bosoms had also hardened. No way now that their size and shape could be altered. Over-large they might be and pendulous, but they would have to do. I laid her gently on her back so that the boobs would not detach, pulled off by their own weight before the mender liquid had time to set. I stuck them on and stood back, head on one side, considering. Not *quite* the image I'd originally had in mind but no one could deny that she embodied the *essence* of an Earth Mother. And was that not the aim of any sculptor, to capture the intrinsic nature of a living creature?

In a glow of satisfaction I set off for the yurt. When everyone had gathered in the farmhouse for supper, I'd put my bag and Gorgonzola in her rucksack in the car. I'd eat quickly and leave before the others, with the excuse that I had to dash to the studio to deal with my sculpture before it dried out. Then a final visit to the studio to collect Earth Mother and carry her off to the car.

CHAPTER TWENTY-SIX

Carol hummed as she stacked the dinner plates in the sink ready for washing and turned on the tap. Tamsin Kennedy's snooping days were over. Dinner had gone more or less as planned. Stu had perfectly staged accidentally catching Kennedy's wineglass with his sleeve, followed by much mopping up and embarrassed apologies. It had been the most natural thing in the world for him to insist on giving Tamsin his untouched glass of wine, doctored, of course, with the heavy sedative. Dolores' planning. A master stroke.

Her humming stopped abruptly at the thought that the whole scheme had almost come unstuck. Stupid Vic had offered Kennedy a quite unnecessary top-up when her glass was still three-quarters full. Kennedy had put her hand over her glass. She'd laughed. 'Trying to get me drunk, are you, Vic?' But her expression had held a hint of unease. That had nearly ruined things. Carol added a vicious squirt of washing-up liquid to the hot water. Only Dolores' quick thinking had saved the situation with her exasperated, 'What *do* you think you're doing, Vic! That's the last of the bottle, thanks to Stu's clumsiness. We'll share it out when everyone's glass is empty.'

Then had begun a waiting game while they'd watched for Kennedy's eyelids to droop and her speech to slur. It had been a bit of an effort to keep up light conversation until the drug had taken effect. When she'd slumped half-conscious in her chair, it had been easy for Vic and Stu to steer her on her wobbly legs to the car park and leave her lying there for the Removal Men to pick up and dispose of, discreetly of course. Good mood restored, Carol's humming resumed. She'd check the kiln when she'd finished the washing-up.

* * *

The Removal Men sat in their van studying the photo of their target for that night. With her spiky blue hairdo, even in the dark there'd be no possibility of mistaken identity. Woozy from a knockout drug in her drink, they'd find her dumped beside her car ready for them to collect, abduction made easy. But they'd charge extra anyway because of the short notice and the additional guarantee of a tidy foolproof disappearance of both target and car.

The leader drew a folded newspaper from his jacket pocket and spread it out on the dashboard. The others craned forward. *MAN DIES IN WILD BOAR ATTACK.* His tattooed finger traced the headline, then stabbed down to draw their attention to phrases in the page-long article... *full-grown wild boar particularly aggressive... four razor sharp tusks up to five inches long... more dangerous than a bear... can't outrun them.*

Picturing the bloody outcome for the target, the others nodded and grinned.

The leader produced a map, finger pinpointing the chosen disposal site. Land hidden from view by a high stone wall and tangled thickets of wind-stunted trees. Land where farmed wild boar roamed free so were likely to attack a body lying still and silent on the ground. Land made for the job in hand.

He looked at each one in turn. 'The target will be discovered with all the appearance of an unfortunate accident, perhaps never be identified. Hungry pigs, it seems, devour everything edible. With luck, only the teeth and shreds of her clothing will remain.'

Wider grins and mutterings of, 'Brill, Boss!'

'A doddle!'

Route checked, map folded, the van moved off, job as good as done.

CHAPTER TWENTY-SEVEN

Ouoooh Ouoooh Ouoooh... ahhhhhhh ahhhhhhh ahhhhhhh...
Groans. Somebody was in trouble... Gradually I realised the groans were coming from me. My head ached, my stomach heaved. As I attempted to lift my head, a fresh stab of pain shot through it. Overwhelmed by a wave of nausea, I sank back and lay still, conserving strength...

Just have to take it little by little. I was lying on something very hard, not mattress, not carpet, not wooden floor... An exploratory movement of my hand detected damp earth, twigs, a thick layer of brittle dead leaves... Not in the yurt then. Outside.

What had happened? Was it important to remember? I thought about it for a long time and decided that it *was*. Mind filled with cotton wool... Where was I? Too much effort to open my eyes so maybe I'd get a clue from what I could hear. Wind in trees, distant breaking of waves... unmistakable hum of car engines approaching, receding... Have I been in an accident? Car gone off the road and I've been thrown out? Yes that was it. Too much thinking. I drifted off once more...

I opened one eye and then the other. Very dark, too dark

to see anything of my surroundings except that I was staring up at a thick tangle of twiggy branches silhouetted against the pale glimmer of the night sky. Raindrops on my upturned face. Headache not quite so bad now. Still couldn't work out where I was, and how I got here. Occasional swish of tyres on wet tarmac, some way off to my left. Rustle of movement nearby… silence… rustle… nearer…

Silence.

Not the wind. Something or somebody creeping closer, trying not to be heard. A nudge at my leg. A loud shout might frighten off whatever it was. I took a deep breath – and produced a weak inarticulate squeak, more mouse than lion. I rolled on my side. The thing poked at my back. Poked again, harder. Flung out an arm to knock it away. My hand felt fur.

At the touch of my fingers, the animal leapt away. Returned, scuffling softly through the leaf litter, approaching closer and closer to my head. With no strength to do anything but lie there, I folded my arms across my face and waited.

It was creeping towards me. So close now that its breath warmed the back of my hands. Too lethargic to move, I lay there in the dark under the tangle of bare branches, heart-pounding, waiting for the animal to attack. Fox? Rat? I tensed myself for the pain inflicted by sharp teeth or raking claws.

A rough tongue made an exploratory contact with the back of my hand. *Purrrrrr.* It took my dulled brain several seconds to register that this wasn't the feral growl of a wild animal. Just a cat, and a friendly one at that. I ran my hand over its back – long fur, patchy in places, especially at the tail. Pressing my elbows into the ground, I slowly raised my head.

Gorgonzola's copper eyes stared into mine.

Muzzily I thought back... Couldn't remember anything after leaving her in her rucksack in the car before going into dinner at the farmhouse. So what was she doing here out in the open? And why was I lying on the ground under a tangle of twiggy branches? I'd put my rucksack in the car, so must have been going somewhere... All too difficult to work out. Too tired. G nudged my hand aside and curled up in the crook of my arm with a satisfied *purr*. Closing my eyes, I sank back and waited for daylight.

CHAPTER TWENTY-EIGHT

The blare of a distant car horn startled me into full consciousness. My head had cleared, nausea been replaced by hunger. Tossed and shaken by strong gusts of wind, the tangle of bare branches overhead creaked and groaned, filtering pale patches of watery sunshine across my legs. Ten o'clock on my watch. I sat up and looked around. Gorgonzola, no longer nestled beside me on the ground, had gone hunting for her long overdue breakfast. I realised I too was hungry. When had I last eaten? Eight o'clock last night, the usual time for dinner at the Farm, but all I could remember was sitting down at the table and sipping a glass of wine. After that, a blank.

Loss of memory, headache, nausea, the predictable aftermath of drinking too many glasses of wine. In this case, that didn't apply. I've never even been tempted to break the rule that an agent's alcohol intake be limited to one glass. So my one glass must have been spiked. Everyone's glass had been filled from the same bottle. How could they possibly have engineered that only *my* drink was doctored? Think, *think*… A hazy memory of Stu spilling my wine… offering me his glass. Yes, that's how it had been done.

I'd known I was under suspicion, but had fatally underestimated how little time I had to escape from the Farm. I sank back. Why was I still alive? Why had they not arranged an apparently alcohol-induced death for me when I was helpless? Why had they not dropped me in the sea, left me on the railway line, thrown me over a cliff near Tantallon? Why, instead, had I been left here alive and uninjured in this thin plantation of trees?

And even more puzzling, why was Gorgonzola here with me? Was it just a dream, imagination, that she had slept beside me in the night? I levered myself up on an elbow. Definitely no dream. That long red hair on my sleeve, that rucksack lying a few feet away under a bush, unzipped just enough to allow G's head and shoulders to force a way out.

I pieced together what must have happened. At the Farm I'd left her in the rucksack in my car ready for a quick getaway after dinner. They'd put me in my car. On hearing unfamiliar men's voices, G would have remained silent and still. They'd dumped me here, rucksack beside me. No sign of my holdall, might still be in the boot of the car.

Of *course* they'd plan a permanent solution for anyone who might be a possible threat to the operation at the Farm. I hadn't seen Neil since he went into the Exhibition to snatch back his stone sculpture. I'd just accepted their explanation that he had gone down South to source more stone. What had really happened to him?

As for Madge, she had patently been very frightened about something going on at the Farm. Had she simply forgotten to switch off her studio door light? The gang would want a fail-safe guarantee that her suspicions couldn't be passed on to the police. There could be a sinister explanation for it burning in daylight.

As for myself, unlikely that they'd just wanted to scare me off. A fright was not how they'd dealt with the handyman Baxter. So what did they have in mind? That sudden alarming thought brought me shakily to my feet. Time for G and me to get away from here. I drew the cat whistle out of my pocket, thankful it was still there. One blast was enough for her to come stalking through the trees, upright tail twitching. I gave her a quick stroke, then stuffed her back in the rucksack before she could dart away to investigate any tempting rustle in the bushes.

Close-by, a grey stone wall too high to climb reared up above my head, blocking out what lay beyond, a busy road, judging by the sound of traffic. There'd be an exit to the road not far away as the gang wouldn't have carried me any distance from the car. Trees stretched away on either side, trunks a few yards apart, tops sculpted into a twiggy interlacing canopy by the prevailing wind, the ground below a mix of churned earth, dead leaves and grass.

Voices. Away off to the right, a flicker of movement, the snap of dry sticks underfoot. Dolores' men checking to see if I'd succumbed to an overdose of drugs, and inject me with a fatal dose if necessary? When my body was found, a 'shocked' McClusky would confirm to police that Kennedy, a drug user had been asked to leave the Farm.

I was still drained of strength and energy by the drug, so there was no point in trying to run. No bushes. Nowhere to hide. Heart pounding, I could only stand and watch two figures running towards me through the closely-packed trees. Relief surged through me. Two women, ramblers judging by their boots, red woolly hats, rucksacks and walking poles? Dolores' hit squad would seem harmless, their knives or guns concealed.

I turned and headed away from them as quickly as my weakened state allowed. If I was their target, they'd change direction. I glanced back. That's exactly what they'd done.

'Hello, there!' Two voices, synchronised.

I broke into a stumbling run.

'Stop! Stop! Have you seen them?' The cry came from close behind.

No point in running. I turned to face them. The two identical faces below the red woolly hats gazed anxiously at me. 'You see, we were walking through the grounds of the Estate...'

'Got lost and–'

'Let *me* tell it, Ruth. We climbed over a fence–'

'Shouldn't have, of course, thought it was safe. Couldn't see any pigs– '

'Not pigs. *Wild boar!*'

The other nodded.

Puzzled, I stared at them. 'Wild boar! I don't think there are any round here.' I laughed, hoping I didn't sound condescending.

'Oh, yes, there are!' they cried in unison.

'They're farmed on this Estate. We *were* warned, you see, that that they were dangerous, could attack.'

'No, Lou, *would* attack, if we went into their enclosure.'

'Don't worry,' I said. 'This can't be their enclosure. I've been here for some time, bound to have seen them.'

Lou looked doubtful. 'Boar dig up the ground looking for food.'

In silence we studied the ground, churned-up under the trees in all directions.

'All pigs root about on the ground. Doesn't mean *wild boar* are here.' I tried to sound confident. But they'd convinced me. It certainly fitted in with why I had been left here, helpless on the ground to be killed by wild boar. Verdict at the inquest, Death by Misadventure.

'If we *do* see one, we know what to do, don't we? We've to move slowly away.'

'Yes, definitely not *run*.' The red woolly hats nodded in synchronised agreement.

That was the theory. I hoped we wouldn't have to test it. 'You'd better keep a good lookout.' I shouldered my rucksack. 'But before you go, could you show me where you climbed that fence. You didn't see any boar back that way, did you?'

Shaking of heads. They looked from one to the other.

'But there could be some ahead,' I said, 'so let's go back to the fence.'

Ten minutes later through the tree trunks a two-metre high mesh fence glinted in the sun. I must have shown my surprise. The twins weren't young, at least in their sixties. How had they managed to climb over it?

They laughed. 'You're wondering…'

'…how we did it, aren't you? Come this way!'

They walked beside the fence for a short distance, stopped and pointed. A tree angled to about forty-five degrees by years of prevailing gales, leaned trunk and branches over to our side of the fence.

'Easy!' said Lou. 'Ruth thought of it.'

Unfortunately neither had thought about how to climb back. Their faces fell as they realised that the lowest overhanging branch was too high for any of us to reach.

'Well, so far so good,' I said diplomatically, knowing what seems to be an inspired idea can be ill thought out. 'At least we've not seen any boar. There must be a gate somewhere. If we follow the fence, we're bound to find it.'

And we did. The problem was the large heavy padlock. Only the work of a moment for my picklocks. If I'd had them with me instead of being in the holdall in the boot of my car.

The twins were looking desperately this way and that, clearly expecting a herd of wild boar to come charging out from the sparse undergrowth.

'We're trapped!'

'What do we do now?'

'STAY EXACTLY WHERE YOU ARE!' A disembodied voice boomed. 'YOU'RE TRESPASSING IN A FORBIDDEN AREA. WE'RE ON OUR WAY.'

The twins eyed each other accusingly.

'Your fault!'

'No, yours!'

A CCTV camera must be concealed among the tangle of branches overhead. Whatever happened now, we were safe. The attempt on my life had failed.

A few minutes later a jeep roared up. Two angry men let us out of the enclosure and re-padlocked the gate.

'What the *hell* were you doing in there? Boar attack faster than…' his eyes assessed the three of us, '…people like you can run.'

'Fred's not exaggerating. If we hadn't moved the herd to another area of the Estate yesterday morning, you could have been seriously injured. Or dead!'

Their obvious consternation drove home the message, the

chilling realisation that there could indeed have been a very different outcome for the twins. And definitely for myself, lying on the ground, semi-conscious.

CHAPTER TWENTY-NINE

From us, repentant apologies. From the two gamekeepers, a stern warning and the threat of prosecution for a repeat offence. We were ordered into the jeep, and sat in subdued silence till deposited on the main road at the entrance to the Estate.

My intention had been to contact Gerry on the encrypted emergency number to arrange for back-up. I felt first in one pocket, then another. Nothing in either. To delay the identification of my body for as long as possible, the gang had emptied my pockets of phone, of money, of everything. The twins offered their phone, and after I'd sent a coded emergency message to Gerry, they strode off, still heatedly arguing which of them was to blame for the unfortunate incident. I watched their red hats dwindle to dots in the distance.

Gerry could always be relied on to have someone in place ready to act when an emergency call came in. Even though rescue would come quickly, as always on a dangerous mission like this, I couldn't wait here in full view of passing traffic with the danger that someone from Pear Tree Farm would spot me. Vital to lull the gang into a sense of false security. I'd have to disappear without trace, make them think they'd got rid of

Tamsin Kennedy and with her any threat from newspaper headlines, police enquiries or inquest. I moved further in among the trees and bushes lining the road and sat with my back against a tree trunk, confident that the GPS device embedded in G's collar would pinpoint my location within a metre or two.

Tamsin Kennedy had outrun her usefulness. Once her cover had been blown, she'd become a liability for the mission. My only regret would be the loss of my terracotta Earth Mother, no doubt already gleefully smashed to smithereens by a vindictive Carol.

G shifted her position in the rucksack. The movement subsided as with no scents of interest to challenge her, she reverted to the Snooze Mode that takes up sixteen hours of a cat's day.

At the sound of a car drawing to a halt, I peered through the screen of bushes. The bearded driver of the large black Mercedes reached over to open the front passenger door, then sat waiting, phone to ear. Gerry's cavalry to the rescue? Or just someone stopping to use his mobile legally? I made no move. Neither did the driver, just sat there, phone to ear. The door remained open.

Poooop poop poop Poop poooop poooop poooop.
Again, *Poooop poop poop Poop poooop poooop poooop.*
Morse code? *Dash dot dot* D. *Dot dash dash dash* J.

I seized the rucksack, ran to the car, slid into the passenger seat, slammed the door and fastened the seat belt. The Mercedes moved smoothly off. I studied the driver. Elderly, grey hair and beard. Hands lightly on the wheel. No point in asking his name, he wouldn't have answered or just given a false one. I relaxed, closed my eyes. The tyres hummed on the road. Safe.

A moment later my eyes flew open. A vital part of an agent's training is taking note of small discrepancies. My tired brain had just registered a mismatch between the grey hair of middle age and the more youthful skin on the back of the driver's hands. I'd fallen into a trap. I fumbled furtively for my seatbelt release, waiting for an opportunity to throw myself out of the car the moment it slowed.

'Don't bother.' Gerry's voice, deadpan. 'You've failed to notice the click of the door lock. Childproof, and of course, agent-proof.'

'Ok!' I snapped, relief and irritation at the implied rebuke an explosive cocktail. 'I missed it! So would *you* have, if *your* drink had been spiked and you'd been left on the ground to be killed by a herd of wild boar!'

His only reaction was a momentary tightening of his grip on the wheel. The only sound the hum of the tyres. Then, 'Tell me, Deborah, why is it that whenever we meet on a mission you are somewhat the worse for wear?'

While I was searching for a suitably crushing answer, my eyelids closed in sleep.

That evening I lay back on the bed in a safe house somewhere in Edinburgh. I should have been finishing my notes in preparation for next day's debriefing, but had found it too emotionally draining when it came to writing up the traumatic events of the last twenty-four hours.

I couldn't settle. If Gerry offered me another undercover mission, would I accept it, or be content to revert to private citizen DJ Smith? A snake sloughs its skin and a hermit crab changes its shell as a change for the better, but it's not as simple for agents to revert to their own identity once they've immersed themselves intensively in a role. G too would be affected by any decision I made, lose her role as sniffer cat, a challenge she really enjoyed. Was that a reason for me to turn down another mission? I sighed. Have to wait and see how things turned out. A decision for another day. With a sigh, I gave my attention once more to the debriefing report.

CHAPTER THIRTY

The digital seconds flicked by on the wall clock. I sat in silence, my mind elsewhere, as Gerry read slowly through my report on Pear Tree Farm, from time to time pausing to make a note. This was plainly the end of the role I was destined to play in Operation Smokescreen. I had mixed feelings, in part relief for at last being out of danger, in part frustration at my failure to uncover the man or woman responsible for the deaths of those agents, the kingpin of the organisation, the drug boss who gave orders relayed to Dolores at the Dirleton Castle meetings.

Covertly I studied him. Hard to tell from Gerry's expression how he rated my performance. From the trouble he'd originally taken to track me down, it was clear he'd thought I possessed the very qualities he needed. But somehow, by action or word, I'd blown my cover. He'd relied on me, and I'd let him down.

As if he could read my mind, he looked up and smiled. 'Don't torture yourself, Deborah. Thanks to you, I think the mission's made reasonable progress. Allow me to summarise: we now know how the drugs are concealed and how they're distributed, thanks to you. What we don't yet know is–' He broke off raising his eyebrows in enquiry.

Damn him! He was playing Finish This Sentence For Me, that oh-so-irritating mind game of his. Normally I would counter with a deliberately obtuse reply, as if I had misunderstood the point he was making. This time I remained silent, adopting the fist to brow pose of Rodin's The Thinker.

A long pause. I was conscious of the faint hum of traffic filtering through the double-glazing. I'm not sure what reaction I was expecting from Gerry, but there was none.

Unnerved by his lack of response, I raised my head a fraction and under lowered brows peered across the desk to see that he had adopted a similar Rodinesque pose. I couldn't suppress a giggle.

Rodin poses abandoned, we eyed each other.

'As you have observed, Deborah, I have been thinking. Let's try again. What we don't yet know *is*–'

In appreciation of his Rodin-Thinker tactic to defuse the tension, I gave him the answer he wanted without further evasion. 'What we don't yet know is the identity of the mastermind behind the Organisation.'

He nodded. 'So, what we have to decide now is how we proceed.' He picked up a pen and began to doodle, another method he favoured to reveal to me what was on his mind.

Puzzled, I watched as the pen moved swiftly across the blank sheet of paper. He'd said, '*We* have to decide, how *we* proceed?' Gerry always chose his words carefully. Surely my role in Operation Smokescreen was over? How could I possibly be of use now?

With a few deft movements of the pen, Gerry's doodle was finished. He held it up for me to see. A stick figure with spiky hair wielding a giant pair of binoculars, and alongside it a large, very black question mark.

I frowned. 'I don't–'

He didn't let me finish. 'I quite understand your surprise, Deborah. I know you were not expecting to see Pear Tree Farm again, but,' he held up a hand, 'just hear me out. The position is this. The gang's attempt to get rid of you shows they are aware they have been infiltrated by a hostile organisation, so now they will lose no time in closing down the Pear Tree Farm operation. After one last exhibition of these hollowed-out art works to distribute the current stock of drugs, they'll go to ground to resurface who knows where with yet another clever scheme.'

'Yes, yes,' I said, 'I know that, but–'

He held up a hand to stem any further objection. 'Time is running out for them, so the insights you have gained from your stay at the Farm will be invaluable to us. With *your* input the mission can still have a good chance of success.'

He had my attention now. An agent hates when a mission fails, and he knew it.

'May I suggest this?' He stabbed a finger down on the doodled binoculars. 'It's most unlikely that they'll have time to stage another large scale exhibition, but they'll want to move out the drugs stored on the Farm in the next couple of days. So my bet is they'll set up a pop-up stall at some local event if they have enough art objects ready. Have you any idea how many they might have?'

'Definitely enough ceramic pots. Those fat cooking pots of Carol's would hold a lucrative amount of drugs. It took me an age to load them into the kiln. Possibly some of Dolores' picture frames. Might be some input too from Stu and Vic's studios.'

'Pop-up stall they'll go for, then.' A swift movement of

Gerry's pen produced a doodle of pots lined up on a stall. 'That will distribute some but not all of the drugs stored on the Farm. Now, the chap who bought and carried off a...' he consulted my report, '...driftwood sculpture, used the name Phillington Carruthers. He's likely to be used again, so he's our strongest lead.'

I nodded. Camel-hair coat or not, I'd have no trouble recognising that quite distinctive plummy accent and spotting his tall figure, easy to home in on even in a crowd.

Gerry was saying, 'My thinking is, Deborah, that for them time's too short to place an advert in the local weekly, so they'll have to advertise their exhibition some other way.'

I couldn't resist joking, 'Well, if they advertise by notices cable-tied to lamp posts, lucky if they stay up for even a day. There's a phantom cutter-down of posters in North Berwick!'

With a wave of his hand as if brushing off an annoying insect, he continued, 'Once we have established where the exhibition is being held, your role would be to latch onto Carruthers and so hopefully lead us to the figure pulling the strings. But...' He removed his glasses and looked thoughtfully into the distance.

I remained silent, sensing this was not the occasion for another quip or question. Some minutes passed.

Glasses replaced, he stabbed his pen down decisively on the pad. 'But from your notes it is clear that drugs sufficient for an upcoming exhibition are brought in via an underwater pulley system on the lake and stored in the hut secured with the heavy-duty padlock. Then your cover was blown, and they've suddenly been faced with the threat of a raid either by the authorities or by a rival gang. The pop-up exhibition will get rid of some of the stored drugs, but their priority will be moving any surplus from the Farm to their main storage base. To find that base we'd need a fly on the wall at their council of war.' He doodled a couple of ears on the pad, then pushed back his chair, walked to the window and stood there looking out. He was taking the pressure off, giving me time to come to a decision.

I understood. He wanted me to plant a listening device. 'It would be reasonably easy,' I said slowly. 'Every night they have an evening meal together in the farm kitchen.' That told him what he hoped to hear, that I was accepting the mission.

He returned to his desk. A large star materialised on the doodle pad.

'Thank you, Deborah. We both appreciate how dangerous it will be for you to go back to the Farm. Stick a listening bug on the kitchen and studio windows but on *no account* are you to set foot in the farmhouse itself, or for that matter, Dolores' studio. That's an order.'

CHAPTER THIRTY-ONE

The last of the day was fading pinkly from the western sky. On the dark landmass on the far side of the River Forth pinpricks of light sprang up marking the string of small coastal towns of Fife. The car assigned to me by Gerry for tonight's mission was a run-of-the-mill Yaris electric model. No souped-up engine this time, the crucial consideration being silence, not speed. A far cry from my beloved old jalopy, eye-catching, memorable for its rattle, its flamboyantly artistic rainbow patches and outrageous addition of metal 'eyelashes' curving above the headlights. I sighed in mourning. Its body had without doubt gone to the great Scrapyard in the Sky, eyelashes and headlight eyes now trophies on some hoodlum's wall.

Supper at the Farm would be underway, everyone gathered round the kitchen table, offering suggestions and counter-suggestions on how to deal with the threatened raid from a rival gang. I checked over the equipment needed for tonight's assignment: head to toe dark clothing, night vision goggles, a selection of professional covert listening devices (Gerry's choice), and Gorgonzola (my choice). On no account was I to set foot in the farmhouse, he had been adamant. But even so, sticking a device to the window glass was high risk: if the curtains were open, anyone in the room happening to glance that way would spot me attaching it. Another consideration was that I might have to remove the device with only a few seconds warning, not even that perhaps, if someone left the farmhouse on their way back to their yurt.

G was already wearing her On Duty collar. Better if I slipped the transmitter into the specially designed pocket and put her in position sitting on the Farm's kitchen windowsill. I stroked her head that was sticking inquisitively out of the rucksack safely fastened to the front seat belt. 'Orders are orders, but sometimes one has to be a little flexible, eh, G?'

A loud purr of agreement. *Flexible* obedience to orders was instinctive, natural, only to be expected. A cat chooses to do what a cat *wants* to do.

Time to make my move. I pressed the ignition. The Stealth Mobile glided silently forward, the *purrr* in my ears, not from the engine but from an approving G, expert in furtive nocturnal hunting.

In this part of East Lothian, the roads are narrow and twisting, offering few places to draw in out of the way of passing traffic. Eventually I came upon a lay-by only a short walk two fields away from Pear Tree Farm. By now the north-easterly wind had increased in strength, whipping up scatterings of fallen leaves, tossing the topmost branches of trees into a frenzied dance, creating a background whispering of rustles and creaks, perfect cover for what I was about to do.

To forestall the anticipated feline escape attempts, I gently but firmly pushed G's head down into the rucksack, ignored her startled yowl of protest, and quickly pulled the zip closed. The expected delights of nocturnal hunting having been denied, the rucksack immediately took on a life of its own, rocking and shaking violently as she threw herself against the sides in a temper tantrum. This also foreseen, I blew the cat whistle, signal to her that she was On Duty. Training kicked in. With a last defiant grumble, the struggles subsided and the rucksack was still.

I stood beside the car. Smoke-grey clouds chased overhead. The surrounding countryside was an undifferentiated black mass with the occasional tree silhouetted against a sky surprisingly light in comparison. I peered ahead in the direction of Pear Tree Farm. Without the night vision goggles I'd have been reduced to feeling my way, stumbling over stones and uneven ground in danger of twisting an ankle. Tonight's mission would have had to be aborted in case a speedy getaway was necessary. With the goggles in place, surroundings eerily illumined in green, I set off, balaclava pulled down, tiny listening devices securely stored in the G's collar.

Dinner would normally be over in an hour and a half from now, and with it the vital to record discussion. Speed was important, but I didn't make the mistake of cutting straight across a field as a passing motorist might spot my running figure. Under cover of the hedgerows, I became one with the other creatures of the night, a human version of Gorgonzola on the hunt, bursts of speed interspersed with several moments of immobility, crouching low when approaching headlights threatened to catch me in their beam.

When I reached the field bordering Pear Tree Farm, I stopped to make a cautious scan of my surroundings. I froze. A foot patrol of four men were standing, not two hundred yards off to my right, an indication of the importance of the meeting now taking place at the Farm. They were spaced out in a line, heads turned to right or left, pale faces probing the dark of the field.

Quick movement attracts attention. Slowly, slowly, I bent my knees and lowered myself, heart thumping, to lie pressed flat between the furrows of ploughed earth. Seconds passed. No crunch of earth under approaching heavy boots. Cautiously I raised my head a fraction. They were standing motionless, their line no nearer, one facing right, one left, leader gazing ahead, last man watching the rear. I lowered my head and let the seconds drag past before risking another peek. First panicky thought, they were waiting for me to make a move. A second more sensible thought, they couldn't have seen me or they'd have come charging over.

Their direction of gaze hadn't changed, and they were standing completely immobile in the field, like... like... scarecrows! I stood up and tentatively approached the figures. Each was dressed in coloured jersey, jeans, and long scarf, gloves dangling from the end of arms. A very effective face was formed by two huge eyes and curved mouth drawn on a white sack. Certainly realistic enough to fool wily seagulls, geese, and myself.

Relieved, but concerned that I'd wasted too much time, I hurried on to the edge of the field. Ten yards ahead, the galvanised wire fence running along the top of the low drystone wall enclosing the Farm car park showed up clearly in the green illumination of the goggles. Unfortunately, there had been too short notice for Gerry to source the state-of-the art night vision technology able to produce realistic daylight imagery, so areas of less contrast appeared merely as dark shapes. Up till now, this older type of goggles had not been a problem in the wide expanse of the open fields, but now, though the car windows showed up clearly, the body and wheel areas remained in deep shadow. If I tripped over a hidden obstacle, the noise might alert those assembled in the farmhouse kitchen that there was an intruder. Just have to take the chance.

CHAPTER THIRTY-TWO

I stood motionless, listening to the sounds of the night: the sough of the wind through the twig tracery of the gnarled pear tree, a faint rustling from somewhere in the grass at my feet, the distant screech of a night bird. All natural, nothing out of the ordinary. No lights on this side of the building from Bev's and McClusky's bedrooms or Bev's office. As far as I could tell, it was safe to proceed.

I put a foot on the wall and was gripping the wire fence to haul myself up and over when I felt light vibrations travelling along the metal strand. Someone or something close-by was touching it. I'd seen no animals as I'd crossed the field. A perching owl? No time to speculate. I dropped to the ground, face pressed against the rough stones of the drystone wall to hide reflection from the goggles. Inside the rucksack, a thump and a muffled outraged *miouw*. A miffed G was registering resentment at her abrupt change of position. I breathed, barely audibly, 'Quiet, G,' and the rucksack was still.

Vision blocked, I strained to catch any sound that might give a clue to what was causing that unsettling vibration. I'd not long to wait to find out. A grunt, heavy breathing, curses.

Male voice. Not far away, too close for comfort. I lay, heart pounding, all too vulnerable to a boot or knife in the ribs if I was spotted. A *twang* of wire relieved of a heavy weight. A faint *thud* from the other side of the wall. Another quiet curse. The barely perceptible *crunch crunch* of receding footsteps on the car park's thin gravel.

Slowly… ever so slowly… I raised my head to peep over the wall. Distinct in the green glow of the night vision goggles, a burly figure was standing between two of the cars. He was looking around as if searching for something.

The *click* of a car door, quietly opened. A hissed, '*Psst!*'

The man swivelled his head in the direction of the sound. A murmured, 'That you, McGurk?'

The figure emerging from the car was undoubtedly Sapphire. What was she doing here at this clandestine meeting? Vital to listen in to what was being said. I unzipped the rucksack, lifted Gorgonzola out, and reached up to place her on top of the wall.

'Go!' I whispered. I switched on the wireless radio receiver in my ear.

She jumped down. I raised my hooded head just high enough to see her disappear under the nearest car before I ducked down again. The voice-activated device would pick up their conversation.

Man's voice, '…bloody stupid idea of yours, Sapphire, to tell me to come across the fields. Couldn't see a thing without a torch, so shut up about me being late!'

'Coast's clear, Trev. Told you they'd all be at dinner in the kitchen.'

Hroooo Hroooo G's triumphant drug detecting croon made

me jump.

From Sapphire a sharp scream cut off abruptly as he clamped his hand over her mouth.

Trev, 'Shut up, McGurk! It's just an over-sexed tomcat!'

The sound of the farmhouse's back door opening.

'*Get down!*' Trev's urgent whisper. A scuffle as they both ducked down between the cars.

Hroooo Hrooooo

Stu's voice, 'Only a cat. Beat it!' The rattle of a small stone rolling across tarmac. The farmhouse door slammed shut.

Hrooooooo

The *thud* of boot against tyre. 'Bugger off, mog!'

Hroo–

A quick blast on the ultrasonic cat whistle summoned G back unhurt. The silky play-mouse, her reward, kept her quiet as I listened in, cradling her in my arms.

'That's seen it off! Don't just stand there, Trev, give me a hand up.' A gasp of effort from overweight Sapphire as she struggled to get to her feet, followed by a grunt, which might have been thanks.

'About that text offering me a business deal, McGurk. The packets carried into your studio early this morning were drugs, that right?'

'Too right. Though just icing sugar supplies for Madge *they* said. Fooled me at first. She's not been around for some days, apparently gone off to some fondant icing competition in London. But I cleared them out of my way, threw them into a corner. How the hell was I to test my dyes and hang wool up to dry while tripping over a stack of packages? Too bad that one of them burst. Then I had a closer look and tested the powder on my tongue. No *way* was it icing sugar. Thought you might be interested in liberating a couple of packages.' A giggle.

'Too right! What's the deal, then?'

'Twenty-five per cent to you,' said with the finality of an expert in steamrollering hard deals, as I knew only too well. During that mission when I'd paid to share her large studio at the Pittenweem festival, her idea of sharing had been to claim ninety-five per cent of the floor area, forcing me into the remaining tiny space, a small table, to display my very large White Lady statue. It still rankled.

'No *way*, McGurk. Don't piss me off! You're a bloody amateur. What you know about dealing is–' Loud spit. 'The deal's on *my* terms. Without me to do the business end–'

'But–' Squeak of outrage.

'Get moving. I've not got all night. You'll do what *I* say or…' Indistinct as they moved out of range.

In celebration I gave G an extra pat before lowering her and mouse into the rucksack. 'I think Sapphire's met her match there, don't you?'

I remained behind the drystone wall, too old a hand at surveillance to climb over the wall on the risky assumption that they had walked off to Madge's studio. Sapphire didn't realise when she was beaten. They could very well have stopped on the edge of the car park to continue the one-sided argument out of earshot of those in the farmhouse kitchen.

I gave them another five minutes before I climbed over the wall, crossed at a crouch between the cars, and stopped on the edge of the car park making sure that Sapphire and Trev had indeed gone off to the studio. I realised now there'd be *much* less time than I'd anticipated to eavesdrop under the farmhouse window and climb back over the wall to avoid Trev returning to the car park, deal done.

When I reached the back of the farmhouse building, it was in complete darkness except for the closely-curtained kitchen window, viewed through the goggles as a bright green rectangle, duplicated on the worn flagstones of the yard. I kneeled under the window beside the refuse bin, eased G out of the rucksack and lifted her onto the windowsill.

With a whispered, 'Stay!' I ducked down.

Through the headphones, loud and clear, McClusky's voice, '...so that's what *I* think we should do.'

Dolores impatiently, 'Definitely not enough time for that! Kennedy's gang will be expecting her to report back any day now. Any other suggestions?'

Silence.

McClusky again, 'Nobody anything to say? Then let me sum up the position. A rival gang is threatening to muscle in on our territory, so our supplies for the next scheduled exhibition have to be moved to safety. We made a start this morning with the dozen packages now in studio C. I propose a pop-up exhibition to dispose of them.'

I flicked away from my face a large brown moth attracted by the thin line of light escaping above the top of the curtains.

A short silence, then an outburst from Stu and Vic.

'But that won't help much...'

'Still leaves the problem of the other ninety per cent in our store here, doesn't it!'

Dolores, impatiently. 'We move all that back to our main storage *prontissimo*, of course. None of the bastards trying to muscle-in are going to find out where that is, are they? The raid when it comes will be on the Farm and studios. So let's concentrate on where to hold a pop-up exhibit–'

The rest drowned out by a clamour of voices.

Bored with inaction and tempted beyond endurance by the moth fluttering against the window, G jabbed at it with her beefy paw.

Thump. Missed. *Thump*.

McClusky, 'What's that? Probably just the wind, but check it out, Vic.'

Scraping back of a chair.

'But more important, check the studio. Can't be too careful with our drugs there. Too easy to break in.'

Hell! I grabbed G, hugged her tightly to me. How long did I have? A lightning calculation. *If* I made it as far as the open countryside the advantage of night vision would give me a chance of escape. But, a very big but, a mere ten steps along the hall from the kitchen would take Vic to the back door. He'd throw it open, couldn't miss my running figure, only too visible silhouetted in the light spilling out over the flagstones. At his shout of alarm, the gang would rush out hot on my heels. The odds were stacked against me.

An ever-widening line of light shone out from the door opening a couple of yards from where I crouched beside the refuse bin. Too late to make my escape. Time had run out.

McClusky unwittingly to the rescue. 'Hold on a minute, Vic. I'll get the key for you. Better go into the studio and make sure the stuff's still there.'

The advancing slit of light from the opening door wavered and stopped.

A vital ten second delay, but all I needed to edge the bin a fraction more away from the wall and hunch down behind it with a warning whisper in G's ear.

There was a slim chance that as Vic passed me, the pool of light from his torch would direct his attention ahead rather than to the side, and that his night vision, already compromised by the sudden adjustment from bright interior to dark exterior, would make it hard for him to pick out any detail of my black clothing and balaclava in the shadow behind the bin.

His footsteps approached... passed... grew fainter... died away. For him to get to the studio, unlock the door, cast a quick look inside, and return, allow to be safe, maximum five minutes.

CHAPTER THIRTY-THREE

Glowering, Sapphire inserted her key in the studio door. Trev thought he had menaced her into accepting a paltry twenty-five per cent, did he! Well, she'd see about that. He wouldn't be able to carry off more than a couple of packets *tonight*. So what if…

She switched on the studio light and locked the door after him. 'Don't want anyone walking in on us, do we?' She watched him walk over to the burst packet and test the white powder.

Then she put her scheme into action. 'I've been thinking, Trev. Why *should* we be satisfied with only *two* packets? Why don't we take the lot? You'll manage two tonight, then you can come back for the rest with a porter's trolley before dawn tomorrow and drop me off at the railway station with my share of the cash. By the time they come to get this stuff for an exhibition, packets gone, me gone! Deal, Trev?'

She didn't trust him as far as she could throw him, of course. She knew how it would play out. At North Berwick station tomorrow when she held her hand out for the cash she was due, he'd just toss her a fiver, laugh in her face, and drive off with the drugs, banking on the fact that she wouldn't dare to attract attention by shouting abuse. But two could play the double-cross game.

Trev wedged a packet under each arm with a grunt that could have meant 'Deal,' or possibly, 'No Deal,' and made for the door.

Footsteps outside and a rattle of the studio door handle. 'That you in there, Sapphire?'

Trev froze in mid-step.

Sapphire recovered first. Quick-thinking was one of her strengths. 'Yes, it's me, Vic. Just preparing some dye for tomorrow.' She snatched the packets from Trev and in one swift movement returned them to the pile in the corner.

Another rattle of the handle and an impatient, 'Well, let me in. Door's locked.'

'Just a sec. Drying my hands.'

She jerked her thumb in the direction of the walk-in cupboard, and mouthed, '*In there, Trev!*'

Cupboard door pulled shut, she whipped on an apron and let Vic in.

'This interruption's not *at all* convenient.' Scowling she wiped her hands on a towel. 'Better be important. I'm just about to start on an *extremely* complicated dye recipe. Needs a lot of concentration.' She walked over to a shelf and picked out a packet of powder labelled *Cobalt*, muttering, 'Let's see... Five teaspoonfuls midnight-blue, or two teaspoonfuls sky-blue?'

'Hey, what's this! Why have these been moved?' Vic was staring at the plastic-wrapped packets heaped untidily in the corner of the room.

Brushing aside the angry question as if of no importance, she spooned the powder into a jar and added hot water.

'I asked you a question. Answer it!' He grabbed her arm.

Deliberately leaving the jar lid only half-tightened, she followed his gaze. 'Oh,' a casual shrug, 'the icing sugar packets? Had to move them. Stupid place to leave them beside my barrels of dye! I've already tripped over the blasted things twice.' She shrugged off his hand. 'They'll just have to stay over there till Madge gets back and can decide where to store them.'

Damn, he was striding over to the packets, ignoring the flow of words she'd hoped would divert his attention. Had to get rid of him before he spotted that split she'd taped up in one of them. Only one way to hasten his departure. She hurried up to him, shaking the jar with excessive vigour. As intended, splashes of dark blue dye leaked from the sabotaged lid to land perilously close to Vic's expensive trainers.

He leapt back. 'Watch what you're bloody well doing!'

'Oops, sure I'd tightened the lid! It's essential to continue shaking the dye for *exactly* two minutes. Better stand back a bit.' He retreated, she advanced, spattering the floor with threatening dark blue drops. Now give him something else to distract him from those packets and get rid of him. 'What was it you came to the studio to ask me?'

'Er...er...' To give himself time to think, Vic made a pretence of inspecting his shoes for stains. 'Happened to be passing and was surprised to see a light in the studio at this time of night. Wanted a word with Madge, thought she'd come back early.'

Sapphire's eyes narrowed. Easy to detect the lie. When he'd tried the door handle, he'd called out, 'That you in there, *Sapphire?*' He wouldn't have called out her name if he'd *really* wanted to speak to Madge. As for his 'happened to be passing by'. At this time of night he'd actually have been halfway through supper with the others.

'Well, she's not come back yet.' She glanced pointedly at the clock on the wall and jotted down the time on a notepad. With masterly aim, a final shake of the jar satisfactorily directed more dye in Vic's direction.

'Goddammit, woman!' The studio door banged shut after him.

'Well that worked just dandy! Piece of cake!' Sapphire turned the key in the lock, strode over to the store cupboard and yanked open the door. 'When we're sure he's gone, Trev, you grab two packets and scarper. Come back tomorrow at five a.m. with the trolley and we'll make off with the rest while they're all still snoring in their beds.'

Barely controlling his impatience, Trev strolled over to count the packets, openly calculating the profit (soon to be all his). Sapphire watched him, covertly calculating the profit (soon to be all hers).

After a few minutes, 'Ok, Trev. All clear to go.'

Studio door safely locked behind him, she flung back her head and laughed. One thing for sure, *long* before five a.m. she and the remaining packets would be gone. She contemplated the dark cobalt stains on the floor. McClusky would be livid. Scrubbing those away would take blood, sweat, and tears. Well, that was somebody else's problem. It sure as damn wasn't going to be hers!

She had the future all planned and it didn't include Trev. She didn't need his porter's trolley. She had her own version liberated from a supermarket to transport her dye-vats to and from her van, fitted with a ramp designed for the loading of heavy wheelchairs. Stroke of luck that the drugs had been packaged in white plastic bags indistinguishable from that roll of pedal bin liners in Madge's kitchen cupboard. But it was no stroke of luck that the van's electric engine would enable the silent getaway, so essential at times to dodge those she'd double-crossed.

All she had to do now was weigh one of the drug packets, fill the pedal bin liners with the same weight of icing sugar, load the genuine packets into the dye vat, wheel them off, and drive away – not exactly into the sunset, or even the first lightening of the sky pre-dawn. No, it would be *well* before that. For the one thing she could be sure of was that Trev would arrive long before five, when he'd be counting on her being asleep in her yurt. He'd break open the studio door, on his face a smile as wide as the Cheshire Cat's at the sight of the heap of packets, apparently just as he'd left them, tested a few hours ago by himself as genuine. Another laugh brought tears to her eyes. Trev's *face* when he eventually opened the packets to find nothing but worthless *icing sugar*!

CHAPTER THIRTY-FOUR

Slowly, cautiously, I extricated G and myself from the narrow space behind the bin, all too aware that the slightest scrape of metal on the uneven flagstones would bring someone to investigate. This took a big chunk of the precious time, much more than I could afford. But an anxious glance in the direction of the studio revealed as yet no dancing beam from Vic's returning torch.

I wasn't out of danger yet. While crossing to the car park and climbing over the drystone wall with its fence, I'd be silhouetted, a dark figure against the paler night sky. No time for the niceties of placing G gently into the rucksack. Under my arm would have to do. At a crouching run I set off, trusting my black outfit would render me indistinguishable from the dark background. Standing on the wall to straddle the wire fence, I was at my most vulnerable. Heart pounding, I released G to let her slip under the wire ahead of me. I reached out to grip the wire with both hands.

'Hey! Who the hell are you?'

Vic had come back from the studio quicker than I'd anticipated. I rolled over the top of the wall, landed with a bone-jarring thump in the field and scrambled to my feet. The field would definitely have a gate. I set off at a run across the ploughed furrows. A backward glance showed that Vic had reached the wall.

I was now out of range of the weak beam of his torch. He'd assume I would run straight ahead, the direction he'd glimpsed me taking. I changed course, angling sharply left, the night vision goggles enabling me to see a long distance ahead. I cursed the red East Lothian clay sticking in heavy clumps to my boots.

Where was he now? I turned my head to keep tabs on his position, only to realise my change of direction had been a bad move. Slowly but surely he was gaining on me, off to my right, alarmingly close. Even as I watched, his torch beam swung in a wide arc, right to left, left to right, right to left. I couldn't keep up this pace for long before his light picked me out. In the middle of a field there's nowhere to hide.

Wrong! Clearly visible to me through the goggles, only fifty yards ahead were the four scarecrows I'd mistaken for a foot patrol. I'd become a scarecrow! A few seconds later, I was lying on my back, stealth-black jacket whipped off to reveal my coloured jersey beneath, last scarecrow in line pushed with adrenalin-fuelled shove from vertical to crazy slant as if partially dislodged by notoriously strong East Lothian gales, a scarecrow's white sack face plucked off and transferred in an instant to cover my head.

With the whispered command, 'Quiet, G', I manoeuvred her rucksack under my jersey to replicate a bulging scarecrow belly. Then confident that she wouldn't stir, I stretched out my arms at right-angles to my body in scarecrow mode, and lay motionless. Taking air in shallow breaths. I waited...

Running footsteps approached. Slowed. Torchlight leaked through the plasticised hessian sack over my face... moved across... passed on. Curses, loud... receding... Weak with relief that his boot hadn't thudded into my head or the rucksack belly in frustration, I gulped in air, deciding fallen-scarecrow mode was quite restful after my exertions. Foolish to risk moving. When he got to the far end of the field, hopefully he'd give up, resigned to failure, and make his way back across the field to the farmhouse to report he'd frightened off an intruder.

Sound carries a considerable distance at night. When at last the faint slam of the farmhouse door indicated he'd gone back inside, I stirred, pulled the sack off my head and got to my feet. In acknowledgement of the farmer's efforts to protect his crop, I folded up the sack and weighed it down with a heavy clod of earth, then with the aid of the goggles set off to make my way back to where I'd left the car. Tonight's luck wasn't going to hold, we'd have to be off.

'And it's all your fault, G,' I grumbled as I skirted round the seemingly endless rows of vegetables.

She began twisting and turning in the rucksack, raucously demanding out to prowl along the foot of a nearby hedge, her idea of well-deserved relaxation after work, so I gave her freedom to hunt. After five minutes the squeak of a frightened rodent indicated her approximate position and with the aid of the night vision goggles she was easy to spot. Dangling the irresistible silky arcade mouse by its tail, I blew the ultrasonic cat whistle. She turned her head in my direction. No need of night-vision goggles for her! Just before she reached me, I held the rucksack invitingly open and cunningly dropped in the mouse.

With G safely zipped up in the rucksack, I drove off, mulling over the info I'd gained. As I'd overheard, the drugs to be passed on at the pop-up exhibition were at this very moment stored in Sapphire McGurk's studio, there tonight but gone tomorrow, spirited away by the undoubtedly double-dealing Trev. I could *almost* feel a twinge of sympathy for her.

As regards the chief purpose of the mission, the location of the gang's main storage base, all I could report to Gerry was that it was on an island, probably one with easy access to the East Lothian coast. On my couple of visits to North Berwick I had seen small boats of all types pass to and fro attracting little attention as to where they put into shore or to what they carried.

Even the Isle of May couldn't be discounted. Other possibilities were Fidra, the Lamb, Craigleith or the Bass Rock, the four small uninhabited volcanic islands close to North Berwick. In theory any of these sites were well-suited for the transfer of drugs to the mainland. None of them, however, was a secure place to hide a large quantity of drugs. Birdwatchers, volunteers clearing vegetation from the puffin burrows, or visits by the Seabird Centre's boats made them unlikely. To discover the whereabouts of the drug cache would need time.

* * *

Pear Tree Farm. 1.30 a.m.
The well-oiled wheels of the liberated supermarket trolley made no sound as Sapphire pushed it across the car park. So far, so good. One by one, careful not to burst the plastic wrapping, she lifted the drug packets out of the dye vat and stacked them in the back of her van.

Clunk. Caught by a sudden gust of wind the lefthand door hit the side of the trolley. Due to the low night temperature Bev and McClusky's bedroom windows were both firmly closed, but for a few anxious moments she held her breath, dreading a curtain pulled back, a face to appear. Nothing. She relaxed. Dye vat loaded, light-weight ramp stowed, rear doors quietly closed. Van lights off, Sapphire McGurk made a stealth exit from Pear Tree Farm. All very satisfactory.

'Who's going to be a millionaire?' she sang. 'I am!' She hummed a few more bars. She had time to disappear. Trev had tested the spilt packet, so no reason for him to suspect that the drugs had been switched for icing sugar. He'd find *that* out only when he tried to sell them on. And saving his own skin would give him *more* than enough to worry about.

The humming stopped abruptly. Not just Trev would be after her, if he survived, but whoever had stored all those packets of drugs in Madge's studio. Her grip on the steering wheel tightened, then relaxed. Not to worry. The value of the drugs just inches away in the back of the van would be more than enough to ensure her safety. New name, new passport, new country. She rather fancied Tenerife, warm but not too warm, English spoken, English *food*. Could even make herself understood. She was proud of her language skills.

'*Boowainas grasseas maanyana olaay.*' The murdered words rolled confidently off her tongue.

And, of course, the money would pay for a new face. A quick glance at her reflection in the rear-view mirror. She'd never liked that nose. Yes... a new nose. And what about...?

CHAPTER THIRTY-FIVE

The magnificent herbaceous borders in Dirleton Castle Garden, so splendid in high summer, were dying back, colours fading, seed heads left as food for birds. Almost gone now the luxuriant colourscape of the Art and Crafts garden, an artist's joy as well as a challenge. The muted oatmeals, buffs, and browns of approaching autumn, yellowing leaves, flowers fading, seed heads forming, were all more in tune with Dolores' mood as she set up her easel in preparation for this week's rendezvous with the Boss, an encounter she was dreading.

A cluster of Crocosmia Lucifer caught her eye, a blood-red splash amid shades of bronze, green, brown, its sword-shaped leaves stabbing at the sky, the sort of composition that would normally have her eagerly sketching, dipping into her paints to select just the right tone to capture the play of light or shade on leaf or petal. But not today. She stared with unseeing eyes at her completed pencil sketch, rehearsing how she was going to break the news to the Boss of the overnight disappearance of those packets of drugs under her care.

She herself found it hard to accept that without suspecting anything she had allowed Kennedy and McGurk, not just one but *two* members of a rival gang to infiltrate Pear Tree Farm. In her defence she would point out that as soon as Tamsin Kennedy had roused suspicion, she had taken immediate steps to eliminate her, calling on the professional services of the Removal Men to make sure of that.

The nightmare had begun with yesterday's discovery of the splintered lock on the studio door. Raid by a rival gang, they'd thought at first – until it was clear that the McGurk woman had done a runner, belongings gone from yurt, van from car park, rubbishy dyed stuff from studio. All that remained of her occupancy, these vile blue stains defacing the expensive studio floor (McClusky had been livid about them, as if that mattered!).

But would the Boss accept that McGurk had fooled everyone into believing she wasn't a threat by pointing the finger of suspicion at Kennedy? She thought not. So what if–? What if the Boss decided that Dolores herself had masterminded the disappearance of the drugs? Neil and Madge had been a threat to the gang's income. And had been immediately dispatched. It would be the same with her. A shiver ran down her spine.

She opened her paintbox to select a colour… Sap Green? Hooper's Green? Perhaps a mixture of the two for the Yucca, and add a touch of black for that giant Phormium, dramatic against the red-brown of the boundary wall in the background. She applied brush to paper. Her shaking hand frustratingly widened the dagger-thin point of a Yucca leaf silhouetted against a depressingly grey sky. Damn! But at least with acrylic paint, mistakes could be easily rectified. For some moments the concentration required for the delicate stroke drove all other thoughts out of her mind.

It switched once more to the looming rendezvous. Twenty minutes and she'd find out if the Boss accepted that it hadn't been her fault. Quick flowing strokes captured the elegant stems of the graceful Pampas grasses. She'd get to grips with the delicate feathery fronds later, after that meeting…

…The paint was dry, time to go. Unfinished picture safely stowed, easel folded, she made her way to the secluded seat in the adjoining Victorian Formal Garden screened by the massive yew hedge, so thick and high that it cut off sight and sound of anyone sitting in that seat from visitors strolling along the herbaceous borders in the Art and Crafts Garden. Failing to still the tremor in her hands, she placed the artist's case and easel under the garden seat. Rehearsing how she was going to break the news to the Boss, she stared across the expanse of lawn toward the clipped evergreen trees standing sentinel over the decoratively shaped arrangement of flowerbeds resplendent just a month ago with bright pink begonias and blue lobelias, now reduced to bare raked earth. Propelled by the stiff breeze a crisp autumn leaf was turning cartwheels across the short grass. The low sun highlighted the dagger-sharp tips edging the trunk of the stately Monkey Puzzle tree, silvering the edges of the triangular scale-like leaves clothing its narrow branches. How she longed to set up her easel right now and capture the fleeting beauty with her paints. But that imminent interview was preying on her mind, blotting out all other thoughts.

How *best* to word the report of the theft of the drugs to the Boss? 'I've to confess that…' Definitely *not*. Would seem she herself was responsible, was the only one to blame. Or perhaps, 'I've bad news. The drugs have gone. I'll explain…' No, too abrupt, too negative. Have to think of something blander, less provoking. What about, 'In my previous reports I told you how I had successfully dealt with a rival gang's attempts to infiltrate us via our residential courses. However, they've changed tactics...' Yes, that might work.

On the lightly-gravelled path, the sound of soft footsteps approaching. Dolores looked up with a start, swallowing nervously as the Boss rounded the end of the hedge and stood before her.

She plunged into her prepared defence, from time to time stumbling nervously over the words in haste to finish. Running her tongue over dry lips, she waited, stomach clenched, for the expected furious reaction.

No reaction. None. Not even a frown. Silence except for the rustle of a bird turning over dry leaves in the interior of the thick wall of the yew hedge. From the adjoining Art and Crafts Garden, children's laughter and the patter of footsteps running along the paths beside the herbaceous borders.

At length she saw his mouth compress in a tight line. Then, 'Let's take a walk. Somewhere a bit more private...' A brusque, 'Leave your easel and paints under the yew hedge for now. They'll be quite safe. You won't be needing them.'

2 a.m. Dirleton

A small van made its way down the gradient of Ruthven Road into the village. The murmur of the electric engine did not waken even the lightest sleeper in The Castle Inn or The Open Arms Hotel. Close to the sixteenth-century Dovecot where the Garden's boundary walls were low and easily scaleable, it paused long enough for the van doors to slide silently open. Two Removal Men flitted over the narrow strip of grass. Thirty seconds later they were inside the grounds, striding along the path in the Art and Crafts Garden to retrieve the artist's easel and case from beneath the yew hedge in the Victorian Formal Garden. Taking collapsible spades from their rucksacks, they set to work in the confined space between the walls of the gazebo tower and the dark sword-like leaves of the giant Phormium.

11a.m.
The early-autumn sun warmed the borders, small ornamental thistles spiked the air, their seed heads mediaeval sharpened throwing-stars. Hoverflies busily harvested the microdots of golden pollen on the prominent dark centres of coneflowers. Tall in the background, elegant Pampas Grasses leisurely swayed their golden feathery plumes in the gentle breeze, and sunflowers wearily drooped their flat saucer heads, heavy with seed.

Beside the gazebo tower the massive Great Plains Phormium brooded over its grim secret.

CHAPTER THIRTY-SIX

Gerry had already decided that the gang would hold a pop-up exhibition to dispose of some of the drugs, but I hadn't learned much more than that at the Farm last night except that their main cache was on an island in the Forth.

'So,' I said to Gerry despondently, 'not much progress, I'm afraid. What happens now?'

He didn't seem to be listening. Then, 'When one door closes…?' A raised eyebrow invited me to complete the sentence.

'It remains *shut*.' I snapped, guilty that I'd messed up.

As if he hadn't heard, 'When one door closes…?'

'Don't rub it in, Gerry. You were depending on me and I let you down, didn't I?' Try as I might, the tremor in my voice was embarrassingly audible.

He sighed. 'When one door closes, another opens, is what I'd hope you'd say, Deborah.'

He'd want an honest response, not glib or too readily produced to be sincere. After what had been to put it bluntly, my unsuccessful mission, he was testing how strong I still was mentally and emotionally. Tightrope walkers on the thinnest of ropes, or Olympic athletes on their run-up to clear the bar, must have *complete* belief in their ability to carry out what they have to do or failure is certain. And it was the same for me.

We sat there in silence. I frowned. The gang must remain confident that I was dead and that all I had learned about their drug operation had died with me. A high chance of being recognised would surely prevent me taking any further part in Operation Smokescreen, wouldn't it?

His murmur interrupted my thoughts. 'A foot in the door could stop it closing.' *Could.* His choice of word significant. He was leaving the decision to me. He pulled his doodling pad towards him, pen conjuring up a dainty stiletto-heeled shoe.

So after all, there was still a chance of continuing with the mission.

I met his eye. 'I'll definitely provide the foot if you tell me what you have in mind. But the combat boot is more my style than the stiletto heel.'

For the first time, the trace of a smile. 'As you know, Pear Tree Farm is merely one of a nationwide network of bases that the Tenerife-led drug ring has established in the UK. The info you passed us about Carruthers has led us to a certain McGillivray Zendersen, a respectable Edinburgh businessman. We suspect he is the kingpin, the Mr Big, of the drug organisation. He's the director of a firm importing top of the range mattresses. And by 'top of the range' I mean eye-wateringly expensive! *Voilà.*' He tapped his phone and held up a picture.

Nothing distinctive about that mattress. Nothing remarkable about it, except the price. 'What's it stuffed with? Bank notes?'

An enigmatic, 'You *could* say that, Deborah.'

'Drugs?'

A shake of the head. 'Try again.'

The silence lengthened. I was hoping he'd run out of patience before I did. He didn't.

I surrendered. 'OK. Give me a clue.'

'Tob–?'

I mimed a Munch scream of frustration.

'Brain a little below par?' Encouragingly, the pen sketched a cigarette, the smoke drifting up.

I couldn't resist. 'Got it! The mattress is stuffed with cigarettes and is a fire hazard!'

He leaned back smiling. 'An agent has to have all brain cells firing. I was worried there for a moment, but you're back on form I see. Yes, with U.K. government taxes on tobacco sure to increase, a mattress filled with tobacco is an innovative and lucrative way of smuggling. Poor quality tobacco is bought dirt-cheap, and once smuggled into the EU can be sold at half the legal price making a hundred per cent profit.'

'A hundred per cent profit on, say fifty cents. Hardly worth the bother is it, Gerry!'

'You're forgetting quantity. The packets arrive at our major ports shipped in forty-foot long containers. So we're talking millions of packets worth many millions of euros. When the cigarettes are counterfeits of major brands, there's more profit, of course. The gangs are concealing tobacco or drugs among goods shipped by reputable businesses, but sniffer dogs, X-rays and a scrupulous check of the cargo manifest often catch them out. And that's how Mr McGillivray Zendersen and his mattresses came to our attention. You told me you'd definitely provide the foot once you'd heard more details. So are you interested in hearing more?'

I didn't hesitate. 'Count me in.'

'To put you in the picture, our Mr Z is at the moment in Tenerife on his private three-decker ocean-going yacht, present location Los Cristianos marina. The *Cheetah* is in effect his head office with all the records and documentation for the drug distribution bases in Europe and the UK. Early this morning we received intelligence from Tenerife's Unit Against Organised Crime that his yacht is scheduled to set off in a couple days for the UK.'

He leaned forward. 'And that is where you come in. When you get on board, if you gain access to Z's office that would be ideal, but a photo record of anything useful will do. I want you to wear this.' He handed me a rubber-strapped fitness watch, the type with a rectangular dark face. 'No, it's not to count how many miles you'll walk, or for you to check how well you've slept. This watch is a spy camera with autofocus, saving photos or videos to its internal micro SD card. Press this side-button to take videos, and that one to take photos. A LED light will flash once to show the camera is ready. That tiny dot like a speck of dust on the face of the watch is the camera lens.'

I fastened the watch onto my wrist. 'Mmm. What about if there's a device in his office that will detect any electronic bug planted there?'

Gerry smiled. 'Not a problem with this little gadget. It hasn't an electronic signal to trace.'

'And if by chance he wants to check if it's really a fitness watch?'

'Just a flick of your finger across the screen and the time will appear, another sideways stroke shows the number of steps etc. And so on… To all intents and purposes this is a genuine fitness watch.'

A day after that meeting with Gerry, blue-dyed hair restored to its natural brown, I was on my way to Tenerife. But without Gorgonzola. More than a bit worrying. Had I not promised her that she'd *never* again be left behind in HMRC kennels? I felt as guilty as hell. But the mission came first and we wouldn't be separated for long. As soon as possible I'd take the first flight home, pick her up from the kennels and we'd be off on a well-deserved holiday, safely out of the way until all those based at Pear Tree Farm had been rounded up.

The plane made its approach to Tenerife South airport. Below, a clear view of Los Cristianos harbour and the white wake of a ferry heading out, destination the cloud-capped island of La Gomera. Several sizeable yachts were moored at the quayside, two at anchor out in the bay. Which was the *Cheetah?* Impossible to say.

I couldn't think how Gerry was going to get me on board the lair of the mega-rich McGillivray Zendersen at such short notice. Various ideas flicked through my mind. Would he arrange for me to interview Zendersen posing as the representative of a well-known yachting magazine? Idea rejected. Security would be too tight, my credentials too exposed as fake by a phone call to the magazine.

How about me slipping into the marina under the cover of darkness in wetsuit and snorkel to climb aboard? Out of the question – spotlit quayside, sensors, alarms, security as tight as Buckingham Palace.

Or perhaps I could mingle with the celebrity-gawping crowds in a daytime visit to the marina. Might get an opportunity to meet him, admire this and that, ask a few artless questions. But the chance of him inviting me, a stranger, onto his yacht? Non-existent.

I sighed. Only twenty-four hours before the *Cheetah* was scheduled to up-anchor. Gerry had better come up with something very soon.

CHAPTER THIRTY-SEVEN

Rays of early morning sunshine glinted and sparked off the crests of wavelets rippling the surface of Los Cristianos harbour. Sunhat on head, camera slung around neck in tourist mode, I'd taken up position on the Muelle des Pescadores with a perfect view of the Gomera ferry loading cars and passengers at the terminal, the cluster of boats in the marina, and moored further out in the bay, sleek sea-going yachts, one of them the superyacht the *Cheetah* with its Helipad.

To whip out binoculars or use the rather battered pay-as-you-view telescope at the end of the mole might be to draw unwelcome attention. Instead, I moved slowly along the deserted pedestrian walkway, stopping now and then for a nosey inspection of a particular cabin cruiser or catamaran, careful not to show any interest at all in those distant yachts. At the far end, I leant my elbows on a railing and stood staring out to sea, waiting for Gerry's phone call scheduled for 7.45 a.m.

When he connected, I said eagerly, 'I've been thinking of ways to get on board the *Cheetah*. How about if I staged an accident? I could fall off a jet ski after a foolhardy manoeuvre! Z would have to rescue me then, wouldn't he?'

A disappointingly long silence. 'Some flaws there, I'm afraid, Deborah. Visualise this… there you are on your jet ski heading towards the towering side of the yacht. You perform your foolhardy manoeuvre and fall off. The jet ski hurtles on, takes about 300 feet to stop, and smashes into a yacht worth forty million pounds. Do you really think Mr Z's going to pick you up? More likely to drop the anchor on your head! And if there's no collision, he might just sail on regardless. And even *if* he dragged you dripping from the sea, he'd just radio ashore for the coastguard to come and get you.'

'Oh,' I said, feeling a bit of a fool.

'However, I've been thinking somewhat along the same lines.' Gerry was ever quick to detect when an agent felt despondent. 'The important thing is not only to get you on board, but to keep you there long enough to do some snooping. And that will mean?'

My pent-up frustration boiled over. 'Oh, Gerry! Just *tell* me!'

'Well, the jet ski is a no-go. However, the idea of an incident is *definitely* feasible, using not a jet ski but a hang glider!'

This time the long pause was at my end off the phone.

'I've never flown one! Only know that I'd be relying on wind direction and thermals. Obviously needs a lot of skill and practice. Anyway there's no guarantee I'd– '

'I'm envisaging a *powered* hang glider, Deborah, with a fabric wing from which is suspended a fibreglass pod that can carry two passengers. Note, *two* passengers, a pilot and yourself. That means an expert will be driving, if that's the correct word, with you as the passenger.'

'You'd make a great used-car salesman, Gerry. You're

persuading me that all I'll have to do is sit back and take in the breathtaking views!' Then a disturbing thought, 'You're not envisaging an *accident*, are you? The powered hang glider isn't going to hurtle into the sea from a great height, is it?'

'An *incident,* Deborah. An event, a *planned* event. Reassured?'

I was. With Gerry, the safety of his agents was paramount.

'And,' he added, 'the advantage of using a powered hang glider is that this incident can take place far enough from land for it not to be worthwhile for the ship to summon help to return you to shore immediately. On the phone you've been issued with you'll find a new app, *what3words*. The app receives three words from a satellite, no wifi or data signal needed. The words are a way of giving the GPS co-ordinates for any location. You tell the rescue services, or myself, these three words and they will be able to locate your position within three metres.' A pause. 'Except, of course if you're down a mine deep underground so not in contact with the satellite. A most unlikely event. By the way, you *are* following my instructions to keep the phone with you at all times?'

'Well, I'll have you know it's in my pocket *now*.' A flash of irritation. 'Could it be you're *assuming* I'd leave it in my room because I'm not at the moment in an active undercover role?'

'*Touché*! Guilty as charged! But when you manage get on board, as I'm sure you will, it's vital that I track your position. Try the app out now. Tell me the words on the screen and I'll tell you *exactly* where you are at this very moment even though you are in Tenerife and I am two thousand miles away in Edinburgh.'

'*Rituals.scoped.submarines*, I read out. 'Ok, *exactly* where am I in Los Cristianos? You've two seconds to tell me.'

'Muelle des Pescadores!' An irritating note of triumph. 'Now that I've demonstrated the wonders of technology, I'll make the arrangements with someone who has a reputation as a Fixer and is a little creative when it comes to ideas.'

CHAPTER THIRTY-EIGHT

'Name's Reg.' The man wearing jeans and a *Water Ski with Reg* t-shirt was tough and wiry, face and arms tanned from years of exposure to the hot Tenerife sun. We shook hands, his grip firm but not bone-crunchingly so. 'Hear you want to write about an adrenalin sport?'

So that was the story Gerry had spun about my role. I nodded. 'Hi, I'm Jess. Micro-lighting's the current craze, you know, and not just for the young. I'm hoping to be able to sell an article about it in a wide range of magazines.'

'But from the flight plan I've been given, you have a much more lucrative aim in mind?' A knowing wink. 'Perhaps you aim to wangle a hard-to-get interview with the reclusive Mr McGillivray Zendersen?'

'Couldn't possibly comment!' I lowered an eyelid in an equally conspiratorial wink.

I had to hand it to Gerry. He had come up trumps as ever, giving me the perfect undercover role of unprincipled journalist prepared to pry in pursuit of juicy titbits.

'Ever been in one of these aerial trikes?' Reg waved a hand in the direction of a strange Heath Robinson three-wheeled machine resembling a motor cycle sidecar with alarmingly cut-away sides. At the rear, a small engine and plane propellor were attached rather too close to pilot and passenger. Overhead, the slender arrow-shaped wing seemed a bit flimsy to support the weight of two people and the engine. Definitely a dangerous contraption. My heart sank. What had I let myself in for? But I didn't have to go through with it. I could still withdraw. There'd be no condemnation from Gerry.

Reg's eyes weighed me up. Sensing my unease, he smiled. 'I'll be in control. Nothing to worry about, nothing at all. You don't have to do anything. I'll be doing the steering, you'll be in the front seat. Just sit back and enjoy the view.' A rather unnerving echo of Gerry's confidence-boosting spiel. 'Ok, let's get kitted up. You'll need these. It'll be breezy up there.' He handed me a zipped flying suit, gloves, lifejacket and visored helmet. 'We'll have radio intercom. Gone are the days when I'd have had to shout to be heard above the engine noise.'

Once we were strapped in, safety drill completed, he switched on the engine. Unprepared for the noise as it roared into life, I clutched the horizontal bar in front of me and hung on grimly as the trike bumped over the grass for what seemed an interminably long time before it soared into the air.

'How does this thing steer?' my voice squeaky with tension.

Loud in my helmet, Reg mission-control calm and reassuring. 'By weight-shift, same sort of thing as with skis, you know.' The horizontal bar tilted as the machine banked gently to the right. 'I have control. You can relax.'

And I did. Gerry and Reg had been right about the views: spread beneath me were small isolated villages dotting the lower slopes of Mt. Teide; as we neared the coast, plantations of bananas and tomatoes under protective plastic sheeting; rocky cliffs white-fringed by pounding sea; finally, Los Cristianos itself and its harbour. I peered down at the cluster of ships in the outer bay. No sign of the *Cheetah* with its helicopter pad. It had sailed on schedule at midnight.

We droned on out to sea.

'How long before we catch up with the *Cheetah,* Reg?'

'We're on the course that Zendersen filed. That should be his ship ahead on the horizon.'

So far so good. Getting permission to land on board was another matter, but I had compete confidence in Gerry's choice of microlight pilot though I had no idea what a guy who was a Fixer and a little creative planned to do.

Reg must have read my mind. 'Get ready for action.'

I don't know what I'd expected, but it wasn't the engine faltering… coughing… I clung desperately to the horizontal bar in front of me, mouth dry, forcing back a scream.

The engine cut out. The trike's nose dropped, sending us into a shallow glide. In my helmet, Reg's voice, calm and confident. 'Not to worry. Just a little bit of play-acting to convince them that we have engine trouble.' The only sound now, the whistle of slipstream past metal struts and the leading edges of the arrow-shaped wing. After a heart-stopping pause, 'Thanks to the construction of the wing, the trike will glide before it stalls.'

'And falls out of the sky!' My feeble attempt at a joke to hide the fear.

'No danger of that, Jess. Just a flick of the switch and…'

The engine burst healthily into life again, the nose lifted, and my heartbeat dropped back to normal. Until, that is, the thought struck me: how would Reg know the moment to switch off the engine so that our angle of glide would ensure the stalling point was over a Helipad only a few metres wide? And if, by some miracle, he managed to do so, surely it would be a *crash* landing.

His voice broke in on my thoughts. 'Of course, to convince them we're in trouble, I'll have to switch off the engine several times when we get closer to the ship.'

'Er, Reg…' I said. 'Come clean. There's no way a motorised microlight can land on a Helipad, is there?'

'What made you think that's what we're going to do?'

I thought back to that last phone call from Gerry. I'd asked him if the powered hang glider would hurtle into the sea from a great height. He hadn't actually denied it, just airily mentioned arranging an incident, a planned event. And I'd assumed that was indeed his intention. Actually *planning* to hurtle into the sea was as crazy as my original idea of the unstoppable, uncontrollable jet ski, instantly dismissed by Gerry. But I tried to convince myself that before giving permission to go ahead he'd definitely have ensured that Reg had the expertise to carry it out. I should be in safe hands.

'So we're going to have to land in the sea, then?' I asked, attempting to sound unconcerned and hoping he didn't see how tightly my gloved hands were gripping the horizontal bar.

'Of course we are. Did you not notice the floats fitted above the wheels? This trike's like a seaplane, will just skim along the surface as it slows. A wind-powered hang glider, of course, is a different kettle of fish. You'd think that someone landing in the sea near my waterski boat would be an easy rescue. I was only a couple of hundred yards away but didn't get to him in time, I'm afraid. He didn't release the parachute harness before he hit the water, got tangled in the lines and was dragged under. I fished him out, but there was nothing I could do.'

To break the awkward silence, I said quickly, 'Understood. I'll release the seat belt just before we hit the water.'

'Bad idea. With the trike it's important we stay clipped in to avoid being thrown out. But don't you worry about being trapped and dragged down. Inbuilt buoyancy enables us to stay afloat long enough to get out and swim away.' In case that wasn't enough reassurance, he added, 'Another plus, our lifejackets are self-inflating, activated by immersion in water, and it won't be long before a boat from the *Cheetah* picks us up.'

The surface of the sea came appreciably closer, much closer than I was comfortable with before it started up again.

The engine coughed… coughed… and cut out.

CHAPTER THIRTY-NINE

By the time we'd splashed into the sea, I'd worked out a strategy that would have the most chance of me being left alone in a cabin to recover – and of course, of giving the opportunity to wander round the *Cheetah*, pretending to admire, but really to snoop and plant a listening device. Gerry had planned meticulously and everything was in place to get me on board. Ferreting out that vital information would now be up to me.

'Don't be alarmed if I act a bit tearful and hysterical,' I said to Reg as we bobbed in the in the somewhat choppy water watching the ship's inflatable speeding towards us. 'Somebody in charge, you see, will feel sorry for me, perhaps introduce me to Mr Zendersen or at least show me round the ship. Even if all I get is a cup of tea, I'll be able to write a first hand account about a microlight crash-landing in the sea. But a famous person like Mr Zendersen will probably refuse to give an interview to an unknown journalist like me, so don't reveal that's what I am hoping to do.'

'Silent as the grave.' A wink. 'I'll make a drama out of our crash-landing and your quite understandable panic. Count on me to lay it on thick.'

*

After my feigned collapse on deck, it all turned out better than I'd hoped. I was given a hot drink and the use of a spare cabin to recover from my dreadful experience. To convince anyone looking in on me that I was indeed in a fragile state, eyes closed as if in sleep, mind busy, I lay wrapped in blankets on one of the two queen-sized beds, no cheap bunks on this luxury yacht.

Through one of the three large open windows, no teensy round portholes here, sounds drifted from the deck above: the clink of glass, the murmur of voices, and cutting through it all from time to time, Reg's voice as he recounted his heroic battle to keep the propellor turning and the trike in the air.

'Passenger panicked… unbalanced the trike… dropped like a stone… fought to regain control…' Reg was doing his bit. Time for me to do mine.

I sat up, and for the first time since I was laid on the bed in the faked state of collapse, had the opportunity to look round the cabin. I could have been in a six-star suite at The Ritz, complete with luxurious furnishings and an armful of white orchids in a golden bowl. Blanket draped round my shoulders, bare feet sinking into the luxurious carpet, I crept to the door in borrowed baggy t-shirt and cut-off jeans, phone switched to silent but ready to take pictures.

Cautiously I eased open the cabin door, clutching at it pretending weakness. No need. The passageway was deserted. Another cabin next to mine, and facing me across the short corridor two cabins, on each door a metal card frame to identify an occupying guest.

Phillington Carruthers. A name definitely associated with Pear Tree Farm's distribution of drugs via art objects. Last seen when he'd collected the seabird wood sculpture from Pear Tree's exhibition in North Berwick. 'Our best lead', Gerry had said. But we'd lost him. Now here he was on the same boat as myself, only a picklock away from finding out more. My heart beat faster.

A great chance to snoop? Not worth the risk. Much more important to pick up useful information on the organisation's drug distribution bases in Europe and the UK, in particular the one linked to Pear Tree Farm. No use secreting the listening device in his cabin. It would have to be in the ship's office or in the owner's master suite. Gerry's plan of the *Cheetah* had shown both of them to be on the main deck.

Taking a deep breath, I started up the shallow carpeted stairs that led to the deck above. Halfway up I paused, eyes level with the floor of the splendid main saloon. Lining each wall, was plush seating together with long coffee tables. Vases of elegant white lilies and expensive orchids added to the luxury ambiance.

Without warning, fingers tapped me on the shoulder.

I swung round with a gasp.

'So sorry to startle you, my dear lady,' Carruther's posh plummy voice, unmistakable. 'Excuse me, but if I can disturb you...'

My first reaction was alarm. Then common sense came to the rescue. At the exhibition I'd been at the back of the people crowding round the stand. So no reason for him to pick me out, no reason for him to recognise me now. I moved aside, pressing against the handrail to allow him to pass, then followed him into the saloon.

He eyed the blanket draped round my shoulders, the baggy

t-shirt, cut-off jeans and bare feet. 'Well now,' he drawled, 'you must be the lady descended from the heavens like Icarus when your wings failed, but unlike that famous chap you were fortuitously plucked from the sea thanks to the good services of the *Cheetah*.'

Here was my chance for an introduction to Mr Zendersen. '*So* grateful,' I gushed. 'Perhaps you would be so good as to introduce me to the owner so I could express my heartfelt thanks for saving our lives. I was so *frightened*. I thought I was going to *die*.' I pressed my hand against my heart in suitably dramatic gesture.

'Well, my dear, only *too* delighted.' He patted my shoulder, allowing his hand to linger just a little too long. 'He'll be in his office just now working out a new course that will enable you to be put ashore in Santa Cruz without delaying the *Cheetah* too much on its way to the UK.'

As Carruthers led me to the far end of the saloon in the direction of the owner's master suite, I looked back. Through the sliding door onto the sundeck, I could see Reg leaning casually against a rail, beer in hand.

'...Yes, today was pretty challenging,' swig from beer glass, 'but nothing compared to what happened only a month or so ago! Water skiing has had its stressful moments too, I can tell you, but in my thirty-five years as a water ski instructor, I've never had such a shock. Never been at such a loss as to what to do...' Dramatic pause for more swigs of beer to be dispatched. 'The tension on the tow rope slackened... She wasn't in any trouble, just floating there waiting for me to pick her up. My God! What did I *see*–'

I switched my attention back to Carruthers as he paused to

knock on a panelled door marked *Private.*

From the other side of the door, a raised voice. 'Yes?' The tone brusque. Not too promising.

Undeterred, Carruthers persisted. 'Sorry to disturb you, Zed. The young lady you rescued is here, anxious to thank you in person.'

From inside the cabin a short, sharp, 'Wait!'

Carruthers shot me an apologetic look. 'Putting you ashore, you see, is going to play havoc with our docking schedule in the UK. Business contracts involved… penalty clauses… Late arrival will have a domino effect.'

For a nail-biting moment, planting the bug in Zendersen's office hung in the balance.

The door opened. Zenderson stood there unsmiling. Close-cropped receding grey hair, bull-neck, muscular arms straining at the sleeves of his black t-shirt, the unemotional assessing stare of a nightclub bouncer.

I didn't make the mistake of revealing I knew the identity of the man standing in the doorway, I stammered, 'Er… Mr… er… Can I thank you for–'

'No, you bloody well can't! You're nothing but a shitload of trouble! Why the hell did you think you could come so far out to sea in a contraption like that? No, don't answer! Stupidity, that's what! Can - I - make - it - *clear* - I - do - not - want - disturbed - by - *anyone!*' The door slammed shut on me and on my mission.

Quick thinking needed. Perhaps there was a chance, just a chance… Lower lip quivering, I gave a strangled sob, followed by several loud watery sniffs.

As I'd hoped, Carruthers took the opportunity once again

to pat my shoulder, this time his hand lingering even longer. 'Sorry about that reception, my dear! Zed doesn't like being told what to do.'

'But I didn't tell him to do anything.' Another sniff.

'Not you, my dear,' his hand commenced a slow but steady journey down my back. 'A radio message came in from the Coastguard alerting us to a motorised microlight with engine trouble in our vicinity and requesting our help, not in fact a request, of course, but an order.'

'Oh, I see,' I said, and I certainly did, much more than he realised. Reg had known that everything would be under control, our engine failure only simulated, and that the *Cheetah* obeying the International Law of the Sea would be obliged to go to the rescue of any vessel in distress. The Coastguard had not become involved through a Mayday call from Reg. The alert could only have come through Gerry, certain that otherwise Zendersen, allowing nothing to interfere with his plans, would ignore the ditched microlight and ruthlessly sail on.

Carruther's hand paused in its journey down my back. 'I don't get the impression you're a stupid woman, so why *were* you taking the risk of flying so far out to sea in a microlight?'

If I played it right, I might still be able to rescue the mission and not let Gerry down. 'Well...' Sniff, sniff. I took the opportunity to disengage from his hand by rummaging in the pockets of my borrowed clothes for a non-existent handkerchief. 'It *was* my fault. Reg wanted to turn back, but I *so* needed an aerial picture of the *Cheetah*. You see, the *Diario de Avisos* has a full page article, ready to print, about the ship and its owner. They were relying on me to get an aerial picture of the ship.' More sniffs. 'This was to be my big chance,' I wailed, wiping my face on the hem of the baggy t-shirt, and rubbing my eyes hard. 'And I've let them down!' Sobbing, I looked at Carruthers with reddened watering eyes.'

'Now, now, my dear,' he pulled me close, amorous intentions somewhat hampered by the folds of the blanket loosely draped round my shoulders. 'Don't take it too much to heart. Just think, you can have an even better picture of the salvaged microlight safely secured on the boat deck, and with it a dramatic report for the *Diario* of engine failure and of how Mr Zendersen came to the rescue.'

'Oh,' I gasped. 'I should have thought of that myself!' I had actually, but it was a photo not of the microlight, but of the charts, that Gerry wanted.

I heard the *thud thud* of rope-soled shoes on the steps from the bridge. A crew member appeared, a sheet of paper in his hand.

He addressed Carruthers. 'Excuse me, sir, Mr Zendersen's not answering his phone.'

'Ah, yes, he's made it clear that he's not to be disturbed.'

'I've a note from the captain for him, sir.'

'Let me see. Perhaps I can help.' Carruthers read the message and nodded. 'I'll have a word with the captain.' He turned to me. 'Care to see the view from the wheelhouse? After that I'll show you the delights of one of the deluxe cabins.'

No guesses as to whose cabin and what delights he had in mind. I'd deal with that problem when I had to. I nodded enthusiastically. With a bit of luck I'd get a peek at the marine charts set aside for the *Cheetah*'s proposed landfall in the UK. The mission was still live.

I let him lead me up the steps to the bridge, spy watch on

wrist powered up in readiness. As expected, the wheelhouse was as state of the art as the rest of the yacht. White-uniformed captain, officer of the watch, able seaman at the wheel, several chart tables, a hundred-and-eighty degree arc of windows and beneath them a bank of screens. Some were monitoring areas of the yacht fore and aft, others displaying essential info such as depth beneath the keel, GPS, weather, and the proximity of other shipping (apparently none).

My objective: get close enough to those chart tables to take photos of the maps on them. First, however, I had to pass as an empty-headed female, and as such no security risk. I wandered in front of the bank of monitors, Oohing, Aahing, and making naive comments.

'All this high-tech stuff, and still the need for a large old-style ship's wheel!' I giggled.

With half an ear I listened with seemingly avid attention to the able seaman's explanation as to why a wheel was still an essential piece of equipment on a modern yacht, and made appropriate comments of 'I see', and 'Really?' to show interest.

All the time, I kept an eye on Carruthers, deep in conversation with the captain. When they seemed to be agreeing on something, I made my move and wandered across.

'The small port of Guïmar, my dear,' Carruther's finger stabbed down on one of the charts, 'is closer than Santa Cruz and would cause us least delay, but is not big enough to handle a super yacht. Captain's going to radio ahead to the port authority at Santa Cruz's super yacht marina which will have the necessary equipment to unload the microlight. Should have the answer in a few minutes whether a berth's available. Then I'll be only too pleased to show you the delights of one of our deluxe staterooms.' He followed the captain over to the radio console.

'MSV *Cheetah* requesting...'

That was my chance. I turned away, raising my hand to fiddle casually with my hair. The lens of the spy watch scanned the cork noticeboard above the chart table and effortlessly saved to its hard disc an annotated schedule of the *Cheetah*'s arrivals and departures at a list of ports.

Now for the few charts laid out ready for the voyage to the UK. Top one would show our present position, lowest the final destination and the stretch of coast, just possibly pinpointing the main drug cache. A quick twist of the watch strap repositioned the camera to my inner wrist. Stifling a yawn for the benefit of anyone looking my way, I picked up the charts, holding them by the left hand corner, dropping them ever so slowly one by one onto the table. With the spy watch on video, Gerry would be able to pause each frame and view the full area of each chart.

With another bored yawn as if losing interest, I turned away. Carruthers and the captain were still in radio conversation with Santa Cruz. I strolled over to the far side of the wheelhouse, and under cover of gazing at the distant shadowy line of the coast, surreptitiously extracted my mobile from under the baggy t-shirt to text Reg.

Be at stairs to bridge. Need help. NOW.

I pressed *send* and slipped the phone back into my pocket.

Captain's voice, 'Thank you. ETA with you will be 14:25.'

Carruthers came striding over. 'That's settled then. Have you safely ashore in a couple of hours. Plenty of time to enjoy yourself...' Long, slow, wink. 'This way.' He held open the wheelhouse door.

Had Reg received the text? Would he be there?

I looked down from the top of the stairs. Hadn't let me down. He was leaning idly against the rails.

I waved. 'Hi, Reg, you'll never guess!' I clapped my hands in mock excitement. 'This kind gentleman has invited you and me to have a look round one of the luxury cabins.' Not quite the seduction scenario Carruthers had envisaged.

And there was nothing he could do about it. Meet guile with guile, is my motto. Checkmate.

That evening I and the spy watch with its sneaked photos were on a plane heading back to the UK. The Revenue and Customs' emergency credit card had covered all expenses incurred in the rescue in the shape of an itemised exorbitant demand from Mr Z due to extra fuel needed for diversion to Santa Cruz, port fees, and transfer of microlight from ship to quayside. Nor had laundry and drying charges for my wet clothing been forgotten. The receipt for the payment was burning a hole in my pocket. I could only hope that the information obtained by the spy watch would justify the outlay.

Something that wouldn't feature on the bill was a last-minute purchase from a souvenir shop at the airport, an aboriginal Guanche terracotta Earth Mother two inches high, with tiny head, huge boobs and massive thighs. Once seen, I couldn't resist. It filled the hole in my heart left by *my* terracotta Earth Mother, so very similar, by now inevitably reduced to fragments by a vengeful Carol.

That same evening, Reg headed in a taxi to the *Diario de Avisos* office in Santa Cruz. In his pocket, his phone with pictures taken by his client Jess, destined for tomorrow's front page: an aerial close-up of the *Cheetah*, sleek, dazzling white, powering through a cobalt-blue sea; a couple of photos taken from the ship by a crew member of their rescue from the ditched microlight; another of the slightly worse-for-wear microlight on the sundeck, the pair of them standing beside it, himself grinning, though Jess must have moved her head as her face had come out somewhat blurred. A pity, but she hadn't seemed too disappointed.

The Diario had offered himself and the crew member a satisfyingly large sum for an exclusive account of the incident. Before rushing off to the airport on an urgent assignment, Jess had scribbled down a few quotes about her personal reaction to the emergency, and he had padded them out with a blow-by-blow account from the moment the engine had misfired, ladling on tension and drama. Jess had assured him all his expenses were covered, even the slight repairs required to the microlight and its transportation back to Las Americas. Leaning back, Reg planned on how to celebrate his unexpected windfall.

CHAPTER FORTY

Despite the late hour, as soon as the plane landed I drove a little apprehensively to the HMRC kennels to collect Gorgonzola. Though a mere seventy-two hours had elapsed since I'd left her, she would undoubtedly have seen it as being Dumped, Deserted, Ditched.

The kennels, reserved for HMRC's sniffer dogs (and now one sniffer cat), are open 24 hours. Light filtered out from behind the edges of the Reception blind. I showed my pass and was admitted.

The sleepy-eyed duty officer consulted the computer screen. 'Let me see… admission number 578, cat, ginger–'

'Cat, Red Persian,' I corrected. 'Name Gorgonzola.'

He consulted the screen again. For some time.

At length, 'Er, it seems that…' Long pause… 'I'm afraid… er… that she's no longer with us.'

My heart missed a beat. 'You mean…?' I gasped, 'you're telling me that she has–' I couldn't bring myself to say the word, *died*. Overwhelmed with grief and guilt, I whispered, 'What was the vet's report?'

'Vet's report on admission was excellent health, no

concerns. But,' he pursed his lips, 'yesterday… it seems your cat …disappeared.'

'*Disappeared*!' I echoed.

'That's right. When one of the kennel staff arrived to put down the cat's breakfast bowl, he found to his alarm the cage empty and the door swinging open. I can assure you the search has been very extensive and, of course, we've left food in the bowl inside the cage. She will be somewhere on the premises. Just a matter of time, bound to come back when she's hungry.'

Time was something I didn't have. The drugs were about to be moved. I knew G was making clear her resentment, wanted *me* to be upset, and she would be prepared to wait it out, intending to steal from food preparation areas for dogs or staff, or more daringly, from a sleeping dog's cage by insinuating a paw through the bars.

Shock followed so swiftly by relief brought on a sudden burst of rage at her antics. So she was expecting a show of remorse from me, was she! Well, what she was going to *get* was a well-deserved bawling-out. Enough was enough.

I rushed outside to my car, calling over my shoulder, 'Just a minute, I think I've an idea on how to find her.' I stuffed the cat whistle into my pocket along with her favourite toy, the realistic furry mouse won at the arcade in Portobello, determined to produce it only when *she* showed remorse.

At my request the duty officer handed over a powerful torch and led me to her empty cage, the door swinging enticingly open, the bowl of food still untouched.

'Are there any tall trees in your grounds? She took refuge high up a tree once when she was upset.'

He thought for a moment. 'There's a big old sycamore in

the exercise area where dogs are running loose during the day. Be a waste of time to look there!'

I wasn't going to be put off. I pointed to the door marked *Kennels and Exercise Yard*. 'She might well have got in there during the night.'

With a yawn to underline how much of a bother it all was, he picked up a bunch of keys and led the way. I stood under the sycamore recalling the mortifying occasion when I had to stand looking up into a tangle of branches to watch her rescue by the fire brigade.

This time it would not be a wheedling, 'Are you there, G? I'm so, so sorry to have abandoned you. Please, please come down.' No, this time it was going to be a Shock and Awe surprise attack. I blew a piercing blast on the whistle, inaudible to human ears, I'm glad to say, and directed the beam of the torch upwards. Like a searchlight seeking out an enemy aircraft, the white beam fingered the highest branches and locked on to a trembling leaf.

'COME DOWN AT ONCE!' I bawled.

For a few seconds, no response.

Then, from the highest point of the tree the barely discernible tremor of a thin branch.

'I CAN SEE YOU, G!' A lie, spoken with utmost conviction.

A slight agitation of leaves followed by the glint of yellow-orange light reflected from the back of feline eyes.

I blew the whistle again, less forcibly, her call to duty, always obeyed. As an added incentive, I thrust my hand into my pocket, pulled out the furry mouse and held it up by its tail, it's soft body oh-so-temptingly spotlit. A loud rustle as leaves were thrust aside, a streak of ginger fur glimpsed as sharp claws cramponed their way down the cracked and peeling trunk in a shower of winged seeds to make a precision four-paw landing at my feet. A graceful aerial leap plucked the coveted rodent from my grasp and carried it off to enjoy at a safe distance. She crouched, a proprietary paw pinning down the mouse, her copper eyes staring at me, challenging, awaiting my reaction. But in the mood she was in, even a conciliatory outstretched hand would be interpreted as preparation for a treacherous snatch and grab.

I asked the duty officer to bring her food and a dish of water and set it down well out of my reach, midway between G and me. The first move would have to come from her. To regain her trust was going to take a long, long time.

CHAPTER FORTY-ONE

Gerry works fast. One day later I stood outside the Zendersen showroom and warehouse. I was holding my 'husband' Gerry's arm in my new undercover role of recently married, somewhat feather-brained wife in search of a mattress (costing an arm and a leg) for the marital bed. To tell the truth, I was feeling more than a little uncomfortable in my fitted haute couture outfit, and tottering along on fashionable spindly heels to match this stylish outfit was proving a pain, used as I was to the comfortable clothes and shoes suitable for most undercover roles.

Somewhat marring, or in some views enhancing, my finery was the across body sling shoulder bag, essential accessory for carrying designer pet, a small dog, or in this case, a non-designer cat. All that was visible of Gorgonzola through the opening, thoughtfully provided for pets to view their surroundings, was soft ginger fur. Cats sleep for about sixteen hours a day, and G was no exception, so it was snooze time to enable her to catch up on last night's vigil at the HMRC kennels, and to digest this morning's very large breakfast of her favourite food.

As for Gerry, his usual wear of casual trousers and open-necked shirt had been replaced by an expensively tailored suit complete with waistcoat and jacquard cravat of blue and green silk.

Clutching Gerry's arm for much-needed support, I teetered up the steps.

'Those steps are not exactly high-heel friendly, are they, darling,' he soothed. Then raising his voice for the ready-to-pounce sales assistant to overhear, added, 'But I'm sure this is just the place we'll find the mattress we're looking for.'

Impressed, I responded with my own contribution. 'But my little Froufrou must show she likes the mattress too, mustn't she?' I cooed, gently tapping the mound of fur to alert G that Duty was about to call. Her face appeared and disappeared in brief acknowledgement. When the time came, she'd be ready. But till then...

'How can I help sir and madam?' Without waiting for answer, the assistant rattled off a rapid-fire sales pitch. 'Are you looking for foam? Springs? Body support firm, medium or soft? Mattress surface cool or warm? Sleeping preference side, back, or as in one in three cases, face? And most important of all, durability and, of course, stability?'

'Stability?' I echoed.

'Yes, madam. How much the mattress moves when your partner turns on it during the night. Very important.'

'*Very* important,' I agreed, recalling those nights of disturbed sleep when G's heavy paws thumped up and down my bed to highlight a grievance. To confirm our undercover roles of living together, I eyed Gerry accusingly.

Hiding a smile, Gerry busied himself consulting the showroom's expensive catalogue. 'We'll just wander around to get a general feel. But we'll let you know if we find something suitable.' He half-turned away, then, as a seeming afterthought, 'We *are* permitted to test a mattress by lying on it?'

'Certainly, sir. Beside each bed, we have full details of what to expect from the mattress.' Spotting new arrivals entering the showroom, he hurried off in the hope of nailing a quicker sale.

Left to our own devices, we worked our way systematically along the rows of beds. Conscious of the danger posed by security cameras, we adopted the tactic of bending over to press a mattress, giving G the chance of a preliminary sniff. Any stirring from within the sling bag was our cue to confer, followed by jotting down a few notes for G to emerge to take a longer sniff. But no head popped out of the bag. No croon signalled a find.

Fifteen minutes later with most of the mattresses inspected, Gerry murmured, 'Time to go about this in a different way.' He raised his voice, 'You're going to have to come to a *decision*, my dear. Try lying down on a bed.'

The perfect opportunity to place G in closer proximity to a mattress. And a welcome if brief respite from those devilish shoes! I kicked them off and lay down on my back, sling bag and its occupant comfortably resting on my stomach. But G took no interest, not the slightest, in this or any of the other remaining mattresses.

I sat up on the bed, and swung my feet onto the floor, psyching myself up to put my feet back into those painful shoes. 'This has just been a waste of time,' I sighed. 'Should have known we'd find nothing *here* to interest us.' Carefully phrased. Lips can be read, and Zendersen would ensure that sharp eyes would later monitor the security camera footage. I eased my feet into the shoes.

'We can look elsewhere for a mattress that suits us.' His fingers pressed my shoulder in warning not to betray surprise at what he was about to say. 'I was just thinking that our boutique hotel is scheduled to open next week, so our priority is not our bedroom but the purchase of mattresses for the eight hotel beds.'

A boutique hotel? What was in his mind? He was studying the notice on a door a few yards away.

WAREHOUSE – NO ADMITTANCE
AUTHORISED STAFF ONLY
KEEP THIS DOOR LOCKED

He summoned the salesman with a wave. 'We've decided on this mattress. We'll require eight for our hotel. How many do you have in stock?'

'Let me see, sir...' He consulted his hand-held device. 'I'm delighted to tell you that there are exactly that number in the warehouse.'

'Good. Reserve them by attaching a label to each mattress. Right now, if you please.' Gerry flourished a credit card, HMRC supplied with name embossed ready for agent signature.

I leapt to my feet. 'One of these mattresses might be selling online right *now*.' I clutched the salesman's arm. 'We must have *eight*. Stock numbers are not always up-to-the-minute accurate, are they? I couldn't *bear* it after all the effort it has taken to find one we really like!'

'You're right, dear. An online order could come in at any moment. Do check in the warehouse *at once*, Mr...er... And if there aren't eight in there, we won't order. We'll have to go somewhere that can supply eight.' Meaningful disappearance of credit card back into wallet. 'Write the name Brydon on the labels. B-r-y-d-o-n.'

The salesman, precious commission at stake, scurried over to the warehouse and punched in a code. The heavy door swung open, triggering a sudden convulsion from the depths of the sling bag. G's head popped out followed by the faint rumble of a drug-detecting croon. No need to give the command, 'Search!' She was already halfway out of the bag.

'I'll have to ask you to wait there a moment. But rest assured, Mr Brydon, I'll count the mattresses and attach the labels in no time at all.' The assistant disappeared inside the warehouse.

In his haste he'd left the door ajar, leaving just enough space for Gorgonzola to slip through towards serried rows of mattresses, whiskers twitching in anticipation of reward.

'Oh!' I adopted a concerned expression for the benefit of the CCTV cameras. 'I think Froufrou must have spotted a mouse in there! Before we pay, we'll have to check our mattresses haven't been nibbled.'

Minutes ticked by. We paced up and down, waiting anxiously for a positive reaction from G rather than a confirmatory call of 'Order ok, Mr Brydon.'

At last, from the depths of the warehouse, a long rumbling *croo-oo-oo* cut short by an angry 'Gerroff!' followed by the *clang* of metal hitting metal. A high-pitched *scre-e-e-e-ch... Waaaah*. The *thud thud thud* of pursuing footsteps. A blur of ginger fur shot out into the showroom. G gathered herself for a leap, extended claws gripped my coat, and she burrowed into the sling bag till only the tip of her tail was visible. How to handle the tricky situation? Attack, or Apology? We had a split second to decide.

The angry salesman appeared in the doorway, red-faced and panting.

Before he could get a word in, I strode towards him. 'You *frightened* little Froufrou! That screech showed she was absolutely *terrified*.' I pointed accusingly at the shaking sling bag. 'Look, she's still trembling.' Indeed she was, but knowing her as I did, it was outrage, not fear.

Gerry added his own broadside. 'You threw a heavy metal object at her, didn't you?' Glaring at the man, he snapped, 'Don't deny it. We heard the clang! Shocking! *Quite* out of order! Consider the order cancelled.'

With that, we turned our backs and marched out of Zendersen's showroom.

CHAPTER FORTY-TWO

'Yesterday's expedition to Zendersen's showroom filled in one of the missing pieces of information needed to wrap up Operation Smokescreen. Plans are already in place for a raid on his warehouse. And thanks to Gorgonzola we now have all the evidence needed to nail Zendersen for tobacco smuggling, so we're just waiting for the *Cheetah*'s arrival in U.K. waters.' Gerry doodled an hourglass, sand trickling down into its lower chamber.

'And G's not the only one who did a good job, Deborah! You spotting Carruthers' name on a cabin door was another breakthrough. It linked Zendersen with the drug organisation at Pear Tree Farm.' He gazed thoughtfully into space. 'But there's still one loose end to tie up…'

'We haven't yet located the stockpile for Pear Tree Farm's drugs?'

'Yes, that's what's worrying. We've raided Pear Tree Farm, rounded up all present. Let me see, that was…' He pulled a sheet of paper from the file on his desk. '…the Course Director McClusky, the young woman claiming to be some kind of secretary, and three creative artists signed up for the Pear Tree

Farm course. Two others, the artist Dolores and the McGurk woman are still to be rounded up.'

'No need to waste time looking for Sapphire McGurk, Gerry. She's not involved with the gang. Just takes unscrupulous advantage of any opportunity that presents itself. Concentrate on finding Dolores. Her weekly briefings at Dirleton connect her with someone higher up the drug supply chain.'

He sighed. 'Failure to arrest Dolores wasn't the only disappointment. The other was the quantity of drugs discovered on site. All but a derisory amount had been moved. A clue to the location could be in the spy watch footage of the East Lothian coastline on the final chart selected for the *Cheetah*'s voyage. There's no port on that stretch big enough to take a super yacht, but Zendersen'll have no problem with that. The *Cheetah* will linger far enough away from the drug cache not to attract attention. Then he'll send one of its powerboats to pick up or deposit a consignment, possibly on one of those islands in your report, or even further south such as a tiny secluded Borders harbour like Cove. However, that's for me to deal with. You and Gorgonzola are both due a well-earned a break.'

That wrapped up my part in the mission.

CHAPTER FORTY-THREE

Now that the drug operation at Pear Tree Farm had been closed down, I wasn't going to waste even a day of my well-earned break deciding on a destination in the U.K. and looking up reviews on Trip Advisor. I knew just where to go, North Berwick. I booked one of the many self-catering apartments, looking forward to long walks along the beach.

It was on the third day of my break that events took an unexpected turn. Freed from the pressures of Operation Smokescreen, I thought I'd enjoy a visit to Dirleton to see it this time through the eyes of a tourist. While waiting for the bus after the reconnoitre of the Castle grounds in preparation for spying on Dolores, I'd popped into The Open Arms Hotel there for a quick coffee and had been most impressed by the comfort, relaxed atmosphere and setting on the village green opposite the castle. This time I'd have lunch. How to get there? Catch the bus, take the car Gerry had conjured up, or walk along the beach?

It was sunny and mild so having checked the tide tables, I wandered along the shore below the West Links golf course, wandering past rock formations, shallow pools, and pausing now and then to pick up interesting shells. Distant Fidra island with its lighthouse marked the point for me to leave the beach, and walk inland to Dirleton. Gorgonzola securely zipped into the rucksack apart from her head, was not interested in scenery, only in seagulls gliding on the thermals, white wings spread. I hadn't walked very far when her frustrated lunges caused the rucksack to bump annoyingly against my shoulders. With no need to hurry, when I came across a sheltered spot in the sun, I made myself comfortable against a marram grass-covered dune moulded by stormy waves into an inviting hollow.

G curled up in the warm sand by my side, restrained against seagull-hunting temptation by my arm resting gently over her. Leaning back against the dune, head resting on rucksack I took sips from my water bottle and gazed over choppy waves to the coastal villages of Fife, tiny in the distance the squat shape of an oil rig and the white turbines of a wind farm. Sun warm on my face, I dozed…

…I became gradually aware of the murmur of men's voices, quite close at hand, coming nearer, drifting down from the Links golf course hole fifteen feet above where I lay on the sand. I yawned and stretched.

Suddenly, louder, 'Well played! You gauged the wind just right. Only inches from the hole!'

Another deeper voice, 'Congrats, Phil! That makes our scores level.'

'Surprised me too.' A laugh. 'Didn't think I'd get so close.'

I'd recognise that plummy voice anywhere. *Phil…* Could only be Phillington Carruthers.

If he looked down from the golf course he'd recognise me. Alarmed, I turned on my side, covered my face with my arm and lay there, ears straining, eyes focused on the variety of patterns imprinted on the firmer sand: a tideline of black bladderwrack; ripples left by waves gently washing up and back; seabird tracks, oystercatcher not gull, thin toe marks clearly visible; blurred hollowed-out paw prints of dog chasing ball, the pattern of its owner's shoe well-defined.

'How about another round tomorrow, Phil? See if you're as good then or if that was just a fluke.'

'Can't do tomorrow. I'll be taking the boat out to the Bass. Make it Thursday. I'll stroll down to the harbour this afternoon to get everything ready. After a dram with you in the clubhouse first, of course.'

The golfers seemed in no hurry to move away. I risked a furtive glance up the grassy dune. The head and shoulders of two men, neither of them Phillington Carruthers, were silhouetted against the sky, backs half-turned, now deep in conversation about tactics for playing the next hole.

The *click* of club hitting ball, another two clicks at short intervals. I played safe as if asleep in the sun, waiting till their voices dropped to a murmur as they moved away.

I sat up hurriedly, abruptly reminded by a startled *miaou* that Gorgonzola was snoozing at my side. Before she could realise she was free to take off, I grabbed her by the scruff of the neck, reached behind me for the rucksack and zipped her securely in. Deaf to muffled sounds of outrage, I scrambled up a narrow sandy track cut steeply slantwise across the dune, dropped flat, and peered after the receding figures. All were wearing similar dark trousers and jackets, but the man with the green tartan cap was definitely Carruthers.

Too much of a risk to follow him when he came out of the

clubhouse. I have a sixth sense that tells me when I am being followed and it might very well be the same with him. Better to wait at a vantage point near the harbour where I could see and not be seen. To be able to track him tomorrow with a powerful pair of binoculars, I only had to know the name and colour of his boat.

He'd said he'd visit the Bass tomorrow. Though to all appearances he'd be bird watching or fishing nearby, perhaps to pick up a floating canister, his destination was somewhere along the coast to the east. The stockpile would definitely not be on its flat treeless top, the nesting site of aggressive gulls and gannets, or in sight of the thousands of tourists, boat trippers and camera close-ups at the Seabird Centre, and in the dark even a pinprick of light on the rock would attract attention.

Deaf to G's complaints from the rucksack, I set off at a leisurely pace towards the harbour. No need to hurry. By the time they'd completed the course and wound down in the clubhouse over a dram at least three hours would pass.

CHAPTER FORTY-FOUR

That evening I consulted a map to find the best place to view the Bass Rock and the surrounding sea. Seacliff Bay directly opposite would be an ideally placed vantage point for tracking Carruther's boat.

At first light the next day, with a still-sulking Gorgonzola gone to ground in the rucksack, I made the short drive along the coast from Dirleton towards Tantallon Castle. At a sharp left hand bend after the castle, I took a narrow side road, paid the toll fee at a barrier, drove down the winding wooded track, and parked on the wide stretch of grass close to the beach. Car park and beach would be busy even as early as this in summer, but my car was the only one here now. And that suited me fine. I could take Gorgonzola with me onto the beach without attracting attention and comment.

As soon as I lifted G out of her rucksack and attached her lead, she sat ears twitching, head turning, to follow the sound of seagulls' cries, sulks gone at the prospect of pitting her wits against them. With bag containing flask, sandwiches and powerful binoculars, we started down a sandy track brushing between head-high bushes. The early morning sun cast long dark shadows narrowing the sandy path to a golden strip. The next turn unexpectedly revealed a short stretch of beach and directly ahead, the Bass Rock, so close it seemed only an achievable swim or quick kayak trip away.

I stood for a moment taking in the curve of the bay, the long sweep of sand, the sea reflecting the blue of the sky. As I set off in search of a comfortable seat, I gave a gentle tug on the lead. G was reluctant to move, eyes fixed on a seabird tossing pieces of the bladderwrack lining the water's edge. Time to assert myself as Alpha Cat. But subtly of course to avoid a clash between two strong-willed females. I stepped behind her and lobbed a pebble into the sea, carefully aimed to miss the sea bird and send it flying off.

'More birds along there, let's go.'

This time the tug on the lead came from G, eager to stalk the now distant bird, and off we set in the direction I wanted to go.

It was an easy stroll in the soft yielding sand. I soon found a half-buried tree trunk, bleached by sun and salt water, something to lean against for what might well be a lengthy wait until Carruthers' boat came into sight beyond the headland. I unrolled my beach mat and lay back against the tree with the wide sandy beach a pleasing foreground to the Bass Rock and its surrounding sea. I'd be able to spot Carruthers' approach from North Berwick and note whether his destination was the Bass as he'd told his friends.

Yesterday evening after I'd identified his boat at the harbour, I'd concealed a tracking device on it for Gerry to activate on a signal from me, so if Carruthers continued past the Rock, there'd be no need for me to rush back to the car to follow the progress of his boat.

Gorgonzola stretched out in the sun beside me dreaming of a very different outcome to her stalking. With the binoculars close at hand, I tilted my face up to the sun and thought my own thoughts. No hum of distant traffic, only the wash of waves breaking on the beach, and the harsh cries of seagulls. Sound carries a long way over water, so there'd be no problem detecting an approaching boat.

Despite my good intentions, I'd slipped into a doze when the faint *throb throb* of a boat's engine brought me fully awake. I rejected an impulse to peer over the fallen tree to see if the boat rounding the headland from North Berwick was Carruthers', definitely a mistake if he was scanning the shore with his binoculars. Instead I slithered down to lie on my side shielded by the massive trunk, giving a restricted view of the sea, yet a clear sight of any boat within a few hundred yards of the Bass Rock itself.

Even without using the binoculars I could identify the boat as his by the black hull, white wheelhouse and the two red pennants tied to the aerial mast, so sent the arranged coded message to Gerry for him to activate the tracking device. At first the boat seemed to be heading along the coast, wake creaming, then with a sudden abrupt U-turn to the left steered straight for the Bass.

I dug my elbows into the sand, held the binoculars to my eyes to focus on the figure at the controls. Surprisingly, Carruthers was wearing a loose cotton shirt rather than a warm jacket needed against the wind chill on a fast-moving boat at this time of year. The white of the wake subsided as the engine slowed and the boat drifted towards the sheer cliffs to the right of the lighthouse. The powerful magnification picked up the slight splash as he dropped anchor.

I lowered the binoculars. 'Merely checking on lobster pots, G. Looks like we've wasted our–'

Gorgonzola stirred, half-opened one sleepy eye, and closed it. Catching a flicker of movement on the boat, I snatched up the binoculars to see that Carruthers was peeling off his shirt, and that underneath was wearing a black neoprene wetsuit. A few seconds later, shoes and trousers discarded, he slipped over the side and waded toward two shadowy recesses on the face of cliffs plunging sheer into the sea. Through the binoculars I could now see that the larger recess was the entrance to a cave. I watched as he clambered over some semi-submerged rocks and vanished inside.

Twenty minutes passed. I dug my elbows deeper into the sand to steady arms trembling under the weight of the heavy binoculars. A quick check of lobster pots wouldn't have taken him so long. At last, far back in the shadowy depths of the cave, I made out the pale blob of his face. As he splashed towards the entrance he was towing behind him what appeared to be two… three… no… four, bulky plastic-wrapped packages. One by one he lifted them into the boat and climbed aboard by the stern ladder. Packages stowed under a tarpaulin, quick towelling of the wetsuit, shirt and trousers restored, he restarted the engine. The boat reversed into deeper water clear of the Bass and set a course, not back to North Berwick, but eastwards towards one of the many coastal villages of East Lothian or the Borders. Not my problem. The tracker would reveal his destination.

Leaving nothing to chance, I remained flat on the sand waiting until Carruthers' boat was a mere speck in the distance.

For many weeks HMRC had been trying to pinpoint the location of Pear Tree Farm's drug cache. And I, DJ Smith, had found it! I closed my eyes envisaging my triumphant return to headquarters, dancing around Gerry's office high-fiving him and my colleagues…

These pleasant self-congratulatory thoughts were rudely interrupted by a raucous *CHAAWK CHAAWK CHAAWK*. The guttural laughter of a scornful seagull. My eyes shot open to see that Gorgonzola had disappeared. Only a light depression and a scatter of sand on the mat at my side marked where she had been lying.

CHAAWK CHAAWK CHAAWK. More strident, more triumphant. Not one, but three seagulls were closing in on her as she crouched at bay under the overhang of a rock. G, the stalker stalked! My first reaction was to laugh. Until the leading gull strutted forward, cruel yellow eyes fixed on her, vicious beak preparing to stab.

I leapt up. The gull turned its head to judge the threat, paused to consider, then continued its predatory advance. Only when I ran across the sand, frantically waving and shouting, did the birds rise up with loud flapping of wings and a chorus of disgruntled *CHAAWK CHAAWK CHAAWK.* I stood protectively over G until the gulls, losing interest, had flown off along the beach in search of easier prey.

I squatted down beside her and drew her gently out from under the rock.

'What *did* you think you were *doing*? You deserve…' Seeing her frightened eyes, the scolding words died on my lips. I caught her up in my arms in an emotional cuddle, rewarded with a grateful mew.

'We all make mistakes, G,' I said soothingly.

The next day I would make one myself, a very dangerous one indeed.

CHAPTER FORTY-FIVE

The sobering thought came to me that evening while I was enjoying a celebratory drink in The Open Arms bar. Was the cave in the Bass Rock merely an emergency store for a small quantity of drugs? Or was it in actual fact the main drug cache we'd been seeking for so long? This morning I had imagined myself dancing around Gerry's office high-fiving him and everyone else, being congratulated as the agent who'd discovered the main drug cache, the centre of attention for wrapping up the mission.

On the other hand, if I told Gerry that the Bass Rock was the main cache, for it to be found later that Carruthers had just been transferring a few packages to further along the coast, my face would be red with embarrassment. Always ready to take me down a peg, Assistant Controller Andrew Tyler would delight in publicising my mistake as a glaring example of false assumption and a warning to all agents. I thought gloomily that he'd undoubtedly make use of it in a training session for years to come. So, absolutely necessary for me to find out if the cave was a temporary store.

That evening I searched the web, found kayaks for hire

nearby, and booked one with enough storage capacity to collect a sample package from the cave.

At Seacliff next morning I lifted down the kayak from the roof rack and carried it the few yards to the beach, then returned to the car to collect two rucksacks. In one, a change of clothes, sandwich and flask of coffee for a beach breakfast; in the other, Gorgonzola, unusually subdued after the previous day's encounter with the seagulls.

With G's rucksack at my feet, I sat munching my sandwich and gazing across at the Bass Rock. About a mile away, I guessed, though it's difficult to judge distance over water especially when there's a light sea mist. To paddle across, add time for a quick look in the cave and return to the beach? Surely, take not much more than an hour.

The problem was what to do with Gorgonzola. Since the seagull incident she hadn't wanted me out of her sight, stayed close to me, curling herself affectionately round my legs as I walked about, wrapping her paws round my neck as I sat, sleeping pressed against me in my bed. So she'd have to be left on the beach. Definitely wouldn't be safe to take her with me in the kayak.

I placed G's rucksack in the shelter of a nearby bush, and satisfied that she was sleeping peacefully on one of my jerseys, curled up with her pink mouse for comfort, I left my rucksack beside hers. Before pushing the kayak into the water, I took off my jacket and stuffed it into the rear compartment, then checked I had all I needed for my trip: mobile in waterproof pouch? Head torch for cave? Buoyancy vest? Left it in the car. Annoyed at the delay, I hurried back for it.

No movement in G's rucksack under the bush. Confident that I could safely leave her, I slid the kayak into the water, stepped in, and pushed off, soon picking up a smooth rhythm dipping the long double paddle, first to one side then the other. Blue sky streaked with cloud, *plash* of blades sliding into the water, wavelets rippling against the bow… This was a fine way to end my holiday, whether I found the main cache or not.

CHAPTER FORTY-SIX

2 p.m.
The kayak centre owner drummed his fingers on the counter. Only one hire today and that young woman was certainly taking a liberty. Should have been back by twelve o'clock. That was the trouble with some people nowadays. She had been pretty vague about where she planned to go, and when pressed for safety reasons, she'd waved a vague hand in the direction of Dunbar. Wouldn't be surprised if she'd been tempted by the good weather and sea conditions this morning to go as far as St Abbs and hadn't taken into consideration the time and energy needed to paddle back. Well, if she thought she'd escape the charge for a full day, she'd another thought coming. He consulted the hire form for her credit card details…

4 p.m
Where the hell was she? He'd be closing up soon. The address she'd given was The Open Arms Hotel in Direlton. He put in a call and left a message for her.

8 p.m.
Gerry Burnside checked his diary. Time for the pre-arranged

call to Deborah.

'It has not been possible to connect your call. Please try again later.'

He frowned. Why was her mobile was switched off? She'd assured him she'd always have it with her. All agents knew the importance of keeping a scheduled contact, so what had happened to prevent her from using the phone to debrief, or even to send in her position using the *what3words* location app. He always made a point of noting of how agents tended to act at a certain stage of an assignment. Deborah, for example, took a pride in not leaving any loose ends, and the location of the main cache of drugs was a big loose end. On her own initiative she'd planted that tracking device in Carruther's boat, but she wouldn't be satisfied with that, so it had been an error of judgement for him to take her off the mission after that successful probe into Zendersen's store. His notes showed that she was staying at a hotel in Dirleton. He picked up the landline phone.

'Open Arms Hotel... Ms Smith? Went off in her car early this morning, sir... Yes, took the cat with her. Didn't say when she'd be back... Important to speak to her you say? The kayak centre wants to contact her too. Yes, I can give you its number...'

The computer details of the boat's route and timings for the previous day showed that Carruthers' boat had stopped close to the Rock for thirty minutes or so, before heading east past Dunbar and St Abbs... But others were dealing with that. His concern at the moment was the whereabouts of his agent. Deborah had activated the tracker signal when the boat was west of the Bass Rock confirming that she had been keeping it under surveillance from Seacliff Beach. She'd have watched it stop, seen it continue along the coast. Curiosity aroused, she must have hired the kayak today to investigate why Carruthers had stopped at the Bass.

Vital to find the kayak, either floating or beached. The RNLI had four bases close at hand from which to launch a search of the coastline, but in the dark it would be very difficult for the lifeboat crew to see a kayak low in the water. The Coastguard helicopter with the advantage of height would find the small kayak easier to spot as she could be drifting with the tide and current. He had a disturbing vision of her slumped in or clinging to the kayak, rapidly losing strength from hypothermia…

Time was of the essence.

8.30 p.m.
With mounting anxiety he listened to the reports radioed in from the North Berwick lifeboat.

'Waves moderate. Visibility poor… Bass Rock in sight… Helicopter reports sighting of kayak wreckage. Between lighthouse and cave entrance…'

Burnside let out his breath in a long sigh.

The lifeboat radio signal faded… static… then, 'Closing in to investigate…'

He stared into space.

The radio crackled. 'No sign of casualty. Sending two of the crew to check the cave…'

He sighed again. Waiting for news when an agent was missing, possibly dead, that was the worst part of a controller's job.

The minutes dragged by…

CHAPTER FORTY-SEVEN

Ten hours earlier
10.30 a.m.
There'd been very little wind, an almost calm sea when I'd set off, but out of shelter of the land, the wind strengthened. Paddling required more effort as wavelets broke against the bow with more force in an increasingly choppy sea, and bigger waves with the occasional whitecap rocked the kayak. Fairly soon the precipitous cliffs, the irregular dark hole of the cave mouth and a pale strip created by the incessant surge of sea dashing against rock were only a few paddle strokes away. In the clear algae-tinged water at the mouth of the cave, a shoal of tiny fish darted to and fro.

Splash. The round head of a seal popped up, its eyes surveyed me. Satisfied that I presented no danger, it submerged, its long grey shape visible below the surface, twisting and turning with easy flicks of is flippers. Strident squawks and haunting cries of seabirds overhead mingled with eerie groans of seals echoing and re-echoing from the depths of the cave.

The wind strengthened even more. As I pointed the nose of the kayak towards a cluster of rocks at the entrance, a sudden strong downdraft from the cliffs caught the raised the paddle blade and for a heart-stopping moment threatened to roll the kayak over. The landing was going to be a lot more difficult than I'd first thought. What had started off as a recreational paddle had become a strength-sapping battle against wind and waves, raising the thought that it might be better to give up and return to the beach.

The decision was taken out of my hands. At that very moment, a rogue wave flung the kayak violently forward, forcing the bow into a narrow gap between two rocks, wedging it fast with an ominous splintering of fibreglass. Another such wave could raise the stern high into the air, hurling me headfirst into the rocks. Have to act quickly while I had the chance. I heaved myself out of the kayak. Thigh-deep in water, holding the boat steady with one hand, I reached into the rear compartment and made a grab for my jacket.

Ouch! Something sharp had dug into my hand. Must have caught it on a rough piece of fibreglass. Cautiously, I reached in again and pulled at the jacket. Stronger tugs slowly dragged out a sleeve, G's pink mouse and the rest of the jacket.

And Gorgonzola, spread claws embedded in the cloth.

Fifty yards out, a white-capped wave was gathering height. In an adrenalin-fuelled flurry, I stuffed pink mouse into jacket, and hugging it and cat tightly to me, turned my back on the wave, bracing to take the impact. The force of the wave lifted up the stern of the kayak and smashed it side-on against the rocks, breaking it apart at the bow.

Before the next big wave could knock me over, I picked my way to the cave mouth, deposited G on a ledge, hoisted myself up, and sat cuddling her, stroking her with shaking hand. When

I'd rushed back to the car, she must have detected my scent on the kayak and desperate not to be separated from me, curled up inside my jacket with her pink mouse. Before setting off, why, oh *why*, had I not checked if she was still asleep in her rucksack under the bush?

Sipping that celebratory drink in the Open Arms last night it had all seemed so easy to paddle across to the Bass, nip into the cave to confirm by the number of packages if this was indeed the gang's main drug cache, paddle back, and make that triumphant phone call to Gerry.

I gazed dejectedly across the white-capped waves towards Tantallon Castle on the headland. All agents need help when they are in danger, but on this occasion the danger had come from my own misguided actions. I could see no way out of the humiliating consequences: phone call begging for rescue, call-out of RNLI, Tyler harping on about taxpayers forced to cough up for the write-off of expensive kayak, Gerry's raised eyebrows…

But no need to panic *yet*. Surely all I had to do was attract the attention of another kayaker, a Seabird Centre boat trip, or a fishing boat passing close to the Rock. Then the reality check. Chance of rescue so slight as to be non-existent. Kayakers faced with these white caps would have turned back, Seabird Centre trips had finished for the season, and I had no idea if any North Berwick fishing boat would pass this side of the Bass Rock.

Only if packages worth millions of pounds were found in the cave could I convincingly rebrand as 'enterprise and vision' that really bad decision of mine to kayak out to the Bass. The problem was where would they be hidden? The cartel certainly wouldn't take the risk of drugs being stumbled on by curious kayakers exploring the cave. The drugs would be quite far back from the entrance, which would account for the time it had taken Carruthers to return to his boat. They'd be concealed, not easy to find. Putting G to work would take her mind off her dreadful experience.

I stared down at her and tried a tentative, 'Search, G?'

Her head burrowed deeper under my arm. I sighed. Perhaps her training would kick in if she actually sniffed drugs hidden in the cave.

A wave lapped over my feet, a warning that the tide was on the turn. With the high tide mark several feet above where I was sitting now, there was no time to waste. I put on my jacket, zipping G securely inside, grateful for her body heat, a welcome feline hot water bottle against the wind chill.

I splashed my way into the cave, switched on the head torch and stood there listening to the regular *drip... drip... drip* of moisture falling from above. High overhead in the gloom mini ferns clung here and there to the walls, disappearing into the darkness thirty feet or so above; below the high water mark, only slimy brown algae flourished.

Judging by the height of the entrance, I'd expected a huge cavity extending far into the heart of the Bass, but to my surprise, the rear of the cave was only a few yards further on. The bright beam of the head torch moved slowly clockwise round the walls... back... up... down. No packages. My heart sank. The four that Carruthers had taken away must have been all there was. I had to accept that this was just a drop-off place, not the main store, the cache we were seeking. Despondent, I turned to go back the way I'd come. Humiliation, not glory, lay in store for me.

After a last glance round, I switched off the head torch, had waded a couple of steps when a muffled *hrwoooooo* came from inside my jacket. The signal that drugs were indeed here, and close by.

G's head poked out. *Hrwoooooo.* A hollow *hrwo-oo-oo-o-o Oo-oo-oo Oo-oo-o-o* bounced round the walls of the cave.

'Clever girl!' I cried. *Clev-er g-ir-ll -ir-ll -ir-ll.* The cry echoed and re-echoed from the hard rock.

I swung round, and saw on the back wall of the cave a grey smudge, missed in the bright light of the head torch. I waded back for a closer look. Daylight seeping in through a fissure.

Spurred on by an encouraging *hrwoooooo* from Gorgonzola, I discovered that a massive slab was concealing a tunnel running through the rock. Some way ahead along the tunnel, past a jumble of boulders, I could make out the reflection of a pool of water and even further on, a circle of daylight. Suitably rewarded with her pink mouse for Duty Done, G retired inside my jacket. Message: I've done the difficult bit. Now it's over to you. I'm in Recovery Mode. Do Not Disturb.

I switched on the head torch again and played the beam over the boulders. Packages were not likely to have been hidden there: the risk of adventurous kayakers like myself chancing on them was too great. Gingerly I picked my way over and between the boulders. Have to be careful, all to easy to trap a foot or twist an ankle. The water in the pool was too deep and dark to see if there were any packages hidden in the depths. Anyway, G couldn't have detected a scent from a submerged package.

But never before had G been wrong. They must be here *somewhere*, probably in one of the recesses worn in the cave wall by thousands of years of seawater forcing its way into the tunnel. Flicking the torch beam from side to side, I moved slowly back the way I'd come.

Another muffled *hrwoooooo*. I must be close. Visible only at an angle, even with aid of the torch, was an opening in seemingly solid rock. Deep inside a small cave I could see disorderly random heaps of what would at a casual glance appear to be a mass of fallen rock, in fact a very large number of packages wrapped in matt-black plastic. With one arm supporting G's weight, I extricated the phone from my jacket pocket, took a photo and turned to go.

Then stopped. What if I brought back an *actual* package and triumphantly placed it on Gerry's desk? I'd gain *much* more kudos than merely showing him the picture on my phone. Holding G firmly inside my jacket, I stooped to avoid the low roof of the side-cave and reached forward one-handed to snatch up a package.

Hrwoooooo. Sensing drugs close-by, Gorgonzola forced her way out of the hampering jacket. I made a grab for her. Pitched forward. My head slammed into hard rock.

CHAPTER FORTY-EIGHT

Shaken, head throbbing, I was lying sprawled face down across a heap of packages. My finger traced the small trickle of blood running down my forehead. Cautiously I felt the lump under my hair. How had that happened? ...I'd taken a photo of the pile of drugs... was stretching over to pick up a souvenir package for Gerry... and then... yes, that was it. I'd made a lunge for G as she flung herself out of my jacket onto the packages...

But no Gorgonzola nestling close. Where was she? No croon, no miaow, no sound except the slow *drip... drip... drip* of moisture falling into the pool in the tunnel. Sudden panicky thought. I'd crushed her when I pitched forward! Heart racing, I ran my hands over the tumbled packages. No furry body. Had she crawled away injured, was now lying somewhere out there in the dark? I levered myself up on an elbow and sat up. Reflected in the beam of the head torch, two copper-yellow eyes stared back at me.

A rush of relief. 'Gorgonzola!' I whispered.

Mia-ouw she whispered back. Then louder, *Mia-ouw.*

She picked her way warily towards me, took a long look, then leapt into my outstretched arms. *Miaouw* Two paws patted my cheeks as I hugged her to me. Her *purrrrrrrrr* vibrated comfortingly against my chest.

I laid G down gently to free both hands for picking up a package. Its bulk and the slippery wrapping made it difficult to hold. I pondered. Should I be content merely with the photo as evidence of the drug cache inside the Bass Rock? No. I wasn't going to be done out of that moment of glory in Gerry's office and the praise from my colleagues at HMRC. Decision made. I didn't take into account that the package might be more of a burden than I expected.

Gorgonzola followed closely behind as I made an unsteady way into the main cave. No use returning to the main entrance. There'd be little chance of a passing boat spotting the wrecked kayak, and the rising tide would already have submerged the ledge where I could stand to wave for help. I set off towards the welcome daylight beckoning at the end of the tunnel seemingly only a short distance away.

With the head torch battery now appreciably weaker, more shaken than I'd realised and hampered by the package, progress over the treacherous boulders covering the floor of the cavern was slow. Very soon I came to an abrupt halt at the edge of the deep pool. There was no way to get to the other side except by swimming. I'd have to leave the heavy package behind and float across on my back holding G tightly on my chest. Idea abandoned as soon as thought. Too risky. I knew she would struggle, jump into the water, and very likely drown. Both exits were inaccessible. I was trapped inside the Bass Rock with the tide rising.

Dismay until I realised that the blow on my head had muddled my thinking. All I had to do was phone for help. I grabbed the waterproof phone from the inner pocket of my jacket and called 999 for the coastguard.

No network connection.

I stared at the message. Of course there wasn't. The signal was blocked by more than three hundred feet of volcanic rock.

'No one is going to find me!' My hysterical cry echoed and re-echoed from wall to wall. '...find me ...ind me... ind me.'

The repetition triggered the memory of Gerry telling me that he could find me. Anywhere. Via the *what3words* app installed on my phone. 'As accurately as giving the GPS co-ordinates', he'd said. He'd found exactly where I was in Los Cristianos, hadn't he? All I had to do was tap the app on the phone. It didn't open. Tried again. Same result...

Head a bit muzzy... harder and harder to think... Difficult to think clearly... In a cave with no satellite signal, so the app wouldn't work. The fog momentarily cleared from my brain. Didn't need Gerry's app. *What3words* was a life saver if you didn't know where you were – kidnapped, locked in a room, dumped in the countryside – but I *did* know exactly where I was, and if I had a phone signal could have told the coastguard the position myself...

In despair I sank to the ground and sat, chin on hand, staring into space.

Back propped against the damp wall of the cave, I listened to the soft *plop... plop...* of water dripping from the roof into the pool, measuring the slow passage of time as relentlessly as the sombre *tock tock* of a grandfather clock in the dark hours of the night. The bright circle of daylight at the end of the tunnel had dimmed to grey. In a futile attempt to keep warm, I shivered and hugged Gorgonzola more tightly. She didn't protest, didn't resent the tight grip.

Gerry's phone call was scheduled for… for… sometime in the evening. Couldn't remember… But it would raise an alert when I didn't check in with him at the scheduled time. Calm for a moment. But only for a moment. How would Gerry know where to search? He wouldn't. There was no reason for him to think I'd hired a kayak or gone to Seacliff Beach. I could be *anywhere*… My eyes closed…

CHAPTER FORTY-NINE

8.40 p.m.

Drip... drip... drip... Waking from a confused dream, I opened my eyes. Slowly I turned my head. Pitch-black in all directions. Couldn't see the hand I held up in front of my face. Could feel movement of air when I moved my fingers but couldn't see them. Head aching, only half conscious, I slumped down among the pile of boulders... cold, very cold...

Splashes... Shouts. 'Hello-oooooo... hello-oooooo.' A man's voice echoing and re-echoing round the cave walls. 'Deborah...'

Someone calling my name... Just part of my dream... Shouts again... Want to sleep... Why can't that man be *quiet*...

I covered my ears and curled into a ball among the boulders. 'Oh, shut up, can't you! You're hurting my head,' I moaned.

Man's voice, 'Control, we've been round the cave as far as the pool with the flashlight. Shining it now along the tunnel towards the west entrance. Nothing... Turning back now.'

I felt Gorgonzola stir in my arms and thrust her head out of my jacket. *Mia-ouw Mia-ouw MI-A-OOOUW.*

'Wait, just heard what sounds like a cat... definitely the

reflection of a cat's eyes… Taking a closer look…' An excited shout, 'Something among the boulders.'

Someone was bending over me. A touch on my arm.

'Casualty found! Semi-conscious.'

CHAPTER FIFTY

A week later.

The mission debriefing with Controllers Gerry Burnside and Andrew Tyler didn't turn out to be the celebratory occasion I'd keenly anticipated. Instead, I was met with serious faces, not the expected smiles and congratulations.

Gerry began by emphasising just how near I'd been to death. 'It was a very close thing, Deborah, and that, I'm afraid, was because in your eagerness to complete a mission, you are prone to what only can be called ill-considered and ill-advised action.'

Only too keen to find fault, Andrew Tyler nodded. 'I agree. That frivolous sight-seeing jaunt by kayak almost cost you your life. HMRC was forced to call out the rescue services, in particular a very expensive helicopter needlessly costing the taxpayer thousands of pounds.' Unsaid but implied, 'And if it were up to me, every single penny would come out of your salary.'

I looked from one to the other. Tyler's attitude was no surprise. There'd always been friction between us. But I'd expected, indeed deserved, praise from Gerry. The side tunnel had been stacked to the ceiling with waterproofed packages. Had I not located what was undoubtedly the main cache for the gang's drugs? But not a mention or iota of credit for that!

Infuriated, I burst out, 'That frivolous jaunt of mine, as you termed it, Mr Tyler, located the main cache of drugs. *And* deprived the drug cartel of hundreds of thousands of pounds!'

His lip curled, 'My dear girl, that unfortunate blow on the head has led you to magnify out of all proportion *your* part in planting the tracking device compared with the importance of *my* discovery of the main store we've been looking for so long.'

I was stunned into silence. Was the Bass Rock, after all, just a short-term store? Was it Tyler not myself who found the main cache?

Taking from my lack of response that I'd been suitably crushed by his humiliating put-down, he smiled condescendingly. 'I'm afraid you've still to learn Smith, not to jump to a conclusion based on flimsy evidence. You *may* indeed have found a *few* packages–'

'But I–'

'I'm making allowances, Smith.' he snapped. Snatching up one of the reports, he waved it in my face. 'Though you played a *minor* role placing the tracker on Carruther's boat, Mr Burnside put *me* in charge of the vital stage of the operation, the follow-up at the boat's destination. Successful, most successful, if I may so. Carruthers led me to an old quarry, and a stockpile of fifty packages! *Fifty!*'

All deference to his rank jettisoned, I cried, '*Only* fifty! I found *more*, many more!' I pulled my phone out of my pocket and switched it on. 'Here's the evidence!'

In silence Gerry studied the photo on my mobile. Then

said slowly, 'I think you'd better revise and resubmit that report of yours, Andrew.'

After Tyler left the debriefing, Gerry went over to a cupboard and heaved out a large canvas holdall. 'Thought you might be interested in this terracotta clay as a souvenir of your time at the Pear Tree Farm.'

A bag of clay! Just his sense of humour. Unfortunately my clay sculpture days were definitely over as I'd lost all interest in working with clay after I had been forced to abandon my Earth Mother to the revenge of spiteful Carol. But it's the thought that counts, I suppose. I smiled as if delighted with the present.

'Have a look.' He pulled open the zip.

I gasped. Smiling up at me was *Earth Mother*.

Gerry was smiling too. 'Something to reward you after all you've been through. She was on sale at Pear Tree Farm's pop-up exhibition, stuffed full of drugs, of course! A fine example, I might say, of this gang's modus operandi using creative art to hide drugs. Often the best way to conceal something is to hide it in plain view.'

He took a bottle and two glasses from a drawer and raised his glass in a toast. 'To celebrate DJ Smith bringing the mission to a successful conclusion.' We clinked glasses. 'And more important to me,' his tone serious, 'your survival.' He held my gaze. 'When the life boat crew didn't find a casualty beside the wrecked kayak, and as a last resort landed two members of the crew to search the cave, you can imagine how worried I was sitting here listening in. They couldn't see you in your dark clothing lying hidden among the boulders and were about to leave.'

'Can't remember anything. So what made them take a second look?'

Gerry laughed. 'Gorgonzola called for help.'

CHAPTER FIFTY-ONE

The perfect end to a mission for me is when there are no loose ends to be tied up, but one loose end from Operation Smokescreen still niggled – the whereabouts of Dolores. Three months later that loose end was unexpectedly tied up when an envelope popped through my letterbox containing a front page of *The East Lothian Courier*.

GARDENER'S SHOCK DISCOVERY
IN DIRLETON CASTLE GARDENS
Giant Phormium yields up grim secret

The grounds of Dirleton Castle have been closed to visitors for the last two days after the body of a woman, as yet unidentified, was discovered close to the Gazebo Tower. It was buried in a shallow grave under the giant New Zealand Phormium, one of the most spectacular plants in the herbaceous border. The head gardener told our reporter how the body came to be discovered.

'We've a constant battle against bindweed and ground elder, you see. The smallest bit of root left in the ground and it regenerates. Best way to get rid of these menaces is to clear all the plants from the border and cover the earth with black polythene sheeting to kill all weed growth. The only plant left in the ground was the specimen phormium, too large and risky to move. Bert, one of our team was gathering into a heap the windblown leaves that had collected underneath the plant when the tines of the rake snagged on what seemed to be a thick surface root. Turned out to be a wooden box of artists' paints. We find some surprising things in the garden, you know. He put it aside as lost property and continued raking. A few minutes later he uncovered a woman's shoe, her leg and the rest of her body.'

According to a police spokesman, the body had been there for some months The cause of death is at present unexplained.

Acknowledgements

MANY THANKS to all who have aided us in the research for this novel, in particular to…

ALANNA KNIGHT MBE, who is always ready to help other writers, and gave up valuable her own writing time to rescue us from the despair of double writers' block at an early part of the novel.

SKI REG who, with his unique Cockney humour, helped with our research, checking details were not only accurate but possible. His amusing anecdotes about his water ski-ing antics in Tenerife and his experience as a microlight pilot gave us ideas for the character, though, of course, incidents involving this character are entirely fic-tional.

AIDAN STRANGE The Steward for Historical Environment Scotland, who was very interested in the idea of a body being found in the Gardens and patiently answered all our research questions on Dirleton Castle and Gardens.

IAN BAILLIE Expert potter who introduced Morna to the delights of clay sculpture many years ago – a hobby used to advantage as an important part of the plot of this novel.

DEREK MALCOLM "Super Mech", consulted for his unsurpassed knowledge of the working of car engines to ensure that Helen's hazy memory of the working of car engines was accurate for a key element of the plot.

EMERALDS CHASED IN GOLD. The Islands of the Forth, Their Story Ancient and Modern With black and white illustrations by John Dickson F.S.A. Scot. Published by The British Library, Historical Print Editions. First published 1899. Modern paperback edition 2011 Also available online from The British Library. The description of the interior of The Bass Rock on pages 150-170 was used in our research. The book is a very interesting read in its own right.

Lightning Source UK Ltd.
Milton Keynes UK
UKHW020052041221
395059UK00010B/2649